A Paradox of Fates

Prevent the Past, Book 1

By

REBECCA HEFNER

Cover Design: Anthony O'Brien, www.BookCoverDesign.store
Editor: Megan McKeever
Proofreader: Bryony Leah, www.bryonyleah.com

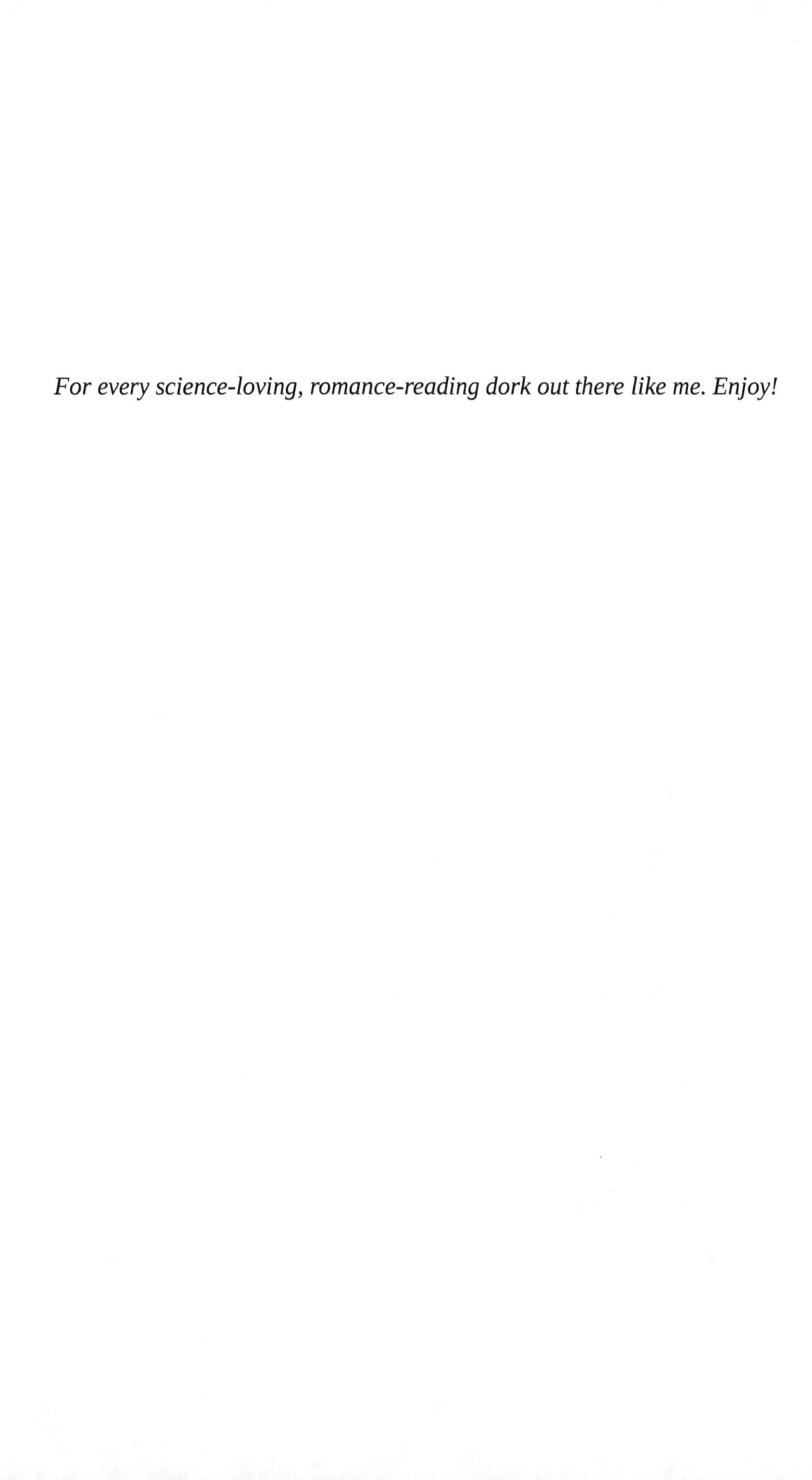

For every science-loving, romance-reading dork out there like me. Enjoy!

Contents

A Note from the Author

I have always been a huge self-proclaimed science dork. When other kids were enjoying time off in the summer, I attended Space Camp when I was fourteen and went to North Carolina Governor's School for Physics between my junior and senior years of high school. Physics has always held special meaning for me, and I knew it was only a matter of time before I wrote a novel with a theoretical physicist female main character. Because geeky scientists deserve love too!

Physics introduced me to the theory of special relativity, which theoretically proves time travel is possible. Time travel stories have always enthralled me, from *Back to the Future*, to *Contact* (which I consider a time travel story since Ellie literally travels through time and space!), to the TV show *Dark*, my newest obsession.

It was important for me to research properly, so this book, even though it's science fiction, is based on solid scientific principles. The Sphere is based upon the theories of Dr. Ronald Mallett as well as Einstein's theories of special and general relativity. Although this novel is science-based, time travel is still, to my knowledge, impossible. Therefore, you will still find some things that make you go, "Hmmm…" and you will have to suspend reality in some instances since a reader's imagination is always much more expansive than reality.

My hope is that this novel can combine my love of science with my love of romance novels and whisk the reader away for a few hours to a world filled with relatable characters and exciting adventure. Thanks for taking this journey with me. Happy reading!

PROLOGUE

The order to destroy the world was given at 17:23 Eastern Standard Time in the year 2035.

From a squalid room set deep in one of the bunkers under the White House, President Randolph gave the command. Surrounded by his wife, the Vice President, and the Secretary of Defense, the president unlocked the nuclear codes and unleashed the atomic bombs. Then, he kissed his wife, lifted the revolver, placed one clean shot into each person's brain, and turned the gun upon himself. No one truly understood his motivation—the cryptic note he left behind explained that he was attempting to save humanity from itself.

The first nuclear warhead hit Russia on a Tuesday morning, the gray light of the clouds giving way to the rush of fire. Russia's population had reached 137 million, and almost one million Russians perished that Tuesday morning.

Many others followed in Asia and Africa. Those countries retaliated, firing warheads of their own back upon North America and Europe. For days, the power of nuclear fission transformed humans back to the stardust from whence they came.

When the smoke cleared and the rubble stopped quaking, Earth was in tatters. Sea levels began to rise as a result of Antarctica's and Greenland's melted glaciers. Coastal cities receded into the ocean, lost to mysticism like Atlantis in the ancient world.

A new landscape emerged, and the survivors fled to higher ground. The Appalachian Mountains formed the Eastern American Isle, while the

Rockies formed the Western American Isle. Separated by the ocean, the two former landmasses might as well have been galaxies apart.

Wanting to ensure no more bombs were launched, a small group of scientists banded together on their respective isles. With urgency, they moved all the energy-harnessing and technological machinery to secure locations, staying in touch by Morse code. Once the technology was secure, they detonated the EMPs.

The Electromagnetic Pulses pulverized every last bit of technology left upon the planet, except for the machinery and knowledge that were preserved at the hubs. Humans were thrust back into the Stone Age, forced to survive on will alone. Those who possessed basic survival skills flourished. Small towns and communities began to form along the isles. Cut off from communication by phone or mail, the towns eventually became communes, protected by walls. Strangers were rarely allowed to enter, and when they did, they were expected to conform to the rules or face exile.

The wicked men who had supported President Randolph continued to crave power. These men banded together to overtake the communes and harness their food and labor. This ensured the malevolent men's families were fed and that they could thrive in the new world. This evil enterprise was known as the New Establishment, and they systematically began to attack compounds and settlements on each isle. Not deeming the scientific hubs a threat—since they housed only a small number of people the New Establishment considered weak, irrelevant relics of the past—they left them alone, underestimating the power of science, as most power-hungry, ignorant men do.

Frustrated that their people were being forced into slavery and oppression, an opposing faction of soldiers known as the Old Rebellion banded together to fight the evil regime. Sadly, this thrust what was left of the world into a vicious, bloody war.

And so it went for many years. During these decades, the scientists continued to huddle on their bases, looking for solutions. The four scientific hubs were located in reclusive, inconspicuous locations, all on separate isles, in a bid to keep them off the radar and unengaged in war.

On the Eastern American Isle's hub, in the year 2037, a girl was born. Possessing the DNA of two trained scientists, she was destined to be a wisdom-warrior in the battle against the New Establishment. Bred to save the world, she grew up looking to the stars, observing the desecration of her tiny planet, and wondering if anyone was looking back.

When she turned twelve and had learned all she could from her mother, a former college physics and calculus professor, she began to study with her father. Formerly a world-renowned scientist, the girl's father was an expert in many fields. He cultivated his progeny into a diligent and determined scientist, hoping she could save them all.

Dr. Lewis Randolph dedicated his life to training his daughter Elaine to comprehend the complexities and mysteries of the scientific realm, for his father, President Edward James Randolph, had destroyed the world, and Lewis was convinced Elaine would be their savior. Before Lewis passed away on a cold day in January 2070, he sputtered a message to his daughter as he coughed upon the bed.

"We're so close, Lainey," he said, his voice hoarse. "Don't give up."

"I won't, Dad," she said, clutching his hand as she sat upon the soft bedspread. "I promise, I'll figure it out. There's no other option."

"That's my strong girl," Lewis said, his chapped lips curving into a hint of a smile.

"Tell God I said 'hi,'" Lainey said, bringing their clenched hands to rest upon her cheek. "I think she'll be happy to see you."

"There is no God, sweet girl. I thought my cold, scientific heart raised you to be an atheist."

Lainey swallowed, her throat tight. "I was until I realized I had to let you go. Now, all I want is for Her to take care of you." Tears streamed down her cheeks, running over the wrinkled skin of her father's hand.

"See you in 2035, my darling girl."

"See you in 2035," she whispered.

Lewis inhaled a sizeable breath, his body quivering, and exhaled a large gasp. Unseeing eyes stared at Lainey, and she knew he was gone. Placing a kiss upon his forehead, she stood, feeling her nostrils flare.

"I swear to you, Dad," she vowed, fists clenched at her sides, "I'll never stop until I succeed." Straightening her spine, she called out for the nurse, who shuffled into the room. "He's gone," Lainey said. "Cremate the body. We'll have a funeral later today and then get back to work. I won't squander time for grief. He'd expect no less of me."

Striding from the room, her sneakers squeaked on the linoleum floor. Dr. Elaine Randolph was going to master the one thing that had eluded them so far. Every ounce of her energy and tick of the second hand would be spent discerning that which had thwarted them for so many decades: the scientific theorem known as time travel.

And then, she was going to transport back to 2035 and prevent her grandfather from destroying humanity.

Chapter 1

Five and a Half Years Later...

Lainey awoke, drowsy, in her double bed, the mattress firm against her back as she preferred. A soft mattress would invite the possibility of relaxing back into the cool sheets, allowing her to daydream for a while. Daydreams had no place in the post-apocalyptic world her grandfather had created.

Tossing the comforter aside, she sat up and touched her feet to the worn rug atop the concrete floor. Groaning, she maneuvered her neck around her shoulders, circling while the bones creaked and popped. Thirty-eight wasn't doing her any favors, and she morosely wondered what forty would look like. Good grief, she might as well have Sara start manufacturing the arthritis medication now.

Sighing, she stood and padded into the small bathroom. After a quick shower, Lainey gathered her thick, wavy mahogany hair into a bun atop her head. It would dry that way, ensuring rings of curls fell down her shoulders whenever she chose to release the bun. Probably not until later that evening, when she would be alone in her room once again.

Staring at her amber eyes in the mirror, she absently rubbed lotion over her face and skin. Grimacing at the stretch marks across her hips and the slight pooch under her navel, she told herself to silence the inner critic. She tried to take walks with Cyrus around the compound each day, as much to exercise as to ensure they weren't being surveilled, and those walks kept the space above her navel relatively flat and smooth. Below her navel? Well, she'd just attribute that little slice of flab to the fact she had other priorities in life besides winning beauty contests.

No, there were a few other things to accomplish, for Dr. Elaine Randolph had been born and bred for the sole purpose of saving the world.

In her mind, that sounded quite dramatic, and Lainey was sure her parents hadn't intended to blaze the path of her life in such a systematic and determined manner. But it had happened anyway, and once she was a teenager, Lainey understood her place in their dystopian world. Whereas many other children were tucked away in the communes that now comprised their deadened ecosphere, Lainey had been raised by her parents on the scientific hub. This had afforded her both extravagances and disadvantages other children would never know.

Lainey had never known starvation, nor had she known true despair as others on the planet did now. She'd been sheltered on their commune, safe from danger, with access to the electricity and education so many other humans craved. She'd understood the equivalent of a high school senior by age twelve, a college graduate by fourteen, and enough to be bestowed a Ph.D. in theoretical physics, calculus, and mathematics by seventeen. In her early twenties, Lainey realized she'd surpassed her father when she solved an equation in three days that he'd been trying to elucidate for years. Lewis had looked upon her with such reverence as he held the solved equation in his hands, tears glistening in his eyes.

"The student has now become the teacher," he'd said softly. "You'll save us all, Lainey. I'm so proud of you."

Elation had filled Lainey as she'd clutched her father in a strong hug, for her greatest wish was to please him. Her father's approval was the driving force of every decision in her life.

Even now, although Lewis had passed away over five years ago, Lainey ached to gratify him. To achieve success with the time machine and travel back to 2035, to prevent her grandfather from detonating the atomic bombs that had set off the events resulting in the death and destruction of so many lives.

It was all she cared about; all she'd ever craved.

She would seek that outcome until her dying breath exited her lungs.

Rolling her eyes as she dressed, Lainey reminded herself not to be a drama queen. Emotion had no place in the sphere of science and was wasted within the walls of their hub. Donning a brown sweater, jeans, and sneakers, she rubbed some salve on her chapped lips and headed to the morning meeting with her staff.

They had a small crew at the compound. Some were scientists, some were former soldiers and drifters. All had been extremely loyal to Lewis. Now, they were unwavering in their devotion to Lainey. Their support filled her with a quiet strength, and saving them helped drive her. She longed to create a new thread of space-time for them all, where they didn't have to live on the squalid hub, searching for answers every day. They were her family, and she wanted so much for them to be happy.

As she entered the conference room, she observed the members of her team already situated at the long wooden table. Zach, the coding genius and overall computer whiz, sat beside Claire, smiling politely as she talked his ear off. Claire had purple hair atop her heart-shaped face, which made her look younger than twenty-nine. She'd figured out how to combine lemon, beets and the dark violet flowers that grew on the outskirts of the nearby forest to dye her hair, and it was usually tinted some shade of indigo or red. Lainey knew Zach had been in love with her since he'd come to the hub several years ago, but to her knowledge, he'd never acted on it.

This could be due to the fact Lainey had a strict "no dating" policy for her staff. Their work was too important, and mouths were too hard to feed in their post-apocalyptic world. Although Marie did a great job with the animals and garden, she had other responsibilities that required her time and labor.

At nearly eighty years old, Marie was the mother figure for the hub and seemed perfectly thrilled to have more people to care for every time a new member entered their ranks. She had a never-ending stream of energy that Lainey envied. Lainey had tried to get her to slow down, now that arthritis had overtaken her joints, but Marie wouldn't hear of it and stayed active on the compound. Tending the livestock, cultivating the garden, cooking and mending—nothing was off-limits to the kind woman who wanted to contribute to their success.

Lainey loved her dearly.

Cyrus stalked in and sat at the opposite head of the long table, as he always did in their meetings. Clad in the ever-present black tactical gear that clung to his two-hundred-thirty-pound frame, his face was a mask of steely-eyed determination. He'd always been as resolute to succeed in their mission as she.

Lainey gave him a nod, and his broad lips formed a faint smile under his brown eyes, their color almost the same as his skin. He was like a brother to her, probably her closest confidant in her small world. As head of security at the hub, his job was extremely important. His two recruits, die-hard soldiers from the Old Rebellion whom Alora had met in her travels and Cyrus had vetted extensively, were now part of their team and helped Cyrus maintain their safety.

Sara and Luke breezed through the doorway, holding hands as they sat beside each other. Even with Lainey's best-laid intentions, the compound's nurse and the kind man had fallen in love. This was why Lainey instructed Sara to keep the infirmary stocked with condoms and had them on recurring order when Alora delivered their rations. If anyone was going to shack up against her mandate, they'd better wear a damn condom. Raising a child was one responsibility the hub just couldn't afford.

"Good morning," Lainey said, addressing her team from her standing position at the head of the table. "As you all know, I revamped the equations yesterday, and Zach tested them. Theoretically, they work."

Zach gave an affirmative nod with his dirty-blond head. "I ran them through the computer model, and they look good. I think we can plug them into the Sphere and give it a go with an apple."

The Sphere was Lainey's masterpiece: the circular machine made of lasers and whirling metal bars that comprised her time machine. It was her life's purpose and a marvel of science and technology. Oh, and it didn't work at all. Yet.

Pushing away her self-doubt, she nodded. "Good. Let's go with the apple, and if that works, we'll try one of the garden cats."

"Or we could try one of the birds that always caw outside my window each morning," Claire suggested, her expression pleading to Lainey not to put the felines in jeopardy.

"We can't use anything that has the ability to fly, Claire, and you know it. We'll just have to get it right so we don't harm Puss in Boots or Garfield," she said, referring to the names Claire had bestowed upon the little beasts that chased the chickens behind the compound.

"Fine," Claire said, crossing her arms over her ample breasts, covered by a t-shirt that read *Heavy Metal is Dead. Rust in Peace.* It had been one of Lainey's mother's favorite shirts, and Claire had thought the corny science joke so hilarious, Lainey had gifted it to her years ago. Shoulders shrugged under Claire's dyed shoulder-length hair. "I just don't want to be a cat murderer."

"Let's remember that the goal is to place a *person* in the machine. Namely, Luke. So, it's in our best interests to make sure the Sphere transports everyone and everything correctly. Are we clear?"

"Yes," Claire said softly, her body language softening. "I didn't mean to —"

"It's fine, sweetie," Luke said, reaching across the table. Claire joined her hand with his. "We all have our roles here, and I'm honored to do my job when you all are ready."

Cyrus had discovered Luke lying in a grassy field among several dead soldiers after a bloody battle with the Old Rebellion several years ago. Luke was hours from death, and Cyrus had carried him back to the compound so Sara could attempt to save him. Thankfully, she prevailed. Luke's injuries had left him with a severe limp and the inability to aim or shoot a gun effectively, due to tremors in both hands. Lewis had allowed Luke to stay on one condition: He must be the first person sent through the Sphere once it was fully functional.

Luke had agreed, since he was already halfway in love with Sara, accepting that his future with her wasn't guaranteed. Volunteering to be the first subject for the Sphere was a choice fraught with uncertainty. Lainey couldn't guarantee the man wouldn't perish, or that he would arrive safely to the designated time.

"Thank you, Luke. You have the most important job of all of us. The first person to successfully time travel. It will be the greatest achievement of humankind."

"You're the genius, Lainey," Luke said in his always affable way. "I'm just here to eat Marie's stew and watch you do science. And to cherish my beautiful wife," he added, winking at Sara.

Sara's cheeks turned a delightful shade of red under her short auburn hair. Pursing her lips, she sent him an air kiss.

"Okay, that's enough PDA for today," Lainey said, shooting them a lighthearted wink. "Claire and Zach, meet me at the Sphere in fifteen minutes."

The team dispersed, and Marie approached Lainey, her long white braid swishing across her back. "You didn't eat your breakfast, young lady," the older woman chided. "Here's an egg sandwich for you."

Lainey eyed the plate topped with a steaming sandwich that made her stomach grumble. "I told you I wasn't eating bread anymore, Marie. The carbs migrate directly to my ass."

"Oh, hush," Marie said, waving the plate as Lainey's mouth watered. "I promised your dear father I'd take care of you, and you never eat. Now, put this sandwich in that smart mouth, girl, or I'll stand here all day."

Lainey stared down, since the woman was several inches shorter than her five-foot, eight-inch frame. "I'm guessing you're not going to let this go."

"Damn straight," she said, her smile blinding, even though one of the bicuspids on her upper-right side had vanished long ago. Somehow, the dark space between the teeth was endearing.

Scowling, Lainey picked up the sandwich and took a large bite. Chewing, she regarded the beloved mother figure of the compound. "Those chickens you keep out back make some damn good eggs." The words were slightly garbled, due to bits of food still in her mouth.

Marie chuckled and patted Lainey's face with her wrinkled hand. "They sure do. I made the bread fresh this morning."

"Thank you, Marie," Lainey said, unable to even pretend to be mad at the loving woman. "Did everyone else eat?"

Marie gave a firm nod. "Today's the day, Lainey. I can feel it. You're going to finally get that hunk of metal to work."

"I hope so," Lainey said, stuffing the last of the sandwich in her mouth.

Marie circled around, empty plate in hand, and headed toward the door. "I'll come looking for you at lunch," she called over her shoulder. "You skip too many meals. Not on my watch. I promised your father, all those years ago…"

Her voice trailed off as she disappeared down the hallway. Marie was known to conduct full-blown conversations with herself, so muttering about Lewis as she strode away was nothing new.

Wiping her hands together to rid them of crumbs, Lainey straightened her shoulders and steeled herself to test the Sphere—again. All set for failure, she had to remind herself to remain unemotional for the team. They needed her to be calm and sure. That feat, at least, was something she could control.

Chapter 2

S everal minutes later, Lainey wished Cyrus a good day and locked the menagerie of security devices that lined the entrance of the hub. He and his two soldiers, Ivan and Steven, would spend the day doing surveillance and ensuring the war was far from their home. Marie would unlock them in an hour, when she went outside to do the week's laundry in the nearby river, but having the door secured always made Lainey feel safer somehow.

The hub was built a few feet into the ground for an extra level of security. There was a large foyer inside the entrance, with a few scattered chairs. Exiting the foyer, Lainey walked down the dimly lit hallway, past the conference room on her right, and then the kitchen. Further down was Claire and Zach's small office on the left, and the entrance to her father's office next door. The large kitchen opened to her right, and that ended their communal space. The rest of the hallway was comprised of doors leading to their sleeping chambers.

The entrance to the Sphere room was completely hidden for good reason. No one on Earth, besides the occupants of the Australian hub, knew they housed a time machine on their premises. The lack of scientific understanding that now pervaded the world actually benefitted their intention to keep their efforts a secret. People in their dystopian existence barely understood how to generate basic power, much less the workings of a complex scientific contraption. Yet it was always good to be cautious, and Lewis had built the bunker in the hopes that if the compound was ever seized, the New Establishment would never find the Sphere.

Lainey closed the door labeled "Supply Closet" behind her as she walked through it. A solitary bulb burned above her head, and she placed her palm flat against the wall. The keypad illuminated under her hand before she typed in the code. A green light blinked twice, then she placed the pad of her index finger against the clear plastic, allowing the scanner to record her fingerprint.

A clicking sound emanated in the confined space, and Lainey reached down, grabbing the small chain that appeared to be attached to a metal drain. With a pull, the hatch door swung open, and she climbed down the ladder. Fumbling for the switch against the rocky wall, she flipped it, causing several yellow bulbs to illuminate where they hung from the ceiling.

Claire and Zach descended the ladder, both of them heading to stand behind the console that controlled the Sphere. Lainey stopped in front of her masterpiece, filled with a mixture of anxiety and resolve. Pulling an apple from the pocket of her white lab coat, her hand clenched the fruit so tight it probably bruised.

"You guys ready?" she asked, turning to look at Claire and Zach.

"Equations locked and loaded, boss," Zach said, his face lit by the glowing buttons of the console.

Bracing herself, she ascended the three wooden steps that led to the center of the Sphere and placed the red apple on the cedar stool in the middle of the large circular contraption.

Stepping back out, she absorbed the scene. Three beams of metal, curved into perfect circles, were hinged together on opposite sides. Lainey gave a nod to Zach, who pressed a button on the console. The metal circles made a loud click and began to slowly rotate. They whirled in differing directions, gaining speed as they swirled, creating a vortex with heightened gravity in the middle of the Sphere.

Hundreds of small lasers sat at each of the four corners of the structure, ready to be ignited. Their light would be shot through small mirrors attached to each corner of the Sphere. This would create constant, unending beams of light, causing the space inside the machine to bend. A fuel rod, absconded by Lewis from an abandoned nuclear power plant decades ago, was attached to the base, the zircaloy sheath that encased the uranium preventing any radiation leakage. The bending of time, the creation of extreme gravity, and a jolt of nuclear energy from the fuel rod would create a wormhole, allowing the object or person to travel through space-time to a desired destination and date.

Theoretically, that is.

Lainey gave another nod to Zach, and he pressed the button to ignite the lasers.

Claire came to stand at her side, eyes wide, still awed by the magnificent power the contraption held even though she was a trained scientist.

The sound grew louder as the Sphere gained traction, circular arms now almost indiscernible as they bled into each other with the speed of their movements.

Training her gaze on Zach, Lainey commanded, "Engage the fuel rod."

Zach lifted the clear cover from the largest black button on the console. With his index finger, he depressed the large orb.

Claire grabbed Lainey's forearm, bracing herself with a wide stance as the rocky walls shook. Unable to look away, Lainey watched a small black void appear from oblivion beside the apple. The point of nothingness grew, ready to absorb the fruit and transport it to 2035. And then, in the blink of an eye, it exploded.

"Shut it down!" Lainey yelled over the commotion from the Sphere. "Now!"

Zach flipped the cover, pushed the large red button, and a loud screech sounded as the metal arms began to slow their rotation. Depressing several other buttons, Zach called, "Shutdown mode commenced!"

Seconds seemed like hours as they waited for the machine to slow to a halt. Tamping down her fury, Lainey wiped a chunk of apple off the white lab coat she always wore during their experiments. Once the apparatus creaked to a stop, she muttered a soft curse.

"It's okay, boss," Claire said, placing a conciliatory hand on Lainey's forearm. "That one was better than last week. The wormhole was stable for two point seven seconds. We're getting there."

Lainey sighed and breathed a laugh.

"What?" Claire asked.

"You have apple all over your face."

"Thought something felt strange," Claire joked, wiping the pieces off with her green-nailed fingers. She was a sucker for the homemade nail polish the vendors sold at the compounds and always asked Alora to bring her vials when possible.

"Goddammit," Lainey said, lifting her hands to her temples. Now was not the time for a migraine, but she felt one forming at the understanding she'd failed yet again. Just freaking great.

"Let me and Zach analyze the data," Claire said, her soothing now a full-on rubbing of Lainey's upper arm. "I'm sure we can make some tweaks to the equations and try again tomorrow."

"Sounds good." Lainey massaged her temples. "Bring it to me when you have it."

"Will do."

Angry at the now pounding splinters of pain in her head, Lainey pivoted and climbed out of the bunker to retreat to her office. Once there, she sat at her desk and opened her laptop to inform Nelson of the debacle.

The ability to communicate with the director of the Australian scientific hub was quite a miracle, something Lewis had ensured during their hub's formation. Lewis had given instructions to build EMP-proof generators, cementing the hub's ability to retain and use power. Then, every computer and laptop had been placed in a faraday cage. The cage protected the electronics from the EMP detonation and allowed them to retain their functionality.

Although most of the world lost power after the EMP detonation, the four scientific hubs retained it. Lainey always wondered if that would eventually make them a target, but so far, their hub had been left alone. Alora, their courier and tactical surveyor, who was a master at getting intel out of drunk New Establishment soldiers at watering holes during her missions, always said the evil regime actually reveled in keeping the planet devoid of a power grid. Having electricity allowed people to connect, and nothing was more detrimental to the regime than millions of angry people communicating about destroying them. No, they preferred to keep the world dark and bereft of hope.

Shuddering, Lainey pushed away the desolate thoughts. Logging on to the secure transmission app, she rang Nelson Longwood, the director of the Australian Isle's scientific hub.

The scientist's face appeared onscreen under his afro of dark hair, peppered with white hairs along the sides. Wrinkles marred the brown skin of his forehead, most likely a result of years of furrowing while trying to figure out a particularly difficult equation. He was in his mid-seventies now and had been close to her father.

"How's it going, Little Brainy?" he asked, his tone affectionate and warm.

"Not so good, Nelson. The apple exploded."

"I'm sorry." He shook his head. "The updated equations you sent me looked legit."

"Yeah. Well, there's still something wrong somewhere. I'm going to work on it today and have Zach run them through the models. We have to figure it out at some point. How's everything going down there?"

"It's going," Nelson said, his expression turning pensive. "So far, we've managed to stay unoccupied and unharmed. At night, I hear explosions in the distance, so the war is getting closer. It's only a matter of time until our hub is seized."

A cold jolt of apprehension ran down Lainey's spine. A few months ago, she'd learned that the New Establishment had seized the Indian and Asian scientific hubs. Although Lainey was in communication with them, she hadn't shared her work on time travel. That was only shared with Nelson, and he was the one other person on the planet working in tandem with her to accomplish that goal. He'd built a concomitant Sphere from the schematics Lewis had sent him and often tested his own equations as well as Lainey's. But their work was dangerous, for if the evil regime raided either of their hubs and figured out what they were attempting, they could force Lainey or Nelson to use the Sphere for their own nefarious purposes. Lainey would sacrifice her own life before she let that happen.

"I was going to try the equations you sent me yesterday in our Sphere, but I'll wait for now," Nelson said, interrupting her thoughts. "Send me the updates once you and Zach are done. Lorna and I will do our best to rework them too."

"How's she doing?" Lainey asked. Lorna was Nelson's wife and a brilliant physicist in her own right.

"Good," he said, white teeth glowing as he beamed. "She still puts up with me for some reason."

"Oh, you're a teddy bear, Nelson," Lainey said, winking. "Give her a hug for me."

"Will do," he said.

As his smile faded and his features drew together, Lainey frowned.

"What is it, Nelson?"

The man sighed, running his hand over his face. "If we're raided, I can't protect you. I promised Lewis—"

"Cyrus and his team will protect me. I have the utmost faith in them."

Deep brown eyes scuttled back and forth on the screen as he seemed to struggle to speak. "There are things I should've told you long ago, Little Brainy. If I die before imparting those things to you, I'm not sure my soul will rest."

Lainey's eyebrows drew together, her heartbeat now a palpable thrum in her veins. "What things?" she asked, her voice gravelly.

Nelson shook his head, gaze dropping to the desk below. "We only wanted to keep you safe—"

"Hi, Lainey," Lorna's sweet voice interrupted from behind her husband. Blue eyes and a brilliant smile came into view as she leaned over his shoulder and waved through the screen. "How's it going?"

"Fine," was her terse reply, gaze cemented to Nelson's. "Your husband was about to tell me something of great importance."

"Oh," Lorna said, face contorting into confusion as she stared down at Nelson. "Sorry to interrupt."

"It was nothing," he said, shaking his head, the tension gone from his shoulders as if it never existed. "I've become dramatic in my old age, Lainey—something my wife here reminds me on a daily basis."

"You missed your calling as a soap star, darling," Lorna said, placing a peck on his forehead. "If only we still had TV, you'd make us rich."

"Quiet, woman," he said, chuckling as he grinned.

Lainey watched their interplay, frustrated to have been interrupted in what seemed like a moment of such importance. "Nelson, if you need to speak to me, it's better we do it now. If there's one thing we know, it's that tomorrow is never guaranteed in our world."

"Wow, and *I'm* dramatic?" he asked, breathing a laugh. "It's nothing, Lainey." Standing, he placed his arm around Lorna's shoulders. "Now, if you'll excuse me, I have to go remind my wife who's boss around here. I'll reach out to you tomorrow. Good night."

Lainey could barely say "goodbye" before he tapped the keyboard and ended the transmission. Sitting in the dim office, she rubbed her upper arms as her busy brain recalled every word of their conversation. Comprehending that Nelson had kept secrets from her, she felt a jolt of frustrated alarm. Secrets didn't further their cause but, more importantly, they were dangerous. The Australian hub was the last free science hub besides her own and remained a symbol that the New Establishment hadn't yet secured world domination. If there was any information contrary to that knowledge, or if her people were in danger in any way, she deserved to know. Lainey would protect her family at all costs.

Sitting back in the chair, she massaged her temples, sighing at the firm pressure. Unfortunately, her mind wouldn't be able to process anything until the pounding migraine abated. Initiating the breathing exercises Sara had taught her, she navigated the path of trying to rid herself of the pain.

Chapter 3

Lainey began the next day frustrated and cranky. She'd spent the rest of the previous day tweaking the equations with Claire and Zach. Each small adjustment altered the power output of the lasers they used to bend space and generate the wormhole. If they could determine the correct output, the Sphere would theoretically function flawlessly. After several hours, she'd given in to exhaustion and headed to the privacy of her room. The migraine had softened to a dull hammer, and she'd eventually been able to fall asleep.

Finished with her shower, she padded to her dresser to dig out some clothes. A chill ran down her spine, and her head snapped toward the window. Squinting at the soft light that filtered through the white curtains, she listened, ears perked.

A sudden shift in the light outside the window caught her eye, and Lainey's heart leaped into her throat. Something was moving outside… outside her *room*. Throwing on her worn jeans, t-shirt, and sneakers, she pulled open the bedroom door, only to find Cyrus standing on the other side.

"Something's outside the hub," she said to the man she trusted above all others.

He gave a curt nod. "The men are armed. Take this." Lainey swiped the gun from his outstretched hand.

"Marie…and Claire and Sara. Cyrus, we have to protect them." Fear laced her tone.

His expression was stern yet calm, reassuring her as blood pounded through her shaking body. "They have no idea what you're doing here,

Lainey. To them, you're just a boring scientist. Just focus on reiterating that narrative and making them believe it."

Inhaling a deep breath, she nodded. Sliding the gun into the waistband at her lower back, she straightened her spine and looked him dead in the eye. "Let's go."

He jerked his head in agreement, and they began the trek down the hallway. They reached the front door of the hub, built from thick metal and protected by several locks. Cyrus freed every bolt, one by one, each click making an ominous sound. Once the latches were all unbound, Cyrus gave her a final glance. Pulling the massive contraption, the door opened, and they ascended the few concrete stairs to ground level.

The first thing Lainey noticed was the smell. One of body odor and sweat, pungent but not overly nauseating. She counted approximately twenty men circling the hub's entrance, each with a rifle slung over his shoulder, gripping the hilts as they observed her. They all stood facing the man she assumed was the leader.

In the gloomy light of dawn, she observed his face, as Cyrus stood between them. Craning her neck a bit, Lainey let her eyes roam. A firm jaw, lined with several days' stubble, led to a strong chin below a chiseled nose and deep-set eyes. Gunmetal gray irises were glued to hers as he stood tall, seemingly unfazed by Cyrus's presence. Although the man's build was thick with muscle and several inches over six feet tall, he was still dwarfed by Cyrus' six-foot, six-inch frame.

Slowly, as if not to alarm them, the leader lifted his hand and plucked the toothpick he'd been lazily chewing from between his thick lips. One corner of those lips curved, transforming the man's face into something almost… seductive.

"Hello, Lainey," he said, the gravel in his baritone shooting daggers of warning through her entire body. *Danger*! her mind shouted, although she couldn't be sure if the admonition stemmed from fear or the tiny pricks of awareness that rose in bumps on her skin. Never had she been so sentient of a man's presence. He seemed to ooze an unidentified energy that encircled every vibrating cell in her body.

"I am Dr. Elaine Randolph, Director of the scientific hub of the Eastern American Isle. We have declared neutrality in the war and have nothing of value to offer you."

The man grunted a laugh and arched a dark eyebrow, the same color as the thick, shaggy hair that slightly covered the tips of his ears. Although not long enough to pull into a tail, the man hadn't seen a proper haircut in some time.

"We are more than aware of your neutrality, Dr. Randolph, and have no intention of violating it. Although we hate the New Establishment bastards with a passion, we believe their lack of understanding regarding your compound is what's kept you safe this long. Unfortunately, those days are coming to an end. Have you spoken to Dr. Longwood yet this morning?"

"Nelson would alert me if anything was wrong—"

"Nelson's hub was seized by the New Establishment a few hours ago," the man interrupted. "Your hub is in imminent danger. I suggest you let us help you."

Worry, thick and smothering, pervaded every inch of her body. "How do you know this?"

A muscle in his jaw ticked. "Let me in, and I'll tell you everything, Lainey."

"First of all," she said, stepping around Cyrus. When he stiffened, she placed a reassuring hand on his bicep, squeezing before she turned to face the leader. "My name is Dr. Elaine Randolph, and I expect to be addressed that way. I would suggest you tell me who the hell you are within the next five seconds, before I have my friend here"—she gestured her head toward Cyrus—"extricate the information from you."

Gray eyes narrowed as he placed the toothpick back between his teeth, chewing thoughtfully. "Lewis did say you'd be resistant," he murmured, studying her with a slight smirk on his face, enflaming her annoyance.

"My father died several years ago, and I'm sure he never met you nor discussed me with you. He would've told me. My father told me everything."

His reaction was a sardonic sneer, causing Lainey to dig her nails into her palms to keep from smacking it off his face. "Lewis was a... *complicated* man. I'm sure you understood that. But there was one thing embedded deep in his soul, and that was his love for you." Spitting the toothpick onto the ground, he reached behind him with the hand that wasn't resting on the rifle sitting atop his thick chest.

Behind her, Cyrus ruffled, drawing his Glock from the holster and aiming it between the man's eyes.

"Whoa, buddy," the leader said, holding up his hand, palm facing out. "I'm just reaching for a letter. It's in my back pocket."

"Slowly," Cyrus said, his tone laced with steel. "I'd really like to eat breakfast before I plant a bullet in someone's brain today."

The man breathed a laugh. "Was just thinking how hungry I am myself. See, my men here, we haven't had a suitable meal or a bath or, hell, anything proper in several weeks. Oh, and I like their chances against you better than yours against me. Twenty-two to one doesn't usually work out that well. But I'll go slow. Relax."

Cyrus grunted, and Lainey could almost feel the tension radiating from his body.

The man reached into his back pocket and pulled out a piece of folded paper. The parchment had faded to a dull yellow, and Lainey could tell it had been folded many times over.

"You can take it," the leader said, hand outstretched to her, the letter between his fingers. "It's not a bomb. Well, not the kind that blows up anyway."

Frozen, she studied the man, frustrated she was unable to get a read on him. "Who are you?" she asked, wishing her voice didn't sound so enervated.

"Captain Hunter Rhodes, at your service, ma'am," he said with a nod, both condescending and respectful—if that was possible. "I'm the leader of this battalion. We're all soldiers, left over from the first war. Every one of us was a ranking officer of the Old Rebellion. Although we lost that war, we still believe in the cause. Still believe in freedom. We're not quite sure the Insurgency or the New Establishment stand for those things, so our allegiance is to ourselves. Your father and I knew each other for many years before his death. He asked that I deliver this to you if I believed you to be in imminent danger, and not before. I'm sorry, but I believe that time has come." He shook the letter at her again. "Read it. Go inside if you want. We'll be here when you're ready."

With shaking fingers, Lainey grasped the letter, feeling tiny jolts at the points of her skin where their fingers brushed. Stepping back, she rubbed the faded parchment in her hand as she contemplated him.

"Captain Rhodes, please don't take this the wrong way, but there's no way in hell you knew my father. I insist you leave this compound at once."

Something akin to sympathy crossed his expression, the gentler emotion making him look ruggedly handsome under the brightening sky. "Go inside and read it, Lainey," he said softly, as steely irises urged her to follow his command. "I'll be here when you're ready to discuss it. I don't mean to sound harsh, but time is of the essence."

Hating that this unwelcome stranger was directing her to do anything, she lifted her chin. "I don't want any movement around the compound. Stay here until I return. I will be sending our soldiers out to backup Cyrus." Pivoting, she gave Cyrus a stern nod, hoping the infuriating man behind her understood that *she* gave the damn orders around here.

After plodding down the steps, she shut the door behind her, clicking the largest deadbolt in place.

"What do you need from us, Lainey?" Steven asked, Ivan at his side. The two soldiers Cyrus had recruited from the Old Rebellion were his right-hand men and extremely competent.

"You saw everything on the cameras, right?" she asked.

They nodded in unison.

"Go outside and back up Cyrus. I need to read this. Lock the door behind you." Clutching the note in her hand, she watched the soldiers trail through the entrance of the hub. Gathering her bearings, she sucked in a deep breath.

Wanting to be in a place she felt secure, she trod to her office. It had been her father's office for so long, the place where she'd sat on his lap while he taught her science and calculated difficult equations. A safe place where they had shared so much laughter and love.

First, she needed to confirm. A scientist's first duty was to verify and corroborate. Reaching for the mouse, she slid it over the desk, causing the screen to brighten. The secure message app was flashing, each slow blink casting a nail of anxiety into her heart. Opening the program, she watched Nelson's face appear. Filled with dread, she clicked the arrow atop his beloved face.

"They're here, Lainey," Nelson said, terror evident in his voice. "Tanner is here with two hundred troops. He's at the door, demanding entrance. I managed to destroy our Sphere, as we'd practiced in our drills. I don't think they'll realize what we've been up to." He glanced worriedly at the closed door of his office. "It won't be long before Eli comes for you. Your father put some protections in place for you—ones I won't detail on this channel since it will soon be overtaken. Trust your gut, Lainey. Be strong and remember that Lorna and I love you."

A knock pounded at his office door, and Lainey could see uniformed men entering. A wave of fear crossed Nelson's face, and then the screen went dark. Holding her fist to her trembling lips, Lainey told herself to remain calm. Nelson had one of the most brilliant minds on the planet. Tanner Cross, the leader of the Australian New Establishment, needed him alive in order to obtain the most from his knowledge. They must've finally begun to comprehend the advantages they could gain by utilizing science in their quest to rule the earth.

Taking the minute she needed, Lainey sent a prayer to the universe, asking numerous gods that she professed not to believe in to ensure Nelson and Lorna's safety. Then, she picked up the faded parchment, preparing herself to digest the information it withheld.

Too restless to sit, she stood firm in the middle of the dim room, the only light shining from her father's old lamp on the desktop. It had been a gift from Nelson. The inscription read, *May the light shine until all your answers are illuminated.*

With trembling hands, Lainey unfolded the paper. Tears welled in her eyes as she read her father's handwriting:

Lainey,

If you are reading this letter then I am gone, and you are still stuck in the timeline that I tried so hard to erase. For that, my darling girl, I will never forgive myself. Leaving the burden of saving the world to you was selfish, although you never saw it that way. You have such a bright energy and a giving heart. This, my child, is why I know you will succeed.

Hunter is a friend. I know this will come as a shock to you since I never spoke of him, but it was imperative that I kept our connection secret. He is no ally to the Insurgency or the New Establishment, but is a strong, loyal soldier and has committed to protecting you and ensuring you succeed in your quest to solve time travel.

There is something Hunter craves with his soul, and I promised him you would grant his request in return for helping you to complete your mission. I won't write it in this letter, but he will certainly tell you upon his arrival. His need to accomplish his goal makes him an ally, and he is a powerful one. He knows many secrets that the New Establishment wants to keep hidden. Learn them, and together, I believe you will succeed.

In the event that you think this letter was written under duress or forged, I have left a corresponding one folded in the pages of Cosmos upon the office bookshelf, for never was my little scientist anything if not cynical. Nelson is also aware of my interactions with Hunter, but I've sworn him to

secrecy until you mention to him that you read this letter. All my love to you, my beautiful daughter. The only thing I did right in my long, failure-ridden life was to love you and your mother.
Dad

A sob broke from Lainey's throat as she read the words. After reading the message numerous times, she threw it on the desk and rushed to the bookshelf. Gulping in air, as she struggled to breathe, she yanked the hardback book from the shelf. The cover read "Cosmos" above the name Carl Sagan, the words overlaying a picture of the Milky Way galaxy. Opening the book, she frantically flipped the pages, a resulting airstream flitting through the air, cold against her cheeks.

Emitting a gasp, Lainey watched the folded note fall to the carpeted floor. As the book fell from her limp hands, she slowly lowered to the ground, resting on her knees. Lifting the paper, she unfolded it, careful and wary. The letters inside were scrawled in her father's deep cursive:

Lainey,
Please trust Hunter. He will ensure your safety. I love you, darling girl.
Dad

Pain, thick and metallic, invaded every pore of her body and bud of her tongue as she buried her face in her hands. Her father, whom she had trusted above all others, had made a secret pact with a rebel battalion leader without her knowledge. How many other times had he lied to her? Who else had he made clandestine arrangements with? Settling onto the carpet, she rested her forearms on her bent knees, contemplating.

Lainey had been under the impression her father told her *everything*. In return, she'd never kept one thought or secret from him—except for her disastrous experience with Dalton, from which she'd learned a huge lesson. Her father had been her most cherished person upon the Earth. Although she'd loved her mother desperately and cared immensely for her family at the hub, her father was her confidant. Her rock. The one person she trusted above all others. Icy rivulets of betrayal swam through her veins as the very notion of the word "trust" was shattered in her soul.

The betrayal turned to anger as she fumed at the notion her father had made a secret promise on her behalf. Lewis would've understood how exasperating that would be to Lainey, as he knew better than anyone how strong-willed she was. Searching her brain, she tried to compute the resentment, knowing it was a waste of time and energy. Still, it burned, and she struggled with the warring emotions inside.

An eternity later, she felt a comforting hand cup her shoulder.

"Sweet girl," Marie said, the woman's frail skin stroking Lainey's hair. "I know it hurts, but he did it for your own good."

Lainey's eyes narrowed. "You knew?" she asked, irritation lacing her tone.

"Yes," Marie said, nodding as she trained her guilty gaze upon the worn carpet. "I promised I wouldn't say anything. Lewis had his ways of keeping us safe."

"How could he promise something of me that I never agreed to?" Lainey asked, shaking her head.

"Once Lewis decided on something, there was no changing his mind. You know that best of all since you inherited his stubbornness," she said, her sweet face awash with sympathy.

"Can I chime in here?" Claire asked, sliding her head around the door.

"Come on in," Lainey sighed, realizing her moment of reflection was over.

"I'm really sorry, Lainey. I'm sure you're pissed," Claire said, tentatively approaching, "but the Australian hub has been seized, and I'm honestly glad Captain sexy-scruff is here. I saw him on the cameras. I mean, if we have to be protected by someone, at least he's easy on the eyes."

All was still for a moment until a laugh burst from Lainey's throat. "Thank god for you, Claire," she said, sighing as she contemplated the gravity of their new reality. "How would I get through this craphole of a world without your sense of humor?"

"I mean," Claire said, gaze darting to the ceiling as she tapped her lip with her finger, "it would be pretty hard. I'm the only one who keeps us sane."

"And I'm the only one who keeps us fed," Marie chimed in. "Speaking of, it's time to get breakfast on the table for the crew, Lainey. I know this is a shock, but we need to get moving. You've got to figure out what to do, and I won't let you do it on an empty stomach."

Sitting back, Lainey observed the two women who were so dear to her. "Okay," she said, running her hands through her hair. "I guess I need to figure out what the hell to do here. I need to have a chat with Captain

Rhodes, but he's got another thing coming if he thinks he's giving orders around here. This is *my* hub, and I run the show. Nothing is more important than finishing my work."

"Damn straight," Marie said, rising and extending her hand to Lainey. "Well, c'mon, girl," she said, shaking her hand in Lainey's face. "Let's get to it then."

Grabbing onto the woman's hand, Lainey let her friends pull her to her feet. After securing both of her father's notes in his desk drawer, she straightened her spine, steeling herself for the day, for in their world, not one day could be wasted. With resolve, she stalked from the office.

Chapter 4

H unter Rhodes stood outside the bunker, doing something he rarely did.

He was waiting.

Hunter had met with Lewis several times in the years before the man's death, and Lewis had informed him that Elaine would be resistant to his help. The older man would always give a wistful smile when he spoke of how stubborn and cynical his daughter was. Perhaps that was the only trajectory her life could have, being that she was bred to save the world. A daunting task to put on the woman's slim shoulders.

But Lewis had also spoken of her kindness and loyalty, her intelligence and diligence in solving the conundrum that was time travel. Hunter was determined to help her accomplish the task, for he firmly believed his future was now inexorably tied with hers.

"No sightings of any New Establishment soldiers or spies within forty miles, sir," his second-in-command said, interrupting his thoughts. "Should we set up camp?"

"Let's wait until Dr. Randolph gives us the okay, Scott," Hunter said, rubbing the back of his neck. "Although we could overpower her in minutes, I want this to stay friendly. Let's give her the appearance of control, if nothing else."

"Aye," Scott said. "I'll inform the troops."

"Thanks," Hunter muttered, his gaze traveling to the wide metal entrance of the hub, which creaked as it was pulled open. Elaine walked up the stairs, chin thrust high, spine straighter than a line drawn against a wooden ruler. Hunter's lips curved into a smile of admiration. She was a tough cookie—something he was grateful for. Weak souls didn't make it far in this world.

She came to stand before him, tall and strong. Hunter guessed her eyes would've been categorized as hazel, but the swirling colors within the amber hue made them so much more. They reminded him of the honey-colored sap that used to ooze from the maple trees on his grandfather's farm, all those decades ago when he was a child. Flecks of dark yellow sliced through the mahogany, causing Hunter to wonder if he'd ever seen the same combination in another's eyes. It was doubtful. They were absolutely stunning.

"I have confirmed that you knew my father," she said, the slight antagonism in her tone reminding him to stay calm so he wouldn't stir her ire. "He says that you want something from me in return for your protection. We have a lot to discuss. I'm prepared to invite you inside."

"Thank you—"

"But," she said, lifting a finger as she interrupted him, "I need to make one thing completely clear. I am the leader of this hub, Captain. I give the orders, and you report to me. A team cannot function adequately when there are two commanders. I need your allegiance and declaration that you accept these terms. If not, we are at an impasse, and you and your soldiers can get off my land."

Hunter pulled the stack of toothpicks from his pocket and thrust one between his teeth, chewing as he contemplated her. He'd picked up the habit years ago when he stopped smoking. Cigarettes from unknown vendors were often filled with nefarious substances and he'd finally beaten the horrid addiction, but the oral fixation never ceased.

"That's an uncivilized habit," Elaine said, face scrunching with disgust.

Hunter breathed a laugh. "We don't all grow up as princesses of fancy scientific hubs. Sorry to disappoint you, duchess."

Those glorious eyes narrowed, causing his smile to deepen. Hunter had a feeling sparring with the intractable woman was going to be a hundred shades of fun. How interesting. He hadn't had fun in so long. An image breezed through his mind of smaller hands in his, clutching, as soft, feminine laughter permeated the air…

Pushing the thought away, Hunter inhaled a deep breath. "As you know, my men are watching, Lainey. I can't concede command to you. It would usurp the entire chain of command in our unit."

He held up a hand when she opened her mouth to argue. "But," he said, giving her a glare, "I will concede that you are the leader of this hub. We are here to protect you and ensure you solve time travel. We serve at your discretion. Now, if that's settled, I'd really like to sit down and discuss our intel with you. The New Establishment has finally turned their sights on the hubs. Lewis was terrified this would eventually happen."

Her mahogany eyebrows drew together, full although she didn't seem to be wearing a stitch of makeup. "We have declared neutrality and are so far off the grid that it's ensured our safety so far."

"There are many private channels and enterprises you're not aware of, Lainey. And if I recall, the Australian hub is also quite remote. The New Establishment craves power and they'll stop at nothing to get it, hence our presence here." He gestured toward his men, all watching their interplay as they each struggled to define the terms of their alliance.

Growing frustrated at her continued silence, Hunter felt his tone grow brisk as he said, "Look, lady, I'm here because of a commitment I made to your father—"

"And because you want something from me in return," she said, arching a brow.

"And because I want something from you in return," he conceded. "But I'm not a saint. If you're going to be this antagonistic during our… *acquaintance*, I'll just pack up my men and leave. Let's see how you do when Eli shows up on your doorstep and my men are gone. Is that what you want?"

The woman's shiver was visible at the mention of Eli Hernandez. The leader of the New Establishment on the Eastern American Isle had a reputation for being cold and unyielding. A tyrant who would stop at nothing to become a supreme dictator and oppressor.

Sighing deeply, Lainey rubbed her forehead. "I welcome your protection and agree to your terms. You serve at *my* discretion, so that we can achieve our common goal."

His grin was back, causing Hunter to wonder if he'd smiled this much in a continuous loop…ever? Something about the prickly woman amused him. Extending his hand, he offered it to her. "Should we make it official?" he asked.

Her gaze was wary as she contemplated his hand. Eventually, she slid her palm over his, the smooth flesh a contrast to his callused skin. As they shook, their grips firm and determined, Hunter was overcome with the feeling this moment would turn out to be one of the most momentous of his life. He'd always been a strong believer in fate and understood the significance of great moments of importance.

Once their alliance was formed, Lainey removed her hand, sweeping it through the air toward the men. "They can set up camp around the perimeter of the hub. We have two outside showers that Marie uses when she's spent too long in the chicken coop. Your men can use those. We'll supply you with soap and toiletries. We'll also supply you with food, but don't expect much. It's basically eggs, stew, and bread around here. We live off the land and harvest what we can."

"We're grateful for anything you can provide," Hunter said. Turning to Scott, he gave the command for the soldiers to make camp around the compound. When they were set, he trained his gaze on Lainey. "Ready when you are. Should we go inside?"

Her nostrils flared as she studied him. Giving a brisk nod, she pivoted and headed down the stairs. Deciding that he should follow her, Hunter descended into the scientific hub of the Eastern American Isle.

Chapter 5

Lainey led the way to the break room, determined to retain the upper hand. The arrogant captain might now be her ally, but he certainly hadn't earned her trust. Breezing through the doorway, she motioned for him to sit in the chair to her right, situated at a round table.

Hunter eyed Cyrus, whose large frame was already stuffed into the wooden chair at her left, and sat down across from him. Claire trailed through the door, notebook and pencil in hand.

"Hey guys," she said, circling them to stand beside the open chair across from Lainey. "I'm Claire,"—she thrust her hand toward Hunter—"and you must be Captain McHotty Pants. Nice to meet you." White teeth glowed from her brilliant smile.

"Hello, Claire," Hunter said, shaking her hand. "It's so nice to actually receive a warm welcome from someone around here."

"Oh, we're happy to have fresh blood, believe me," Claire said, lowering into the chair. "Let the boys know, the window that looks out to the showers from the back storeroom is placed high enough that Marie and I can only see their chests. Promise." Giving a sly smile, she traced an X with her finger across her thin sweatshirt.

"Okay." Lainey shot her a glare. "We've got a lot to dissect here. Let's get to it. Claire will take notes, and Cyrus is here as my head of security, to ensure your men and his are on the same page."

Claire lifted the back of her hand to her mouth and whispered loudly to Hunter, "She only *seems* super-serious. I promise, once she relaxes, she's really great."

"Enough, Claire," Lainey said. Gathering her bearings, she trained her gaze on Hunter's. "First, I want to discuss whether you believe the New Establishment has discovered I'm trying to solve time travel. If so, I can only imagine they wish to seize the Sphere and use it for their nefarious reasons. They probably want to go back in time and create a world in their image from the very beginning."

"I don't know yet," Hunter said, "but we can't rule it out. If they do want to go back and alter time, they could take over the hub and systematically torture and kill everyone you love until you turn over your work to them. Then, they'd kill you. I'm sorry to be so blunt, but we don't have the luxury of sugarcoating here."

Lainey's eyes trailed to the surface of the table, and she traced her fingers over it, realizing the moment was substantial, and her life would never be the same. Whether she liked it or not, the hub had moved from inconspicuous anomaly to target in the span of a day.

"I'm a fan of bluntness, Captain Rhodes."

"All right then," Hunter said, swiping his fingers through his hair. The color was an amalgamation—not quite black, not quite brown—and a few tresses at his temples were just beginning to gray. It should've made him look old. Instead, it made him look incredibly handsome and wise. Small wrinkles extended from the corners of his eyes, more pronounced when he smiled, as he'd seemed intent on doing during his assessment of her when they'd spoken outside. It infuriated her that the man would take her anything but seriously. She was the foremost physicist on the planet and held more intelligence in her little finger than he probably did in his whole being. Jerk.

Smart people don't belittle others, Lainey. The second they do, they become ignorant. Her mother's sweet voice filtered through her head, reminding her that extreme intelligence didn't equate to greatness. Her parents had always instilled the belief that compassion, loyalty, and honor were all vastly more important than genius. Clutching onto that, she resumed listening to the man who'd shown up only an hour ago and proceeded to upend her entire life.

"Obviously, the most important thing is that you get your contraption to work," Hunter continued. "Where are you at in the process?"

She gave him a sardonic smile while rapidly blinking her eyelids. "Yes, because it's so easy to travel through time. You know what?" she said, snapping her fingers. "I think I'll just walk into the Sphere room and command the machine to work. Enough stalling, right?"

His resulting glare was acerbic. "I understand your undertaking is massive, Lainey. I guess what I should've asked is, how can I help you solve time travel faster?"

The question was so benign and asked in such good faith that it pissed her off. The man seemed incapable of reacting to her jibing. Although it was irrational, she wanted him to be as off-balance as she.

Attempting to get a rise out of him, she said, "My name is Dr. Elaine Randolph. You can call me Dr. Randolph or Elaine. Only my friends call me Lainey. Are we clear?"

Claire muttered a whispered, "*Oh snap!*" from across the table as Hunter's eyes drilled into hers. Then, those infuriating lips curved again. Damn it! Never had she seen a more mocking expression—or one on a face so ruggedly attractive. Deciding he was a bastard, Lainey gritted her teeth and tamped down the urge to tell him to go to hell.

"I understand, *Elaine*," he said, eyes rolling slightly as he sat forward in his chair. "What do you need to get that heap of metal working?"

Exhaling a huge breath, she sat back, feeling defeated. "The equations all make sense on paper. Unfortunately, we haven't been able to generate a wormhole that retains stability long enough to create a portal to send any object or person to 2035."

Hunter nodded, the hunch of his shoulders contemplative. "Your father informed me that you only have one nuclear fuel rod here at the hub. If I could supply you with more, do you think that would help generate the energy needed?"

Grinding her teeth at the reminder Lewis had secretly met with the man numerous times, she shook her head. "The fuel rod we have is enough to create the portal back to 2035. I only need to create it a few times. Once to test the apple, once for the cat, once for Luke, and once for myself and my team. When everyone at the hub has been transported back to 2035, I'll close the wormhole, and the machine will no longer exist, as this thread of space-time will be erased after I prevent my grandfather's actions."

"How many will you be transporting back?"

"Ten, counting our test subject Luke, Cyrus and his two men, my scientific team, Marie, Sara, and our courier and tactical surveillant Alora."

"They're all currently on the compound?"

She tilted her head. "All but Alora. She's out performing reconnaissance and gathering supplies at the moment. We expect her back any day. She's been gone for months, and her missions rarely last longer than that."

"What intel do you have on the New Establishment?" Cyrus asked.

Hunter laced his fingers together atop the table. "They're systematically taking over each settlement and compound on every isle. The Insurgency is doing a good job of fighting back, but with their lack of supplies and technology, it's only a matter of time before they're defeated. Solera and Terrum remain unoccupied, but the war grows closer to their borders every day," he said, referencing the largest two communes on the Eastern American Isle.

"Why don't you fight with the Insurgency?" Cyrus asked.

Hunter's brows converged as he studied his thumbs, circling them over his clenched hands. "The New Establishment has seized communes on many isles too easily. I think the Insurgency has defectors in their ranks who are working with the New Establishment to ensure their success in exchange for guaranteed safety once they rule the world. Sadly, I don't think the New Establishment leaders plan to honor those agreements, but in times of war, people make decisions they deem best."

"So, you'd rather be a rebel? Someone who fights on the fringes with allegiance to no one?" Lainey asked.

White teeth peeked from behind Hunter's lips where he bit the full bottom one as if tamping his grin. "If I'm not mistaken, *Dr. Randolph*, I just pledged my allegiance to you. Outside, when we shook hands. I'm sure I remember us agreeing to terms. Do we need to pull it up on the security cameras—?"

"I remember *exactly* what was said," she replied, struggling to keep the frustration from her tone. "I'm just clarifying your position."

He studied her, unmoving, for a long while before the features of his face fell into a pensive expression. "I don't much enjoy fighting for other men or causes anymore. I've learned it's best to fight for myself, so that's what I choose to do. My soldiers are good men, and I expect them to be treated with respect. Each one of them is willing to die for the rest, and now, they're ready to die for you. It's an honorable stand."

Lainey felt the contrition in her bones before it even registered in her mind. Her father had made a pact with this man to keep her safe, and he was here to honor that promise. Although she hated the circumstances, her ungratefulness was unwarranted. Realization washed over her as she recognized she was directing her frustration toward Hunter instead of the actual culprit: her father. The handsome captain was an easy target but he didn't deserve her ire. Although she didn't trust him and vowed to remain wary, she would be unwise to not take advantage of his skills, soldiers, and intel.

"Thank you," she said, her tone devoid of irritation or sarcasm toward Hunter for the first time. "We appreciate your help. In the interest of accomplishing our goal, I need to get to work for the day. We have some new equations we need to try in the Sphere."

"Fair enough," Hunter said. "Cyrus, I'd like to introduce your men to mine and send them out on some small scouting missions together, so they can begin to trust each other."

"Agreed," Cyrus said. "I have two soldiers who trained with the Old Rebellion, Steven and Ivan. We'll be outside at eleven hundred hours to meet your soldiers."

"I could supply you with a list of my men if it will help you learn their names and ranks quicker," Hunter said.

"That won't be necessary," was Cyrus's gruff reply. "I have a photographic memory and never forget a name, face, or rank."

"Well, all right then. I'm going to head out and grab one of those outdoor showers calling my name. Don't look at my back too hard," Hunter said, winking at Claire. "I've got some nasty scars."

"Ohhhh," she said with excitement, causing Lainey to imagine heart symbols appearing in place of her eyeballs.

"You forgot to tell us," Lainey said, attempting to steer the meeting back on the right track before Claire started drooling.

"Excuse me?" Hunter asked, shifting his gaze from Claire to her.

"What you want from me. What's so important that you secretly met with my father and pledged your protection and loyalty to him and to me?"

"Oh," Hunter said, the smile evaporating as he nodded slightly. "Yes, I guess that would be significant."

"Okay?" Lainey said, giving him an irritated glare as he sat silent. "So, what can I do for you, Captain Rhodes?"

"Well, Dr. Randolph, it's actually very simple." Sitting taller in the chair, he shot her a pointed look. "I need you to transport me back to 2063 so I can save my wife from being murdered."

And then, as if he'd asked her to pass the salt instead of dropping an epic bomb, he stood, gave her a nod, and stalked from the chamber.

Chapter 6

Hunter spent the rest of the morning checking on his men, ensuring their tents were stable around the hub and that their spirits were high. They all seemed fine, secure in their orders and their duty to protect the compound. Thankful for their loyalty, he set up his own tent directly outside Lainey's bedroom window. The men had established a perimeter around the hub, but he'd instructed them to leave that spot open. He took his vow to protect the duchess of the compound seriously. It was imperative that she succeed.

Once his tent was set, he pulled off his tattered clothes, excited to be in a stable spot with a nearby river where they could do laundry. To state it plainly, he and his men smelled like the bad side of a pit bull.

With a towel wrapped around his waist, Hunter located the outdoor shower, ecstasy thrumming in his veins as he stepped underneath. The water was cold but it was clean, and that was more than he'd had in a while. Using the last of his shampoo rations, he washed his hair and body, grinning to himself as he wondered if Claire was sneaking a peek. Unconcerned, he slid his hands over his nakedness. Modesty was a luxury that had left him long ago.

Once clean, he wrapped the towel around his waist and dressed in his tent. His ears perked as he heard a rustling by the door. Unzipping it, he pulled back the fabric, only to find a morose-looking Dr. Elaine Randolph standing outside.

"What's up?" he asked, understanding he'd opened a can of worms she most certainly was here to grill him about.

"I…um." She glanced at the ground. "Can we go somewhere and talk for a minute? There's a thicket back there with some chairs where I sit when I need fresh air."

"Yeah," he said. "Would you rather I put on some clothes first?"

Amber irises darted over his chest, covered with a smattering of dark hair and a fair amount of scarring.

Lainey cleared her throat. "Yes, please." Nose slightly upturned, she looked like a regal queen trying not to be offended at his state of near-nakedness. Interesting. Was Dr. Randolph a prude?

"Okay," he said, taking pity on her as her cheeks enflamed from peach, to pink, to red. "Give me a sec. I know the clearing."

Lainey paused, scrutinizing him, and Hunter realized his slip. He shouldn't possess knowledge of the spots where she sought solace. Mentally cursing, he arched a brow.

"Or I could just come like this…" He reached for the hem of the towel, ready to yank it from his hips.

"Fully clothed will be fine," she said, giving him a glare. Chin lifted, she scurried off, spurring a huffed laugh from his throat.

After throwing on black pants, a t-shirt, and boots—his standard technical gear—he walked past the showers situated behind the hub and through the thicket of bushes. Lainey sat in the high-backed wooden chair, eyes closed, the back of her head resting on the seat. She looked so peaceful—young, even—and it was evident the spot held reverence for her.

"This is where my father and I would sit and discuss our theories," she murmured, lids still shut as she gestured toward the open seat beside her. "Parallel universes, different versions of space-time, was Carl Sagan the greatest scientific communicator who ever lived? That sort of stuff."

"Sounds heavy," Hunter said, lowering into the seat.

"Actually, the opposite," she replied, opening her eyes and genuinely smiling at him for the first time. It caused his heart to skip, if only a beat. "It's when I felt most connected to him. We shared a love of science that was embedded in our souls. It was our religion. Our reason to be, so to speak. It's one of the purest phenomena I've ever felt."

"I understand that. I felt that with someone once."

She sighed, soft and breathy. "So, you had a wife."

Hunter tilted his head. "I had a wife."

"And she was killed by the New Establishment."

He felt the muscle tick in his jaw. "Yes."

Silence stretched between them, connecting them as they mulled until words could take its place.

"I won't ask for details. I'm a very private person and understand the need to hold things inside." Turning her head so that her temple rested against the chairback, she continued, "But do you understand what you're really asking here? It's not as simple as you think."

Hunter's eyes darted between hers. Inhaling a large breath, he let his gaze rove to the thick tree in front of him, the intensity of her stare too deep. "I discussed it at length with your father. I understand my success is most likely impossible." Cementing his gaze to hers, he said, "But I have to try, Elaine. I won't forgive myself if I don't."

She blinked rapidly, and Hunter could almost see the gears shifting in her brain. "There's a paradox that occurs with time travel that's called the 'fate paradox.' Essentially, it states that if a person is meant to die at a certain moment of their life, nothing can prevent that from happening. So, for example, if I had a friend who died in a fire in 2050, and I wanted to go back and save her, I could save her from the fire, but she would then soon perish in a different accident. Does that make sense?"

"Yes," Hunter said. "You're assuming Kara's predetermined date to die was April 9, 2063."

"It's a possibility. It's hard to comprehend, especially for a scientist like me who doesn't believe in fate or religion or any of that pish-posh. But," she said, holding a finger in the air, "I do believe in energy, and the fact it can neither be created nor destroyed. Each person's soul has been calculated to carry a small amount of energy. Therefore, I can plausibly make the argument that a person's soul, and the energy it contains, is predetermined to leave the Earth at a certain time to allow the entrance of an equal amount of energy. Perhaps a baby that's born at that moment, or something else to the like." Lifting her eyebrows, she asked, "Am I being an over-explanative scientist at the moment?"

Hunter laughed. "No, I get it. There's a possibility that no matter what I do, she'll still die. I've lived through that before, and it would be devastating to do it again. But I owe it to her to try."

She nodded. "I understand. I really do. If I could go back and save my father, I'd do it a thousand times over."

"Do you believe his death was predetermined?"

"I do," she said with a conceding shrug. "He was sick, and it was time for his soul to leave this part of the universe. And still believing that, I would try."

"But you have a more important mission."

"Yes. I have to go back to 2035 and prevent my grandfather from detonating the apocalypse."

"But your grandfather died that day as well. How can you ensure you'll still be born if he perishes in your attempts to stop him?"

"Ah, the perplexity of time travel," she said, squeezing the flat arms of the seat with her hands. "Since he died in this reality but still, I was born, scientific theory states I would still be born in the new reality. My father and mother were already married when he set off the nukes and they still had me. I should be okay. But," she said, giving a slight shrug, "I can't guarantee it. Honestly, I have absolutely no idea what will happen."

"That must be tough for a smart-mouthed scientist like you who has all the answers."

Lainey shot him a look.

"Sorry," he said, holding up his hands and chuckling. "Just an observation."

"What I *think* will happen," she said, glaring at him as she continued, "is that once I stop him, it will create a new thread of space-time. One where the Speaker of the House will assume the Presidency, and President Randolph and his supporters will spend the rest of their lives in prison. The Speaker's name was Anita Rohan, and she was said to be an amazing public servant with a kind and generous heart. Hopefully, she will guide the world to greatness and live in a thread where this dystopian future never existed."

"And you'll be stuck there, in a time that isn't yours."

"Yes," she said, her expression thoughtful. "It's what would happen to you too."

"What do you mean?"

"If you go back to save your wife. You're twelve years older now. You'll go back as your present self. Even if you save her, she would continue her life in the new timeline with that younger version of Hunter, not the version you are today."

"Yes, your father explained that to me. I recognize I'll be saving Kara for my younger self. I accept that. I can live a good life off the land, somewhere secluded and quiet. I don't need much. I've already had everything a man can dream of. Although, maybe I could have a conversation with my younger self about not being such a dick about the little things. I used to get so pissed at Kara when she'd forget to clean her hair out of the bathtub drain. Now, I'd give anything to see that wet gob of hair." His smile was sweet but sad, spurring a flare of compassion in her cynical heart.

"You obviously can't approach or converse with that version of yourself. You do know that, right? Having direct contact with a younger version of yourself would completely destroy the space-time continuum."

"Got it, Doc Brown," he said, giving her a good-natured salute.

"*Back to the Future*," she said, surprised he knew the movie. "One of my Dad's favorites."

"My grandfather was a huge fan. He raved about Marty McFly and Doc. Seems like we have our own real-life version. He'd be tickled all shades of pink."

Lainey laughed, surprised the hardened soldier liked old time travel movies. What other secrets did he hold inside? Between that and the bombshell revelation about his wife, he'd already shocked the hell out of her.

"Well," she said, rubbing her palms over her jean-clad thighs, "looks like we're a bunch of martyrs, resigned to go back and change history and live in a world that isn't ours."

"Looks like it."

The song of a nearby bird blanketed them as they contemplated the gravity of their future choices.

Finally, Lainey said, "You know, I'm not a field trip director here. I hadn't really planned on sending any other people back besides my team. I can't guarantee your safety. It's possible you might die on the trip back. Wormholes are extremely unstable."

Reaching over, he grasped her hand with his. "I won't sue you, Dr. Randolph. Rest assured."

She gave a *pfft* and waved her free hand through the air. "You and what lawyers? I don't think our isle has had a functional courthouse since 2038."

"Then you're safe." Releasing her hand, he gave her a half-grin. "Please, Elaine. I know your father made this promise for you, but I need your help. Please, do this for me."

She stood, rotating to face him, and placed her hands on her hips. Hunter gazed up at her, unable to not notice the small swells of her breasts under her brown V-neck t-shirt. She was tall and lanky—so different from Kara, who'd been petite and curvy. And yet there was a feminine air to her, something earthy and undecipherable, causing him to imagine what secrets her body held. Was she a quiet lover? Did she moan or scream? Whoever had those answers was a lucky man.

"I'll send you back, Captain Rhodes, but I'll caution you with this warning. Be careful what you wish for. Changing the past isn't for the faint of heart. It comes with a thousand unanswered questions and a lifetime of loneliness. Take time to think about it before you commit. In the meantime, I've got to get the damn Sphere working if we have any hope at all. With that, I'll leave you to your men." With a firm tilt of her head, she breezed past him and headed back toward the hub.

Hunter sat for a moment contemplating the magnitude of their discussion. He was so close to achieving a goal he'd spent years contriving. Intent on maintaining his commitment to protect Elaine while she worked, he stood and stretched, readying his muscles for the day. Glancing at his watch and noting it was almost eleven hundred hours, he called to his men to gather around the entrance to the hub.

Cyrus exited through the massive door, followed by two hulking soldiers, one tow-headed, and the other one with jet-black hair. Their expressions were serious and unyielding.

"These your two holdouts from the Old Rebellion?" he asked Cyrus.

"Yes," the man said, his features expressionless.

"You two willing to do what it takes for the cause?" he asked, tilting his head so he could see the recruits behind Cyrus's massive body.

"Yes, sir," they responded.

"Good," Hunter said, reaching into his pockets to find his toothpicks. Placing one in his mouth, he trained his irises to Cyrus's dark ones. "I think we should divide into three groups. You and a third of my men can canvas the river. I'll go with blondie back there and another battalion to scope out the perimeter." The tow-headed soldier scowled. "Enrique Iglesias can hang back and work with the rest of my men to guard the compound."

"I have no idea who that is," the dark-haired man muttered to the blond soldier.

Hunter shrugged. "Early twenty-first-century singer. My wife was obsessed with his music...and maybe other things. Didn't mean any offense."

"Ivan and Steven will carry out those orders," Cyrus said, a warning in his tone. "And you will address them with respect."

"Y'all are a barrel of laughs around here," Hunter grunted. "Fine." He waved his hand. "Let's get to work. C'mon, men," he said, addressing those that surrounded him. "Brigade one with me, Brigade two with Cyrus, and Brigade three will stay here with *Steven.* You have your orders. Let's go."

The men dispersed, and Hunter was thankful he had a task to consume the next few hours. Elaine could work on the Sphere while he got to know Ivan better and safeguarded the hub. Being busy was good. Hunter did his best to stay occupied at all times, even at night, once the sun had set and his men had long fallen to sleep. When one was busy, they didn't have time to focus on all their previous failures and heartache.

Chapter 7

Lainey worked with her team for hours trying to recreate the wormhole they'd generated the previous day. Unfortunately, the efforts were a disaster, and the reworked equations produced subpar results. After several attempts, they couldn't even get the wormhole to form, much less transport anything of note.

"Okay, guys," she said, massaging her temples and giving a silent lecture to her impending migraine to stay the hell away, "enough for today. It's after seven o'clock. Go grab some dinner and head to your chambers. We'll resume in the morning."

Zach gathered his notebook and tablet, giving her a soft smile before climbing out of the hatch. Sighing, Lainey shook her head at Claire.

"I'm worried about them," she said softly.

"Nelson and Lorna are fine, boss," Claire said, gripping Lainey's shoulder and imparting a reassuring smile. "The New Establishment would never murder the *second* smartest person on Earth. They need his brain."

"If they threaten Lorna, he'll turn over every piece of work to them," Lainey said, the thought shooting spears of dread through her exhausted body. "Even though he destroyed their Sphere, the regime could steal the work and use it on ours. They most likely wouldn't understand it, but anything's possible."

"We can't live in hypotheticals, Lainey," she said. "One day, this will all be a bad memory. In the meantime, you need to eat."

"My stomach feels like it's digesting gravel," she muttered, running her fingers through her hair, which had been released from its practical bun hours ago. "You go on and grab something. I'll see you in the morning. I want to study my father's letters and rewatch Nelson's transmission. The more information I have, the better."

Claire's light green eyes darted back and forth.

"What is it?"

"I just…" She seemed to be searching for words—something that was rare for Lainey's talkative friend. "It's just that sometimes, I feel Lewis was unfair to you."

"How so?" Lainey asked, feeling her forehead furrow.

"He instilled so much in you, but he never taught you how to *live*." She shrugged, the shoulders of her sweatshirt moving under her the ends of her purple hair. "I mean, don't you ever want to dance? To kiss a sexy man? To feel someone's hands run over your skin until you're sure your body might explode?"

Lainey observed the woman's wistful expression. "I can see you've been reading my mother's old romance novels again," she said sardonically.

"Oh, posh," Claire said, shooing her with her hand. "You're such a stick in the mud, Lainey. And those novels are hella awesome, by the way. Oh, my god, there's this one series where they're all vampires in this black dagger brotherhood and they do all sorts of sexy things to human women. I swear, I'm hot just thinking about it." She fanned herself with her notebook.

"Yeah, I'm all set. I tried my hand at that once, and it was a disaster, in case you've forgotten. As a scientist, it's important I remember love and emotion are just a manifestation of chemicals being released in the brain. Sexual pleasure is merely a stimulation of nerve endings until they release serotonin and dopamine. It's all rather boring and functional if you assess it rationally."

Claire faked a yawn, opening her mouth to show slightly crooked teeth. "I'm sorry, what? I almost fell asleep from boredom. You need to get laid, boss. I bet you could get into Captain McDreamy's pants. He looks ready for a tussle."

"Yeah," Lainey mumbled, still stunned from Hunter's earlier admission. "He told me today that he aligned with Dad because he wants to go back in time and save his wife from dying."

"I was definitely shocked when he blurted that out earlier," Claire said, eyes wide with surprise. "Are you going to do it?"

"I'm open to it," she said, expelling a frustrated breath. "But at this point, I can't even send an apple back. He might be staking his alliance on a complete failure of a human."

"Enough, Lainey," Claire said, the soft lilt of anger creeping into her tone. "I won't let you disparage yourself like that. Go on and work in your office if you need to, but you can't think that way. I need you to be positive. We all do."

"I know," she said, granting a smile she hoped relayed confidence she didn't feel. "We'll get there. Good night, Claire."

"Night." She turned and reached for her weathered yet functional laptop that rested atop the console. "Hey," Claire said, glancing over her shoulder, "can I open one of the bottles of wine Alora brought home from her last trip? It's been forever since we had wine, and I feel like a drink. I plan to work for a few more hours and run the equations through the program Zach created. Maybe I'll find an anomaly that indicates why they're not working."

"Sure. Just not the Malbec, okay? I'm saving that for something special."

"Sexy times with Captain Sex-on-a-stick?" Claire asked, waggling her eyebrows.

"No," Lainey said, unable to control her laugh. "For a toast when we finally send Garfield through. Malbec's my favorite, and we'll certainly need to celebrate."

"Okay, boss," she said, playfully saluting her. "Hands off the Malbec. Got it."

Lainey spent the rest of the night holed up in her office, completing the various tasks her busy brain required before she could even think about sleeping. She replayed Nelson's video over and over, searching for clues, but found none. She read both of her father's notes, trying to convince herself his actions weren't a betrayal but instead were attempts to secure her safety. She revised the current equations multiple times, coming up with a few new ones they could test tomorrow.

Once those tasks were complete, she sat in the high-back leather chair mulling over the fact Captain Hunter Rhodes had once had a wife, whom he'd obviously adored, and how awful it must have been for him to see her perish. The thought stirred up memories of her own that she kept buried deep inside. Closing her eyes, they hummed through her brain...

Lainey trailed along the base of the mountain, knowing her father would be livid if he knew she was so far away from the compound. She'd ridden her bike here, telling her father she needed a break from the equations for a few hours.

Having nothing that was truly hers, this spot held significance. She'd only managed to escape here a few times, but it always reinvigorated her soul. Living at the squalid hub and working to solve time travel every day was no picnic, and she just wanted a few morsels of freedom.

A gun cocked behind her, and she froze.

"I'm armed," she said, reaching for the pistol at her waist.

"Won't do any good against my Glock and the rifle I have, but you can try. Otherwise, I suggest you turn around and tell me what the hell you're doing on New Establishment territory."

Lifting her hands, palms-out, she slowly pivoted. The grass behind her swayed in the wind, the swooshing sound barely noticeable above the ringing in her ears as she studied the man. Dark hair, deep green eyes, and a prominent chin. He was handsome, although his expression was menacing.

"My name is Lainey Winters," she said, the false name rolling off her tongue. "My father is sick, and I come to the base of the mountain to gather herbs to make his medicine."

Eyes with thick black lashes narrowed. "Are you a citizen of Terrum?"

"We live on the outskirts of the compound. I have no money, if you're wondering. Robbing me would only rob you of your energy. All I have are these." She reached for her pocket and held up a reassuring hand. "Just reaching for the herbs."

He nodded, and she pulled them from her pocket. Thank goodness she'd already picked them. They did actually have healing properties, and she liked working with Marie to create various concoctions and teas they could drink to boost their immune systems.

Opening her palm, she took a tentative step toward him. "See? Just boring old flowers."

He approached, inspecting the buds, and finally lowered the weapon. "I appreciate that you're out here to find medicine for your sick father, but it's dangerous for a woman to be walking alone on New Establishment land."

"It is," she said, her shoulders lifting. "I just needed some space. I know that probably sounds weird."

Assessing her, he secured the gun in the holster on his belt and inhaled a deep breath. "Actually, it doesn't sound weird at all. I walk along this path to find solace too."

"Why do you need solace?" she asked before realizing the words that were leaving her mouth.

His lips curled into a smile, contorting his face into something wickedly handsome. "Because I'm not who I appear to be."

"You're not a New Establishment soldier?"

He glanced down at the uniform covering his muscular body. "Not all things are as they appear."

Her eyebrow arched. "That's vague and quite dramatic."

A laugh escaped his lips. "It is, isn't it?"

Biting her lip, she studied him. Lainey had never interacted with an attractive man her own age—except Cyrus, whom she saw as her brother. Standing in the thicket, curiosity overwhelmed her. She'd often wondered about sex, tried to imagine it but never really understood how something so...functional could be pleasurable. The scientist in her had always strived to find out, but there was certainly a lack of candidates as partners, that was for damn sure.

Yet here she was, in the path of a handsome stranger who'd apparently decided she didn't pose a threat. Did he pose one? Or could she take a chance and befriend him? Could her practical brain wrap itself around that idea at all?

"I usually come here at night, once the troops are sleeping," he said, interrupting her thoughts. "I was only patrolling today because we got word of some deserters passing through. I have to get back to camp. Could you meet me here one week from today at midnight?"

"I..." Lainey swallowed, understanding the danger of his request but simmering in uncontrolled curiosity. Agreeing to meet him would be the most impractical decision she'd ever made.

"Please?" he said, inching closer. "You're... Well, you're beautiful, and I need to make amends for greeting you with weapons blazing." White teeth flashed as he smiled. "Say you'll meet me."

"Okay," she whispered, the word escaping her mouth, burning her throat with equal parts worry and excitement. "I'll see you next week, uh..."

"Dalton," he said, extending his hand. "My name is Dalton."

"Pleasure to meet you, Dalton," she said, enfolding his warm palm...

A knock on her door jolted her from her musings. "Lainey?"

"Yeah?" she called, annoyed she'd been lost in the ancient memory.

The door creaked open, and Zach trailed through to hand her a stack of papers. "I updated everything. If Claire's still working, she can run them through the program."

"Thanks," Lainey said, taking them and placing them on her desk.

His kind eyes regarded her. "You okay?"

Pasting on a smile, she nodded. "My compound's been seized, I suck at time travel, and I'm never going to get to drink my damn Malbec. Otherwise, I'm great."

Chuckling, he squeezed her shoulder. "One day, you're going to chug that Malbec, and it's going to be so good. I promise, Lainey."

Clutching his hand atop her shoulder, her lips curved. "I hope so, Zach. I really hope so."

Chapter 8

Claire sat at her desk, furiously typing while Ann Wilson belted "Barracuda" in her earbuds. The iPod was a dinosaur, previously owned by Lainey's mom and lovingly restored by Zach. It was one of her favorite possessions in the world, and the heavy metal and rock music Mrs. Randolph had uploaded decades ago was amazing. Tapping her foot against the desk leg, she ran the equations through the program Zach had designed. Lainey had popped her head in an hour earlier, handed her some updated calculations, and asked her to scan them with the software. It was designed to look for errors Lainey or Zach might have missed. So far, nothing.

Glancing at the clock on her desk, Claire realized it was almost nine p.m. Holy crap. Where had the day gone? Her stomach gave an angry grumble, and she looked down at it and scowled.

"Okay, you win," she muttered. Divesting her ears of the buds, she stood and stretched, groaning as her limbs creaked and popped.

"You're too young to have bones that crack like that, grandma," a deep voice said from the doorway.

Claire turned and shrugged, feeling her lips curve into a smile. "I'll be thirty this year. That's pretty old in the scheme of this post-apocalyptic shithole, don't you think?"

Approaching Cyrus, she stopped half a foot in front of him. At five-feet, four-inches, she was about eye-level with his pecs, defined under his tight black t-shirt. Daaaaaamn, but he was fine. His nipples protruded under the cloth, making her want to close her teeth around them.

Tilting her head back so she could look into his deep mahogany eyes, she grinned. "We can't all live to be a hundred like you, old man."

He scowled, eyes narrowing as he glared at her. "I'm forty-three. Hardly a hundred. Although, sometimes, I feel that way."

"I think we all do," she said with a chuckle. "Did everything go okay with the troops today?"

Cyrus nodded. "As much as I hate to admit it, Rhodes is a competent captain. His men are well trained and add a level of security here that my team can't provide."

"Well, you're nothing if not practical, Cyrus. I'm glad it went well. And what did you think of today's word? Verisimilitude. Want to go over it?"

"Sure," he said with a nod. "Want to go to the kitchen? I'm hungry."

Claire nodded. "Thank god. I'm starving. Let's go."

Always the gentleman, he offered his arm to her, and she settled hers in the crook. They began walking to the kitchen before she stopped short.

"Crap," she said, yanking her arm from his. "I forgot the book. Go on and get cookin'. I'll be right there." Pivoting, she ran back to her desk and grabbed the novel that lay on top.

When she entered the kitchen, Cyrus was popping the cork on a bottle of wine.

"I set that out earlier, when Lainey said I could open a bottle. Looks like you need a drink too," Claire said. "Lainey is pretty punctilious about letting us raid the wine stash, but I caught her in a weak moment."

"Punch…ill…ee…us…?" Cyrus repeated, slowly pronouncing the word.

"It means she's protective of the wine and rarely lets us touch it," Claire said, waggling her eyebrows. Taking the now-open bottle, she lifted one of the glasses he'd set on the table covered by a cheap tablecloth in their utilitarian kitchen. Once both glasses were filled halfway, she placed one in his hand. "I should've made that one of our 'words of the day,'" she said, clinking her glass with his and taking a large gulp as she maintained eye contact. "Maybe I will one day, and then, you'll have a leg up."

Large, gorgeous lips formed a smile as he reached for the book she'd placed on the table. Lifting it, he read the words slow and unhurried. "Where the Red Fern Grows."

Claire almost shivered at his deep voice. "It's a classic. Really good. It's at a fifth-grade level, but I think you can do it."

Gazing into her, he sipped the red liquid. As his Adam's apple bobbed, she felt her own throat stiffen as she swallowed. His russet skin seemed to glisten under the staid light of the old kitchen bulb. What would it feel like to run her fingers over it?

"Claire?" he asked, jolting her from her musings.

"Huh?" She shook her head to clear it.

"Do you mind if I try to read a few pages while we eat?"

The way he said "we," Claire thought her heart might burst from her chest. Boy, would she love nothing more than to have his silken voice read to her at every possible opportunity. But not in the kitchen. No—that was boring. Perhaps in his bed, which she knew to be king-size to accommodate his massive frame. Whoa, nelly… That would be awesome. To slip underneath his covers—which she imagined were silk in her daydreams, although she knew his practical ass probably only had cotton— and have him draw her into his warm body. God, the fantasy seemed so real.

Clearing her throat, she said, "Um, yeah, let's do it. And remember, there is no 'try,' only 'do.' Yoda would kick your ass." She sat at the table while he set his glass down and turned to the stove.

After dishing out the eggs he'd scrambled, courtesy of the always generous chickens Marie tended behind the hub, he placed two steaming plates on the table. Handing her a fork, he sat down and opened the book, holding it apart with his broad hand.

In between scooping eggs through his plump lips, Cyrus would read a sentence, his words always cautious and halting. She'd been teaching him to read for two years now, but the compound was busy, and their sessions were intermittent. When she'd discovered he was illiterate, he'd seemed slightly ashamed, although illiteracy rates were high in their post-apocalyptic world. Claire had wanted nothing more than to reassure him and had begun teaching him immediately. Every morning, she would surreptitiously slip him a word of the day so he could improve his vocabulary. She thought him a fast learner and enjoyed their discussions immensely.

"Scribbly," Claire said, sounding out a word he was having trouble with.

"Scribbly," he repeated slowly.

"Means it's hard to decipher," she explained. When he just stared at her, she said, "Hard to read."

"I know," he said, smiling. "'Decipher' was one of our words of the day a few months ago. Don't you remember? You slacking on me, Finch?" he asked, calling her by her last name.

"Sorry," she said. "You were just looking at me weird."

"You have a…" Lifting his hand, he rubbed his thumb under her bottom lip, wiping away what must've been a piece of scrambled egg. Claire wanted to melt into the floor. Maybe she could figure out how to make that happen. She was a scientist after all.

"There I go again," she said with a nervous chuckle, determined to will away the tears in her eyes. "Messy as ever when there's good food in front of me. I should start watching what I eat—I'm getting fatter by the day in this place."

His eyebrows drew together under his bald head. "You're perfect the way you are," he said, wiping the egg on the napkin beside his plate. "There's nothing wrong with having a good appetite." Taking a sip of wine, he regarded her.

Claire wanted to trust his earnest words, but her embarrassment made her feel small as a bug on the bottom of his shoe. "You're being scribbly right now," she said, trying to lighten the tone.

"Huh?"

She cursed her heart as it pounded in her chest. "Enough slacking. The eggs are good, and the wine is awesome. Keep reading so I can pour us another glass." Ignoring his stare, she lifted the bottle and poured a hefty amount into their glasses.

Confident she'd averted a crisis of extreme embarrassment, she relaxed, soothed by his calm voice and the rich wine. After he'd read two chapters, she felt her eyes droop.

"Cinderella's got to crash, chief. Sorry." Yawning, she took their now empty glasses and plates to the sink.

Cyrus came up behind her, his brawny arm reaching around her side. Claire gasped, only to realize he was reaching for the dishtowel and not for her breast. Good lord, like he would reach for her breast. What a freaking dolt she was!

He was absolutely gorgeous, a perfect specimen of toned muscle who oozed masculinity. What in the hell would he ever see in her? A chubby girl with crooked teeth, weird-colored hair, and minimal experience with men as a whole. Claire wasn't sure if he was still banging Alora, but she knew he used to take her to his room when she visited the hub to deliver supplies. She was absolutely breathtaking, with smooth, creamy skin, and almond-shaped eyes. Most likely courtesy of her parents, whom Lainey had informed her were from the South American Isle.

Alora was everything Claire wasn't: tall, stunning, witty…sexy. God, she was sexy. Claire couldn't even blame Cyrus for being with her. The woman had something.

"I think you can turn the water off. Lainey would kill us if she knew we were running the faucet."

"Shit," Claire muttered, snapping off the nozzle. "You're right about that. I was woolgathering. Thanks for drying the dishes, and for the eggs—they were great. See ya tomorrow."

Before she could escape, Cyrus grabbed her forearm. Hesitantly, she turned to stare up at him.

"Can I keep it?" he asked.

"Keep what?" Her skin burned under his calloused fingers.

"The book. To read before bed. I'd like to practice before our next session."

"Sure," she said, pulling her arm from his grasp. "We'll have another one soon. You're doing great."

Brown irises darted over her face. "Thank you, Claire. Not many people would teach a washed-up soldier like me to read. You're giving me such an amazing gift. I'd like to repay you one day."

"There's no need for that," she said, clutching his hand and squeezing. "I'm honored to help you." Unable to find a reason to justify touching him any longer, she dropped his hand. "See ya tomorrow."

"Good night," he said. Affection for her swam in his eyes, making her want to cry all over again. It was friend-zone affection, and she couldn't stand the sentiment. Needing to escape, she bolted from the kitchen.

Chapter 9

The rest of the week dragged, each day as repetitive as the last. Cyrus and Hunter were amalgamating their men while Lainey worked with her team to get results from the Sphere. Unfortunately, they seemed to be backtracking, and by mid-afternoon on Friday, Lainey was at her wits end.

"Goddamn piece of crap!" she screamed, seconds after the apple exploded, sending shards of wet pulp flying across the room. "I swear to god, I'm going to destroy the damn thing myself!"

"Hey," Zach said, rushing from behind the console to clutch her wrist as she marched toward the Sphere. "Calm down, Lainey. It's been a long week for all of us. Edison failed a thousand times before he invented the lightbulb."

"Well, at least he got it to work," she said, head shaking in frustration. "And Tesla was a much more prolific scientist than Edison. At least compare me to him, will ya?"

Zach grinned as his shoulders released their tension, and Lainey reminded herself to stay calm. It was vital to her team's mental wellbeing. "Sorry," she said, smoothing Zach's shaggy brown hair behind his ear. She'd never wanted children of her own but had always felt maternal toward Zach. Although he was in his late twenties, he reminded her of a scraggly teenager, gangly and sweet. She wished Claire would pull the wool from her eyes and realize he was madly in love with her, but for some reason, her best friend had a blind spot where the whip-smart mathematician was concerned.

"I've been a pretty big a-hole this week. Are you guys over me?"

"No way, Lainey," Zach said, so endearing as he smiled down at her from his six-foot, two-inch height. "It's been tough for all of us. We're so close—I feel it. Just a few more tweaks to the equations, and we'll have it."

"I appreciate your confidence," she said, glancing at Claire, who stood behind the console. They were both so young, both still in their twenties. Zach had come to live with them when he was still a teenager. His mother had noticed he had unusual abilities for calculating the right amount of grain to plant for harvest and the exact quantities it would produce. Lainey was grateful for her foresight, as the man was a bona fide genius. The woman had left him at the hub in exchange for bushels of food and fuel for her gas lamps, understanding he would have a better life. She'd returned to her home on a small compound hundreds of miles north, with her five other children, and Zach hadn't seen her since. Lainey often wondered if he missed her or felt abandoned in any way, but if so, he never seemed to show it.

Claire was actually a distant cousin of Lainey's, and Lewis and Mara had taken her in after her parents died when she was sixteen. Lewis had trained her in the same scientific methods as Lainey, and she was an exceptional scientist. Perhaps it was embedded in their family's DNA.

Observing them both, she felt such sadness in her heart. They'd never truly gotten to live. Never gotten to thrive or love or exist anywhere besides the utilitarian scientific compound. If it was seized tomorrow, they might perish having never experienced the freedom they all craved.

A sudden rage enveloped Lainey's body, vibrating through her as an insane idea formed in her mind. Why should they cower to the enemy? Didn't that mean they'd already lost? Rebelling against that idea, the words escaped her lips before she could stop them.

"What do you say we take the night off? Claire says I'm an old fuddy-duddy who never has any fun."

Claire stiffened behind the console, staring at her as if she'd just announced she had three heads. "Sorry, boss, but it sounds like you just said we should take the night off and have fun. Do you want to try that again?"

Lainey sighed, rubbing her forehead with her fingers. "I'm so tired, guys. Tired of living in fear, tired of failing…hell, I'm tired of seeing you guys work yourselves to the bone and never get to experience normal human activities. Mom and Dad used to take me to visit your parents at Solera when you were just a baby, Claire. I remember the music they played by the bonfires and how everyone would dance and laugh. We never do anything like that around here, and I'll be damned if we keep living as if we're already dead. Tomorrow is never guaranteed. I want to live a little today."

Her two protegees gaped at her, infuriating her even more by proving they thought her incapable of having one night where they acted like *humans* instead of scientists. Spurred by their disbelief, Lainey cemented what was, perhaps, only the second spontaneous decision in her life.

"We're going to open the alcohol rations and light the bonfire tonight. Not just for cooking this time, but to give us light while we take a few hours to have some damn fun."

"*Ohmygod*," Claire exclaimed, rushing to Zach's side. "Really, Lainey? Can the soldiers hang with us too? I could hook up your mom's old speaker to my iPod so we can dance!"

Lainey almost chuckled at the sincere plea in her friend's eyes. Encouraged she was doing the right thing, she grinned. "Let me talk to Cyrus. His report this morning was that no one was within forty miles of the hub, but I think a speaker might be a bit much. But yes, we'll invite Hunter's men. Tell Marie to whip up a big batch of stew, and we'll open the vodka and whiskey Alora delivered on her last visit."

"Woo-hoo!" Claire yelped, jumping up and down as she clapped, alternating green and orange fingernails glowing under the soft lighting on the Sphere room's ceiling.

Happy she could grant such happiness to her dearest friend, Lainey headed to find Cyrus. He was outside, in the large meadow beyond the dense trees and foliage surrounding the hub, leading target practice with several of the men.

"Hey," Lainey said, approaching his side. "How're they doing?"

"Good," he murmured, arms crossed above his firm pecs. "They're good soldiers. I like our chances against a possible occupation."

"Glad to hear it." She bit her lip and attempted to look contrite. "Soooo… I kinda just had a brain fart of epic proportions. After yet another failure with the Sphere, I had a moment of intense realization that we waste a lot of time attempting to save humanity without really taking the time to be human."

"I don't like where this is going," Cyrus muttered.

Lainey kicked the grass with her sneaker, attempting to look penitent. "I kinda promised the team we could take the night off. Claire wants to hook up the speaker and have all sorts of dancing and debauchery. How much do you want to kill me right now?"

Cyrus glanced down at her, lips pressed together as an incensed eyebrow arched. "You do know we're in the middle of a war, and you're the most valuable asset on the planet, right?"

"My *brain* is the asset, and it's tired, Cyrus. I think we all desperately need this. But if it's too dangerous, I'll put the kibosh on it. Safety always comes first. You know that."

Hunter chose that moment to approach, toothpick firm between his teeth. "Everything's been surveilled," he stated in his smooth voice. "Nothing for miles. We're safe for now." His silver irises darted between them under the late-afternoon sunlight. "Uh, am I interrupting something?"

"Lainey wants to have a party," Cyrus grumbled.

Hunter's eyes swung to hers, then to Cyrus's, then back to Lainey's in a maddening dance. His firm lips pursed, and his shoulders began to quake as he struggled to hold in his laughter.

Observing his amusement, Lainey felt her exasperation grow. "Excuse me, but what the hell is so funny?"

He shook his head and rubbed his forehead with his fingers. "Sorry, you're just the last person I expected to request a party. You're kind of serious, in case you hadn't noticed."

"I'm perfectly capable of having fun," Lainey said, hearing the pout in her voice. "I'll have you know, my mom and I used to sing and dance all the time."

"Really?" Hunter asked, arching a brow, the gesture adding a mischievous glow to his handsome face. "Did you sing about equations or rocket fuel?"

"Oh, screw you," she said, infuriated at his chiding. Dismissing him, she redirected her attention to Cyrus. "So, what do you think? Yea or nay?"

Cyrus sighed. "As much as I'd like to tell you no, I honestly see the logic. We're all tired and on-edge, and that's definitely not conducive to your work. Getting out of the rut of failing with the Sphere each day, if only for a few hours, might actually help."

"Ouch. Thanks for the failure reminder," Lainey teased.

Smiling, Cyrus cupped her shoulder. "You say your team needs this, Lainey, but I think you need it most of all." He studied her for several moments. "Fine. Tell Claire I'm sorry, but no speaker for the music— although she can play it softly through the speaker of the iPod. That will be low enough to still allow people to hear. And we can do a bonfire, but only one. More than that will alert the enemy we might not be using it for cooking. Clear?"

"Got it. But you have to be the one to tell Claire about the speaker."

Cyrus shot her a glare. "Fine."

Joy consumed her, as it so rarely did, and she beamed at the man who'd protected them for so long. "I love you. You know that, right?"

"Go on," Cyrus said, motioning toward the hub with his head. "Tell Marie to use the wooden spoons and bowls. Less noise."

"You're a saint," Lainey said, blowing him a kiss. "See you in a bit." After surrounding him in a warm embrace, she almost skipped back to the compound, her footsteps lighter than they'd been in years.

Hunter crossed his arms and tilted his head up to address the man who'd just made Lainey's year. "You did a good thing just now," he said, tongue rolling against the toothpick.

"Yeah, it's not often we see her happy. She carries such a burden. If I can help ease that, even if only slightly, then I'll consider it a win."

"Have you two ever…?" The words trailed off as the question lingered in the air.

Cyrus's full lips turned up as amusement entered his eyes. "No way, man. She's like my sister. I couldn't see her that way if I tried."

"Really?" Hunter asked, slight surprise in his tone. "It's obvious you have a deep connection. Just figured I'd ask."

"Lewis recruited me from the Old Rebellion when she was still a teenager. I'm only a few years older than she is. I was still a child myself in so many ways when he brought me here, but she never got to be one. She was bred from the time she was born to save the world. Sometimes, I feel sorry for her. She's determined to go back in time, prevent her grandfather's actions, and live in that timeline for the rest of her life. Alone, in a time that isn't hers, surrounded by strangers. I think the least I can do is grant her the ability to let her hair down for one night."

Hunter thoughtfully ground the stick between his teeth as he looked upon the field where the men were shooting at various targets. "Has she always been resigned to that? Doesn't she want more? Kids? A family? A partner?"

"She never has," Cyrus said, shaking his head as he kicked the ground with the toe of his army boot. "She swears it's her choice, but I sometimes wonder if she even had a choice. I'm not sure Lewis ever gave her one."

"A damn shame, if you ask me," Hunter said, spitting the toothpick on the ground. "A woman as fiery as her should be taken to bed as often as possible."

Silence stretched, causing Hunter to glance at Cyrus. "What?"

"I just…" Cyrus shook his head. "It's weird to think of her that way."

"Sorry, but in my mind, it's weird not to. I'll always love my wife, but I would joke with her that I was married, not blind. A gorgeous, passionate, intelligent woman is hard not to notice for any warm-blooded man."

"I guess," Cyrus said, shrugging.

"How about you? Any sordid affairs in your past?"

Cyrus gazed across the meadow, features drawn together as he considered. Finally, he said, "Not to be an ass, but none of your business, man."

"Fair enough," Hunter said, patting him on his back. "One day, I'll get you to tell me. For now, I think we have a festivity to safeguard."

"That we do," Cyrus said. Inserting his thumb and forefinger into his mouth, he gave a loud whistle, calling the men back to the hub.

As the sun set over the distant mountains, they headed back to the compound, both sensing their tentative respect was growing. Hunter would count that as a small victory. Hopefully, in time, he might even befriend the massive, brooding soldier.

Chapter 10

Lainey spent some time getting dressed for the party that evening. *Not* because she wanted to impress Captain McHotty Pants, as Claire called the infuriating man. No, she didn't give a fig what the man thought of her appearance.

At all.

In reality, she hadn't actually taken the time to feel feminine in so long. Rolling through life as a staid, unexciting scientist didn't incite the need for makeup and perfume, but for some reason, she just felt *different* tonight. Maybe it was the urgency spurred on by the knowledge the Australian hub had been seized. This meant the war was closer than ever. They could be so perilously close to losing their freedom, they might as well enjoy some moments of happiness.

Spending time on one's appearance represented a massive waste of time in her book. It seemed pointless to someone as practical as she, but tonight, the desire to expend some effort was present in her gut, and she saw no harm in honoring it even if she couldn't quite place her finger on why it was there.

Her closet was full of boring sweaters and comfortable jeans, but she did manage to find a flowy deep brown sweater dress her mother had passed down to her. It was casual, and the fabric was light. Pairing the dress with sandals, she located the small box that held the handmade cosmetic palettes Alora had gifted her over the years. Frowning, Lainey wondered if she even remembered how to apply them. The last time she'd worn makeup was most likely when she'd been with Dalton. Red lights of warning flashed in her mind at the remembrance of that disaster, and she pushed the dark thoughts away. Lifting the eye shadow palette, she tentatively began to apply the powder atop her eyelid as she stood in front of the rectangular bathroom mirror.

A few minutes later, she'd had enough. Studying her reflection, she wondered if she looked like a goddess or a clown. Or maybe both. She'd applied eye shadow, mascara, and blush. More than enough, in her opinion.

Throwing her long, wavy hair in a bun atop her head, she left her chamber to join the festivities. Upon exiting the hub, the sounds of laughter and soft music could be heard. Lainey observed Hunter's men, most with cups in hand that she assumed held some of their alcohol rations. Some sat around the scattered tents, eating the stew Marie had lovingly prepared. The woman flitted back and forth between the men, scooping out large helpings from the massive pot attached to her hip. Every so often, she would pat one of the soldiers on the cheek, informing them they only had to ask if they wanted extra helpings. Such was the way for Marie with her generous heart.

Lainey spotted Cyrus speaking to Sara and Luke and strolled over to join them.

"Wow, Lainey," Sara said with a warm smile. "You look terrific."

"Thanks," she said, shrugging. "I don't get many occasions to lose the casual attire. Figured I'd switch it up."

"This is great, Lainey," Luke said, hugging Sara to his side as he motioned around with the cup in his hand. "I think everyone needed a break from…well, life, I guess."

"We did," she said, taking the cup Cyrus thrust toward her.

"It's not the fancy Malbec, but it tastes pretty good," Cyrus said.

"I'll take it," Lainey said, imbibing a sip from the wooden cup. The thick liquid doused her tongue, reminding her how much she enjoyed wine. Perhaps when she lived out the rest of her days in the 2035 timeline, she'd buy a winery in Italy and cultivate the vines as she passed the time. The image evoked a warm feeling of contentment in her chest.

The sentiment was dashed, however, with the approach of Captain Rhodes. Sidling up beside her, he extended his hand to Luke.

"I don't think we've met yet. Captain Hunter Rhodes."

"I'm Luke Sondham," he said, shaking his hand. "And this is my wife, Sara."

"The nurse, right?" Hunter asked. When she nodded, he said, "My wife was a nurse. You're a tough breed. I'm sure she keeps you on your toes,

Luke."

"Every damn day," was Luke's good-natured reply, and Sara elbowed him in the side. He responded by placing a peck on her upturned lips.

"Nice to meet you, Captain Rhodes," Sara said. "We're all thankful for your protection, especially now the rest of the hubs have been overtaken. We know Lainey's going to solve the equations and save the world, and we appreciate your help in getting her there."

"Hopefully," Lainey muttered, sipping the wine as frustration bloomed inside. "Sometimes, I think I'm working backward."

"You'll do it, Lainey," Sara said, reaching over to squeeze her hand. "We all believe in you."

That's what makes each failure so hard. The words flitted through her brain before she could stop them.

"Well, if you all don't mind, I'm going to dance with my wife. She *might* be able to keep up if she tries real hard."

"Oh, you've done it now," Sara said, laughing as she tugged him toward the area where Claire had situated the iPod atop an old stump in the brush.

Lainey watched them trail off, so happy they'd found each other. Even though she was skeptical of love herself, their connection was palpable.

Cyrus mumbled something about refilling his glass, and suddenly, she was left alone in the company of the man she didn't quite trust or like—yet. The bombshell about his wife and their subsequent chat had softened her a bit, but she was still a cynical scientist. Only time would tell if his intentions were really true.

"Cheers," he said, lifting his cup to hers.

"Cheers," she replied, taking a drink as she maintained eye contact.

"So..." He cleared his throat, causing Lainey to wonder if he was nervous. "I'm sorry about today. I didn't mean to make fun of you for throwing the party."

"Is that so?" she asked, arching a brow. He looked quite uncomfortable, and she realized that suited her just fine. He'd shown up unannounced and thrown her world into chaos. Finally, he was a bit off-balance. Good.

"The truth is, you've got every right to be serious and wary, but you also want the best for your family, which I'm assuming is what you consider everyone who lives here. I admire your loyalty to them."

Well, crap. The man was actually offering her a genuine apology. The petulant side of her wanted to remain detached and aloof toward him due to the fact he'd secretly met with her father and essentially seized military control of her home. But the compassionate part was deeply moved by the loss of his wife and his commitment to help Lainey accomplish her goal. Deciding to choose compassion, she gave him a slight nod.

"Apology accepted," she murmured. Turning her gaze toward the area where Sara and Luke were dancing along with a few others, she felt his presence at her side. He seemed comfortable with silence, which was welcome, as she often thrived in it as well.

"So, does this mean we're friends?" he asked. Lainey could sense the amusement in his tone.

Latching onto his gray eyes, she gave him a lighthearted glare. "Not yet. It's still Elaine to you, Captain Rhodes."

"Ouch," he said, chuckling as he stole a sip from his mug. "I'll keep working on it."

Lainey couldn't stop her resulting laugh. "You do that."

She resumed staring at everyone who'd gathered, now a mashed-up amalgamation of soldiers and scientists, rebels and survivors. "It's so nice to see everyone *living*, even if it's only for tonight."

Hunter nodded, thoughtful and serene.

They stood there, side by side, enjoying their drinks and mutual solitude. It was rare for her to be so relaxed in the presence of someone she didn't know, but she chalked it up to the hint of wine that now thrummed through her veins.

Eventually, Marie skipped up to them, her imperfect smile threatening to blind them with its joy. "Your men are such good boys, Hunter," she said, setting the large pot on the ground and rising to pat his cheek affectionately. "They remind me of my sweet George."

"George was Marie's son," Lainey said. "Sadly, he passed away while he was fighting with the Old Rebellion."

"I'm so sorry, Maire," Hunter said, his features drawing together. "What isle did he serve on? It's possible I knew him."

"His father was British, so he joined the Old Rebellion on the European Isle. Gave me a hug so deep before he hopped on the ship to cross the ocean, I knew in my bones it would be our last. My dear boy died protecting freedom and goodness. I'll always be so proud."

"As you should be," Hunter said. "I only served on the American Isles, so we most likely didn't meet. You raised a brave man to fight for the cause."

"I sure did," she said with an affirmative nod. "I see his face in each one of your boys. I've promised them all, Sara and I will sew all their tattered clothing back together by the end of next week. You can't have your men running around in rags, Hunter. You should know this." She wagged her finger at him while fisting her other hand on her hip above her flowing ankle-length skirt. Lainey always imagined Marie was the late twenty-first-century embodiment of a hippie if there ever was one. With her long white braid and the flowing skirts and moo moos she wore, along with her occasional headbands, she would've fit right in at Woodstock. Lainey's mother was a fan of classic rock and had educated her about the music festival at length.

"Now, tell me, young man," she continued, scowling up at Hunter, "you've had several minutes to ask this beautiful young woman to dance. She even put on makeup tonight, which is something less probable than the moon sprouting wings and flying away. Are you going to squander this opportunity? I pegged you to be smarter than that."

Lainey's face enflamed with a thousand sparks of heat, and she wanted to melt into the ground. Marie was always meddling, and although it was well-intentioned, it was also highly annoying at times.

"Marie," Lainey said, vowing to keep her voice calm and free of the extreme embarrassment she was suddenly experiencing. "I'm not in the mood to dance. Captain Rhodes has been in the field all day, and I'm sure he's exhausted."

"Actually," Hunter said, smiling down at Marie, "I haven't danced in a long time. I've already pissed Dr. Randolph off several times"—he spared Lainey a sheepish glance—"and don't want to fan the flames by stepping on her feet."

"Oh, nonsense," Marie replied, waving her hand through the air. "Lainey doesn't mind refreshing your memory. She's actually a wonderful dancer. Isn't that right, Lainey?" The woman grinned up at her expectantly, and Lainey wondered if attempted murder was still a crime since the desire to strangle the woman was high on her list at the moment.

"Of course, I don't mind," she said through gritted teeth, "but as I said, Captain Rhodes is tired. I don't want to tax him any further."

"Wow, she must be some dancer," he said to Marie from behind his hand, which he'd lifted to his cheek to feign the appearance of speaking secretly to her. "How much energy does she expend while dancing?"

"Oh, for god's sake," Lainey said, giving them both an exasperated glare. "Fine, come on then." Setting her now-empty glass on the ground, she encircled Hunter's wrist and pulled him toward where the others were dancing.

"Have fun!" Marie said, waving to them with laughter in her eyes. Looking over her shoulder, Lainey gave her a death glare, causing the woman to emit several more lingering cackles.

When they approached the stump near the rear of the hub where everyone was dancing, Hunter slid his palm to hers and grabbed her hand. Pulling her toward the showers, he said, "At least let me set my drink down. I know you're anxious to dance with me, but give me a sec."

Lainey snatched her hand from his grip, furious Marie had maneuvered her into this situation. Once he'd set his cup on one of the ledges near the outdoor showers, he sauntered toward her, lips curved in an ultra-sexy smile. She noticed he'd changed into jeans and a black t-shirt and now sported sneakers instead of army boots.

Determined to appear unfazed, she let him slide his arm around her waist and fit his hand in hers. Resting her free hand atop his shoulder, she felt him begin to sway.

"Wow, you're pissed. Is Marie always this good at manipulating people? I might need to recruit her for witness interrogation."

Lainey breathed an unexpected laugh. "She'd be an asset, for sure. I don't think I've ever met anyone as tough as Marie."

Willing her body to relax, she moved in tandem with his strong frame. "You're not a bad dancer," she said.

"That doesn't mean I'm good either." The whites of his teeth flashed in the moonlight, and Lainey begrudgingly admitted he was extremely attractive. "You're passable."

She squelched the urge to roll her eyes at his teasing. "Thanks," she muttered.

"How's it going with the Sphere?" he asked.

Inhaling deeply, she shook her head. "Not great. I swear, Zach and I have calculated every possible equation to make it work. At this point, I'm beginning to lose hope."

"You can't," he said, the tone of his voice so sure, so encouraging. "There's something happening here, Elaine. I feel it."

The words combined with the musky scent of his skin, sandalwood and cedar, sent a jolt of arousal through her veins. As the wine pulsed through her blood, and she swayed with his warm body, the words didn't compute inside her brain.

"Feel what?" she asked.

"That you're going to get the hunk of junk to work," he said, giving her a reassuring grin. "Kara said I was born with a sixth sense. She believed in psychics and horoscopes and all that jazz. Not sure if it's true, but I do listen to my gut, and it's kept me alive this long. Now it's telling me, you're going to whip that contraption's ass in gear."

Nothing to douse your arousal like the mention of a man's long-dead beloved wife, Lainey thought. Instantly feeling like an idiot, she cleared her throat.

"That's a nice story. I hope it's true."

"It is," he said, squeezing her hand as they danced.

Lainey bore into him, unable to look away. The orbs of gray gave way to tiny flecks of silver and black. They seemed…endless. Would he look at her that deeply if they made love? Would she get lost in the depths of his eyes and become unable to cling to the practicality that kept peace in her measured life? Worried at the turn of her thoughts, she abruptly stopped moving.

"Elaine?" he asked.

"I, um…" Glancing around, she withdrew from him, needing to separate her body from the heat of his. "I need more wine. Thanks for the dance." Uncaring that she probably looked like a stupid teenager with an unrequited crush, she fled to her chamber inside the hub, needing a break from the revelry. It seemed everyone on the compound was able to let go and live a little. Everyone but her.

Clutching the sink in her small bathroom, she gazed at her reflection and remembered another time when she'd danced with a man under the glistening moon…

"How much longer do we have?" a low-toned voice chimed into the shell of her ear. "It must be midnight by now."

Lainey glanced at the watch on her wrist before placing her hand back around Dalton's waist. "One more minute until I turn twenty-six. I feel so old."

Chuckling, he pulled her closer. "You're such a baby. Now that I'm twenty-eight, I have a whole new perspective on life."

Lainey rolled her eyes at his romanticism. She was definitely the practical, cynical one between them. "And what is that?"

"You and I will get married and have babies while I change the New Establishment from within. They'll never suspect I'm a spy for the Old Rebellion. I'll assume power, and they'll become peaceful, and we'll live happily ever after."

She stiffened in his embrace. "You know I don't want those things, Dalton," she said, her tone gentle to ease the sting of her words. "I don't want marriage or children. I have other priorities and want to make other choices. Besides, love is just a chemical reaction our brain misconstrues as something more."

He pulled back, eyes narrowed as they glimmered in the shallow light. "You only say that because I haven't convinced you yet. One day, I will. Every woman wants to get married and have babies."

Lainey felt her brows draw together at the misogynistic statement. "Is that what you honestly think?"

"What else could a woman want in this world? They need to be taken care of by a strong man and no one is stronger than me. You and I will have gorgeous children and you'll look so striking on my arm as my wife."

"Those are your choices, not mine."

"Those choices were made for you when you were born. All women are put here to bear children and build a home with their husband."

Stepping from his embrace, she lifted her hands in a slight shrug. "Not this woman. I've been honest with you from the beginning, Dalton. You don't really know me—my fears and dreams. I enjoy our time together so much, and making love to you is physically pleasurable, but I have one purpose on this Earth, and it's all I care about."

"To take care of your dying father," he murmured.

"Yes," she said, never indicating she was lying to him and had a much more important aspiration. He could never know her secret, but for once in her stark life, she'd wanted something for herself. Something that was hers. Dalton had showered her with affection and praise and taught her the intricacies of making love. Now, she realized how selfish she'd been. Not only had her actions put her life's work—her life's purpose—in jeopardy, but she'd entered a romantic relationship knowing she had neither the inclination nor desire to truly love him back. She'd only ever loved science and her parents, and her only goal was to solve time travel.

Extending her hand, she flinched when he batted it away. "Dalton—"

"What the hell have we been doing here if this means nothing to you, Lainey?"

"I didn't say it meant nothing. You'll always mean so much to me."

"Bullshit!" he spat, causing alarm to tingle up her spine. She'd never seen him this angry, and it was frightening. "I thought this was real. What do you mean, I know nothing about you? What are you hiding from me?"

Terror choked her as her heart pounded in her chest. The last thing she needed was a soldier sniffing around. As far as Dalton knew, she was a young woman who lived on the outskirts of Terrum with her sick father and mother. It would be disastrous if he discovered her true identity. Her efforts to solve time travel must remain hidden from everyone on the planet, lest it fall into the wrong hands.

"Nothing," she said, determined not to telegraph any of her inner turmoil. "It was rash and I didn't mean it. I've told you everything about my boring life."

Green eyes glared at her, filled with disbelief. "We'll see. Don't forget, I'm a spy, Lainey. If you're hiding something from me, I'll find out." Glancing at the moon, he noted its position in the sky. Lowering his gaze to hers, he said, "It's midnight by now. Happy Birthday. I find I've lost my appetite for celebrating, since we obviously were only meant to have a clandestine affair and move on. I'd give you my best wishes that your dreams come true, but perhaps a cynic like you doesn't have any. Goodbye."

He turned to leave, and she reached for him, wanting to comfort him—but before she touched his broad back, her hand fell to her side. The smartest option was to let him leave. It was a natural break in their relationship. An organic end. Her practical brain knew that.

Once he'd ambled out of sight, she began her own trek home, riding the bike her parents had given her for her sixteenth birthday a decade ago, procured by Lewis during one of his trips to Solera. Would she live another decade without achieving her goal? She didn't know, but Lainey knew one thing for sure: Extricating Dalton from her life would rid it of distraction. Terminating their relationship was for the best. She'd also seen a dark side to her lover tonight and it frightened her. There was no place in her sphere for a man with Dalton's views of world domination and misogyny.

She'd been bred to save the planet, not bred to have dreams or romantic love. Her scientific mind would never understand those concepts. She wouldn't begrudge herself for the affair—after all, she'd been quite curious about sex and it had been...well, it had been fine. Not earth-shattering, but what she'd expected. Now she'd experienced a relationship and sex, she could resume her life's work.

When she eventually reached the hub, she snuck inside, understanding her father would be furious if he knew of her clandestine rendezvous. He was insistent that every ounce of her time and energy be spent on the Sphere. And it would be, from now on. Lainey had completed her experiment, proving she was incapable of romantic love and furthering what she already knew to be true.

Lainey's purpose was to prevent the past, and it was time she resumed acting like it.

Lainey stared at the porcelain of the sink as the memories washed over her. They seemed like a lifetime ago yet remained so vibrant. Dalton had taught her an important lesson: She couldn't focus on anything but solving time travel. Passion and arousal were base instincts she recognized but brushed off as insignificant. Yes, her reaction to Hunter was visceral, but that was her animal brain responding to chemicals. It might feel nice in the moment, but it in no way meant she had the capacity to understand love, much less the desire for romantic love. What a folly and incredible waste of time.

No, she had something so much more important to accomplish, her attraction to the handsome captain be damned.

Hunter scowled as Cyrus came to stand beside him, the mug of whatever concoction he was drinking dwarfed in his large hand.

"Saw you dancing with Lainey," Cyrus said. His voice held a soft warning that would make any man cringe.

"We got roped into it by Marie," Hunter said, awkwardly rubbing the back of his neck. "Man, that woman's something else. Where did you find her?"

The corner of Cyrus' lips twitched. "She's an old friend of Lewis' from back in the day. Been a staple of this place ever since I showed up."

"She would've made some soldier."

"Indeed." Cyrus took a drink and sighed. "Lainey's a brilliant scientist, but she's been sheltered here. She took a chance on a romantic entanglement once, and it almost cost her everything. You're both adults, and it probably isn't my place, but I need to make one thing clear."

Training his gaze on Hunter, he said, "If you hurt her, even a little bit, I'll break your fucking neck."

Hunter expelled a breath through puffed cheeks. "That's pretty clear, bro."

"Good," Cyrus said, scowling as he resumed staring straight ahead.

"Becoming *romantically entangled* with anyone isn't a priority of mine, just so we're clear," Hunter said. "My goals are to destroy the New Establishment bastards, restore freedom, and help Elaine go back in time to prevent the apocalypse. That leaves me with a pretty full plate."

"Understood. But even the best of intentions can be broken."

Hunter mulled that sentiment, remembering the feel of Lainey's soft body as he'd held her. His hand had rested on her hip, smooth and warm beneath his palm. He'd be a liar if he claimed he hadn't imagined running that palm over her navel and then trailing it down to cup the hidden place situated between her supple thighs…

Shaking his head to rid it of the image, Hunter thought of the abstinence he'd experienced since losing Kara. It was self-induced, since he had no desire to sleep with anyone else. There were other priorities to focus on, of much greater scale.

Liar. The word flitted through his head, imparting a truth his conscience wouldn't admit to. He was extremely attracted to Lainey.

His body had hardened as he'd held her, and he'd been unable to stop the visions of having her sprawled naked before him. Visions of her mouth held open in a silent wail as he kissed every inch of her skin… Judging by Cyrus' words, she hadn't had many lovers. Had any man truly taken the time to love her properly? If given the chance, he'd relish the opportunity to make her body burn with endless pleasure.

Knowing he had to stop the maddening thoughts, the head attached to his neck gave a stern command for the head below his belt to calm the fuck down. There were things in play that were greater than any one of them individually, and he'd be damned if his libido screwed it up.

After chugging his drink, Hunter was ready to call it a night. Dr. Elaine Randolph was off-limits, and he had plenty of important shit to focus on.

"Your scientist is safe with me, Cyrus. I appreciate you looking out for her. I'm going to round up the men. We have early drills tomorrow."

Cyrus gave him a curt nod. Intending to honor his word to stay away from the prickly, stunning physicist, Hunter began the task of shutting down the party so his men could get some rest.

Chapter 11

The new week began, fraught with an urgency to test the different laser energy output parameters Zach and Lainey had calculated the previous week. Worried for Nelson and Lorna and unable to contact them, Lainey called her team to the bunker promptly at eight a.m.

The first few settings they tried were a bust, the wormhole only generating for milliseconds before it collapsed. Glancing at her watch, Lainey realized they'd been at it for hours. Deciding to try one more setting from their equations, she adjusted the lasers.

Zach set the metal arms of the Sphere whirling, glancing toward Lainey with his finger above the red button on the console. She gave a nod, and he pressed it firmly.

The portal appeared, small at first, then growing slightly until it was the size of a basketball. Lainey stood transfixed, Claire's mouth hanging open at her side, as the black orb floated in the center of the Sphere, above the stool where a red apple rested.

Lainey's heart surged into her throat as she realized the wormhole was stable. "Engage the fuel rod!" she screamed, head snapping to lock eyes with Zach. He flipped open the clear cover housing the large black button that controlled the nuclear fuel rod attached to the base of the Sphere. Releasing just a small speck of its energy would give the wormhole the jolt it needed to open the portal to 2035. Zach depressed the button as the room vibrated around them. Suddenly, the apple began to shake atop the stool. An intense sucking sound pervaded the room as the apple was drawn into the wormhole and disappeared.

"Shut it down!" she yelled, eyes transfixed on the now barren stool.

The arms of the Sphere slowed to a slight whirl, eventually coming to a standstill. With measured steps, Lainey walked toward the metal machine, the pounding in her ears so loud she wondered if it would render her deaf. Approaching the stool, she slowly extended her hand, rubbing her fingers atop the smooth wood.

"We did it," she whispered, barely able to breathe. "Holy shit. We sent the apple back in time."

"Boss?" Claire called softly, stunned disbelief in the uttered word. "Are you confirming what I'm seeing?"

Rotating slowly, Lainey gazed toward Claire, then Zach, her eyes suddenly dry from the amount of air they were being exposed to due to her wide-eyed expression. Sparing a glance at her watch, she noted the time and cleared her throat.

"Time of first completed time travel with an inanimate object, eleven forty-two a.m. on August 29, 2075. Zach, please double check the equations before you confirm."

Agile fingers ran over the keyboard of Zach's laptop as he computed. Then, an astonished Zach lifted his head and said, "Confirmed," from behind the console. "Scientific probability of success is statistically equivalent to one hundred percent."

Claire thrust her arms above her head, hands in fists as she cheered, "Holy shit, Lainey! You did it! You just solved time travel."

The woman rushed her, and Lainey encircled her with limp arms, still in too much disbelief to clutch her firmly. Zach came over and enveloped them both in a massive hug. Feeling her eyes well, she cupped both of their cheeks.

"We did it, guys. Oh, my god."

Claire began to jump up and down, clapping as she broke into a chant of a thousand unintelligible words, speaking mostly to herself. Lainey heard snippets of, "I knew we were close!" and, "We showed physics who's boss around here!" inciting her to laugh with joy. As they celebrated and congratulated each other, Lainey expelled a large breath, reminding herself this was only their first step.

"Okay, guys," she said when they'd regained some composure. "The apple is great, but we need to test a living subject. Let's break for lunch and meet back here at one o'clock. Zach, you've locked in the equation that worked, right?"

"Locked and loaded, Lainey."

"Good. Go on and grab something—I think Marie made bread this morning. I'll be in my office. Great job, guys!"

"Hell yes, Lainey," Claire said, squeezing her hand. "You're a freaking genius."

They all but skipped from the hatch as Lainey headed to her office. As soon as her still-stunned body was seated in the weathered leather chair at her father's desk, she grasped the picture encased in a metal frame atop the mahogany surface. The bright smiles of her parents stared back at her, Lainey in between them, as they stood in front of the hub. Running a reverent finger over both of their beloved faces, she whispered, "I did it, guys. I'm not sure I ever truly believed I could." Something cold and wet slipped down her cheek, and she swiped at the tear.

Her parents stared back at her, faces glowing with their love for her. For the first time in her life, Lainey finally felt she deserved it. Clutching the picture frame to her chest, she allowed herself to cry tears of joy.

An hour later, the hub was abuzz with the news the apple had been successfully sent back in time. Marie was rushing around, gathering clothes from the soldiers staked outside the compound, cheerfully explaining that they couldn't go back in time with worn and ripped clothing. Lainey didn't have the heart to tell her she had no intention of sending Hunter's twenty-two men back. She already had enough on her plate with her commitment to send her own people back. In a perfect world, she would transport everyone, but not only was it a daunting task, she feared it would cause too much imbalance in the space-time continuum. Sending her entire team was already a huge manipulation of universal consistency and order. Reminding herself that Hunter's men had designated themselves to a life of service for the cause, she tried to tamp down the small bugs of remorse in her belly.

Cyrus and Hunter returned from the daily scouting mission shortly before one p.m., and Lainey rushed outside to her dear friend.

"We did it, Cyrus!" she exclaimed, excitement oozing from every pore. "The apple successfully traveled back through the wormhole."

His thick arms surrounded her, clutching her as he spoke softly into her ear. "I'm so proud of you, Lainey. You've worked so hard."

Pulling back, she smoothed her hand over his cheek. "Don't congratulate me yet. We still need to send one of the cats back, and if that's successful, test it on Luke."

"I'd urge you to get to it," Cyrus said. "There were boot tracks in several spots a few miles away, where we've never seen them. We're being surveilled."

Terror clenched her throat. "We can't be overtaken by the New Establishment when we're this close."

"Hunter and I will hold down the fort. We're still clear for now. Let us worry about the regime. Focus on your work."

"Thanks," she said, sparing a glance at Hunter. The man looked delicious in his tight and functional tactical gear, with an aura of strength emanating from his weapon-clad body. Hating that she'd acted like such an idiot the other night after their dance, she gave him what she hoped to be a detached smile. "Thank you as well, Captain Rhodes. We're on the verge of us both getting what we want. I appreciate you keeping us safe."

Ivan called Cyrus's name from behind the hub, and he strolled away to see what the soldier needed. The tick of Lainey's heart grew more pronounced as Hunter approached. He sauntered so close, she swore she felt the heat emanating from his body.

"Elaine," he said, eyes drilling into hers. "I have a really important question for you."

Clearing her throat, she lifted her brows. "Yes?"

Leaning down, his eyes narrowed. "Are you ever going to call me Hunter?"

Torn between the need to laugh, scowl, and run away, she felt herself freeze. Damn it, what was wrong with her when she was in this man's presence? It was as if her body lost all ability to function. It was extremely annoying.

Lifting her chin, she responded, "I believe Captain Rhodes is just fine. Remember, we're not friends. We're two allies working toward a common goal."

Her answer must've amused him because he straightened a bit and pulled a toothpick from his pocket. Placing it between his teeth, he hit her with a grin so sexy she actually thought her knees might buckle.

"I thought you'd committed to not mocking me anymore, Captain," she said, feeling her nostrils flare.

"Oh, I'm not mocking you," he said. Wetness glistened on his tongue as he rolled the stick, and the vision of him sliding that tongue across her nipple flashed through her brain. "I'm just wondering why you're fighting our friendship so vehemently. There must be a reason."

"I don't have time for this," she snapped, wanting to rush inside before she did something insane like beg him to kiss her. "I have to send a cat through the Sphere. Excuse me."

She stomped toward the hub entrance, making it a few feet before he said, "I'm going to win you over, Dr. Randolph, and that's a promise."

Plodding down the stairs, she closed the hub door behind her, the action filled with irritation. Deep inside, in a place she wouldn't acknowledge, she had a nagging fear that she wanted his declaration to come true.

Chapter 12

Lainey, Claire, and Zach reconvened in the Sphere room at one p.m. sharp. Claire had lured Garfield into the cat carrier with some cold chicken, and the lazy feline seemed unfazed that he was about to become an extremely important part of scientific history. Placing him on the stool inside the Sphere, he meowed from the carrier as he observed them.

Zach stood behind the console, initiating the Sphere's startup sequence. The circular arms began to rotate, and Lainey observed Claire tense out of the corner of her eye.

"He's going to be fine, Claire," she murmured, wishing with all her might that it was true. Claire was a gentle soul and quite attached to both their garden cats. If something happened to Garfield, it would break her heart.

The carrier had been lined with zirconium so the feline would survive the radiation blast from the fuel rod. All safety precautions were in place, and Lainey had the insane urge to pray even though she was a staunch atheist. Sometimes, even the biggest skeptic needed an extra jolt of faith.

The Sphere slowly built up to its full speed, and a minute later, it was ready.

"Begin sequence," Lainey called to Zach.

He pressed the red button, causing the lasers to ignite. Seconds later, a small wormhole appeared above the cat carrier. Claire clutched her hand, and Lainey squeezed back. The black orb grew, overtaking the cat carrier and the stool.

"Engage," she commanded, urging him to ignite the fuel rod and generate the nuclear energy needed to send the cat back in time.

The next events seemed to happen in slow-motion. Garfield began to meow loudly, the sound discernable from the whirling of the sphere. The black carrier seemed to stretch, half of it sliding through the black hole, while the other half remained atop the stool. Lainey's stomach fell to the floor as she realized what was happening.

"The nuclear energy is too high. We're creating a singularity instead of a portal. Shut it down, Zach!"

With hurried movements, he depressed the black knob and then the red one, effectively shutting down the machine. Claire's face was a mask of horror as she stared ahead.

"Garfield!"

"Wait," Lainey said, halting her from running toward the Sphere. "It needs to shut down completely."

Claire tugged her arm free. "But he's dying!" she screamed.

I know, Lainey thought, feeling quashed and defeated. There was very little possibility the feline had survived.

"Damn it, Lainey!" Claire said, pointing to the Sphere.

"I'm sorry," Lainey warbled, feeling her throat close as she fought back tears.

Claire's chin quivered as she glanced back and forth between the contraption and Lainey. Never had she seen such disappointment in her friend's disconsolate expression. It was soul-crushing, and Lainey wanted nothing more than to soothe her.

When the machine was still, Claire approached the center. Lainey let her go, understanding her friend needed to process the events in her own way. Emitting a soft wail, Claire unzipped the front of the carrier. Placing her hands around the feline's limp body, she hugged it to her chest.

"No," she moaned, lowering to the floor and burying her face in the cat's mane. "Oh, god. We *murdered* him." Rocking back and forth, she sobbed into the animal's fur.

Lainey tentatively advanced, heartbroken at her friend's pain. Sliding her hand over the soft fabric of her thin sweatshirt, she rubbed the woman's shoulder.

"I'm so sorry, Claire."

Claire's head snapped up, anger and hurt swimming in her wet eyes. "You're sorry? How can that be enough? We killed him in the name of what? Saving the world? A world that was never ours and that doesn't give a crap about us? Sorry, Lainey, but your apology means jack shit. I'm so tired of all of it."

"Claire," she said, feeling wetness cloud her own eyes. "I know this is hard—"

"It's always hard!" she screamed, causing Lainey to jump and stiffen. "What the hell are we doing? I can't. I just can't be okay right now. Let me up." Struggling to hold the cat to her generous bosom, she stood and shot Lainey a glare. "I'll be outside. Someone needs to bury him. He deserves that at least." Wiping her nose with her forearm, she left the bunker, awkwardly clutching the animal.

Sighing deeply, Lainey rested her face in her hands, struggling not to sob.

"It's okay, boss," Zach's calming voice said behind her. "She's upset and took it out on you. She's human, and so are you. Let her process this on her own terms."

Turning toward him, Lainey let the sweet man comfort her. Squeezing him tight, she nodded against his neck.

"I'll let her stew for a while. Thanks, Zach."

"Hey," he said, leaning back and palming her cheeks, "this isn't your fault. Science is a bitch. The settings on the fuel rod were perfect for an inanimate object, but we need to use less for something living. It's the entire reason we use test subjects. Now we know."

"Now we know," she said, nodding into his warm skin. "I'm so sorry, Zach. That cat's been here for years. He deserved better."

"Hey, that's enough," he said, smiling compassionately. "He died valiantly, serving his purpose for science. If we could all be so lucky."

"Oh, Zach, you're such a good man. I hate that you're trapped here, forced to spend your time in this dark hole of a room all day. I know I'm adamant about the 'no dating' policy, but if you want to pursue Claire, I'd be okay with it."

Something flitted across his face, and his eyebrows drew together. "Where did that come from?" he asked after breathing a laugh. "I mean, don't get me wrong, Claire is great. But I don't have romantic feelings for her."

"You don't?" she asked, puzzled. "I could've sworn you did. Man, I'm really terrible at reading people."

His lips curved as he shook his head. "I can see how you made the inference. She and I spend a lot of time together."

"Has there ever been anyone you wanted to pursue? You deserve to be loved, Zach. You have such a good heart."

Red splotches warmed his cheeks, and his sheepish gaze fell to the floor. "Thanks, Lainey. That means a lot. I, um…" He rubbed the back of his neck, the movement relaying his awkwardness as he struggled to speak. "There really hasn't been anybody. We don't meet a ton of eligible women around here. The times I've gone to the market on the main compounds have been few and far between. Sometimes, I daydream"—his gaze traveled north as he contemplated his words—"I'll meet a woman who'll fall desperately in love with me, but she probably wouldn't want a full-blown nerd like me."

"Nerds are sexy, my friend," Lainey said, giving his hand one last squeeze. "Don't doubt yourself. Hopefully, once we're back in 2035, you can find said woman of your dreams and live out your days together."

"That would be nice," he said softly.

"Okay, I need to check on Claire. Thanks for consoling me."

"I'm going to clean up around here and record the session notes."

Thanking him, Lainey retreated to her office for a moment, needing to digest Claire's breakdown before she confronted her. Feeling defeated, she slumped in the chair and allowed herself to mourn the loss of the furry tabby cat who'd so often rubbed against her calves when she returned from her late-afternoon walks. To state the obvious, saving the world sucked most of the time.

Chapter 13

Lainey wracked her brain, struggling with something that would help comfort Claire. When the brilliant idea appeared, she approached her team, rounding them up one by one to soothe their beloved counterpart.

With Sara, Luke, Marie, and Zach in tow, she found Claire in the back thicket near the garden, where Garfield liked to laze in the stray rays of sunlight. Puss in Boots nuzzled her side as she held Garfield to her chest, slowly stroking his fur.

"We've come for the funeral," Marie said beside Lainey, thumping the end of the shovel she held on the ground. "We all loved that little fleabag and we aim to give him a proper burial."

Claire lifted her gaze, allowing it to settle on each person, slow and wary. Finally, she said, "We need to bury him here. It was his favorite spot."

"Well, move your butt so I can dig the hole," Marie said. "Luke, go grab the empty wooden box on the right shelf of my shed."

The man nodded and headed into the nearby shack, returning with the empty box. Lowering beside Claire, he held out his arms.

"Let me take him, honey," Luke said.

Claire regarded him for a moment and then released the feline. Luke lovingly placed his body in the box, pulling a nearby flower from the ground and placing it inside before he secured the lid.

Standing and clutching the box to his hip, he extended his hand to Claire. Latching on, she let him pull her to stand. Marie walked over and thrust the shovel into the soft ground, displacing the dirt. Silent and thoughtful, she continued to dig.

"Let me," Claire said, taking the shovel from Marie's hands. As she started to dig, Lainey could see the tension ease from her shoulders, if only a bit. Manual labor was an easy way to release her anger, and Claire methodically dug until the opening was large enough to bury the cat.

"I think that's good," Claire said, stepping back and surveying her work.

Luke stepped forward and placed the box in the ground. Slow and sure, Claire began to replace the dirt on top, until all that remained was a large brown patch of soil.

Lainey gave a nod to everyone, and they stepped forward and encircled Claire.

"I'd like us all to go around and say something about Garfield," Lainey said. Glancing at Sara, the woman cleared her throat and spoke first.

"He was such a sweet cat and always meowed a greeting to me each morning when I stepped outside to do my yoga stretches. I'll miss him terribly."

They continued, each saying something, until only Marie and Claire were left.

"He was a heap of fleas who was always hungry, but the darn thing grew on me after a while. He ate all the mice in my shed. Hard thing to replace, since the other one's even lazier," she said, gesturing her head to Puss in Boots, who meowed loudly at her feet. "Oh, you hush," she said. "Garfield, may you find a hundred cats in heat across the rainbow bridge."

Lainey heard a snort and realized Claire's shoulders were hitching. Wanting to soothe her tears, she placed her arm around her shoulders. It only took a moment to realize her friend was laughing—quite uncontrollably, in fact.

"Claire?"

Shaking her head, she wiped a tear of mirth from her eye. "Only Marie could say something terrible and still make it sound endearing. Thank you, Marie."

"You're welcome, sweetheart," the woman said, pulling Claire in for a hug. "I'm so sorry, my dear girl. You have a kind heart, and those are always most open to heartache."

"Thank you, guys," Claire said, reverently smiling at everyone in the gathered group. "I know this must seem stupid. I just loved the little bugger."

"We know," Lainey said. "We all loved him too."

"I'm going to build a headstone for him once we're done today. He deserves it."

"Actually, Zach and I need to play around with the intensity of the fuel rod jolt. Take the afternoon to do what you need. We'll resume in the morning, eight a.m. sharp." She didn't address the words left unspoken, feeling it best to not highlight the fact they were going to try the same experiment with Puss in Boots tomorrow. Lainey hoped it didn't end up like today's fiasco. She wasn't sure her team's morale could take the blow.

For now, she left Claire to mourn by the garden as she and Zach headed inside to compute the exact energy output that would stave off another disaster.

Cyrus returned from the scouting mission around four p.m. He and several of Hunter's men had traversed a multi-mile perimeter around the hub in the hours since they'd departed after lunch. The scientific compound was set in the foothills of the mountains, in what used to be rural Virginia, when the world still retained recognized and accepted borders. Now, it was a free-for-all, each compound protected and reclusive. Those stragglers who did live a solitary life outside the communes were subject to capture and enslaved labor by the New Establishment. Most had learned to live in the communities and accept the rules, lest they be banished.

Cyrus had met a fair amount of compound leaders. The large settlements of Solera and Terrum were both within two hundred miles—one north of the hub, and one south. The leaders of the large territories were ethical men who proclaimed to only want peace and freedom. The hub's proximity to the two largest communes was most likely what kept it safe, as the settlements produced many strapping young men who eagerly signed up for the Insurgency to protect their families and way of life. They were formidable even if they were outnumbered by the New Establishment, and their efforts kept the evil regime's soldiers busy.

For now.

Striding into the hub, Cyrus immediately sensed something was wrong. Approaching the kitchen, he found Marie stirring a large pot of something red and simmering.

"What's going on, Marie?" he asked, alarmed. "Something's not right."

Marie sighed, nodding over the pot. "They tried to send Garfield back in the Sphere. He didn't make it." Her arm rotated slowly as she dragged the spoon through the sauce. "Claire's all torn up about it. She loved that little devil."

Cyrus's heart slammed in his chest as he envisioned Claire's reaction to the cat's demise. She had such a tender demeanor and would need comfort. She'd done so much for him, and he yearned to ease her pain.

"Where is she?"

"Out back, by the grave. We held a ceremony for the little critter. She made him a headstone."

With that information, Cyrus pounded down the hallway, past the residential chambers and outside the small back entrance. Claire sat on her knees, stacking dirt around a gray stone that had been erected beside a mound of dirt.

"Hey," he said, lowering beside her. "That's a really nice headstone."

"Thanks," she muffled into the arm of her lightweight sweatshirt as she wiped her runny nose. "I carved his name into it. One day, when we're long gone, someone can stumble upon this and remember him, although they might never know he sacrificed his life for science." The words trailed off as she began to sob. Burying her face in her hands, her shoulders shook as she wept.

Cyrus slid his palm over her shoulders, the tips of her soft hair brushing against his forearm as he pulled her into his chest. Turning toward him, she buried her face in his pecs and cried while he stroked her hair, murmuring soft words of comfort.

"This is so stupid," she said, lifting her head to latch onto his gaze. "I don't know why I'm such a mess about this. It just..." She shrugged and sniffled. "It just seems so unfair."

Cyrus stared at her wet face, her peridot-green eyes bursting with vibrancy from the moisture. They contained small shards of blue, seeming to swirl together, and Cyrus realized his body was beginning to tense. Not from stress, but from arousal. It was something he'd always promised himself he'd lock away. Claire was too young for him and would build a new life with a man who could give her everything she desired once they traveled to 2035. He would never be able to offer her the life she deserved.

Needing to push her away, he focused on her ripe lips. Full and red, he imagined kissing her just once. She was a passionate little thing and would most likely curl into him, much as she was doing now, and rock his world. Damn, but he wished he could taste her.

Embracing his practical side, he smoothed the dampness on her cheek with the pad of his thumb. "It's okay, Finch," he said. "We all know you're a sap."

Her features contorted into something so beautiful as she laughed, and his throat swelled at the image. "I really am. How the hell do you all put up with me?"

The corner of his lips curved, and he shook his head. "Not sure. I think we're just stuck with you."

Emotion-filled irises roved over his face as she studied him. "I was a bitch to Lainey. Like, full-blown, See You Next Tuesday. I feel terrible."

"Lainey's tough," he said, smoothing his hand over her hair. "She'll forgive you and move on. She loves you."

"I know. That's why I feel so ashamed. I need to find her and apologize."

"You're human, Finch. It happens. Just throw some wine her way, and she'll forget about it in a second."

Claire chuckled. "True story." Disentangling from him, she stood, extending her hand to pull him up. Once he was looming above her at his full height, she asked, "What did you think of today's word?"

"Super…flu…iss…" he said, sounding it out.

"Superfluous," she said, the word rolling off her tongue. "It means unnecessary."

"Got it. I'm almost finished with *Where the Red Fern Grows*. It's kind of sad."

"Yeah. All the great ones are." Her shoulders shrugged.

"I want to try something harder next time. I want you to challenge me."

Her expression changed, becoming wistful, and he wondered what she was envisioning in her busy brain. "Okay, let me think. I'll have something for you tomorrow."

He offered her his arm, and she bypassed it, placing her arm around his waist instead. Settling his thick one across her shoulders, they shuffled inside.

Cyrus was thankful she'd discovered his illiteracy. It was the one reason he had to connect with her each day. Otherwise, they were worlds apart. He'd do well to remember that.

Chapter 14

That evening, Lainey sat in her office, eyes forced shut as she commanded the impending migraine to stay away. Claire had knocked an hour ago and enveloped her in a smothering embrace after Lainey gingerly pulled open the office door. Thankful her friend's spirits seemed to be rebounding, she still couldn't shake the feeling of dread. What if their test with Puss in Boots failed tomorrow? She and Zach had determined what they believed to be the exact output from the fuel rod, but who knew, really? These things could only be proven with experiment, and Lainey didn't know if she'd survive killing another living being.

Hating the morbid musings, she headed outside into the warm night, to the high-back wooden chair in the spot she used to sit with her father. It held a certain reverence for her, and she hoped the energy would calm the ache that was growing in her brain.

Lainey sensed his presence behind her while she sat in the broad-backed seat. His sandalwood scent overwhelmed her, filling her nostrils, and her body tensed. Clenching her eyelids together, she tried to will away the pain.

"I'm not in the mood for conversation right now, Captain," she said, not wanting to be antagonistic but unable to offer any niceties due to the dull throbbing in every crevice of tissue inside her brain.

Hunter rustled behind her, and Lainey felt his warmth even though they lacked any physical contact. "My wife suffered from migraines too," he said, his tone laced with sympathy and a trace of hesitation. "I used to help her."

"How?" she asked, not understanding how anyone could ward off the evil bouts of murderous pain that invaded her mind.

He was quiet for a moment. "Can I touch you? By your temples?"

Lainey's eyes snapped open, although she couldn't see him since she was staring into the darkness before her. "Why?"

"I… It's hard to explain. If you'd rather I not—"

"Honestly, I'd let Lucifer himself touch me right now if he could ward off this monster. Go ahead."

Firm arms slid tentatively over the back of the chair, coming to rest on each side of her neck. The warm pads of his fingers pressed against the soft skin of her temples. Closing her eyes, Lainey sunk into the ministrations as his fingers began to swirl small circles, the pressure steady but gentle.

"Oh, my god…" she breathed, her body relaxing in the chair, lithe as a cat on a sunny windowsill. Each pulse in her brain was soothed by his strong, agile fingers. "You're a saint. Don't ever stop. I'll give you all the riches in the world."

His throaty chuckle encircled her like a fluffy blanket. "I know how badly these things hurt. Kara used to wail in pain when one took over. When I would massage her like this, it seemed to help."

"It's heaven," Lainey sighed, not even caring she sounded like a doe-eyed weakling. There she sat, while he stood, feeling true relief from a migraine for perhaps the first time in her life.

Eventually, his fingers shifted south as he tried to move the ministrations to the base of her head and neck, although his standing position stilted his reach.

"This will probably sound all sorts of wrong, but it's easier if you sit in my lap. That way, I can reach your neck better. Those muscles hold a lot of the tension during migraines."

Lainey immediately stiffened, lids flying open as she digested his words.

"Whoa," he said, sliding his fingers back to her temples. "Don't tense up. If that's too uncomfortable, I understand. Just trying to help."

Lainey sat up, turning to stare into his eyes, the silver surrounding the pupils almost the same color as the moon. "I don't think that's a good idea."

He held up both hands, palms facing out. "No worries. I swear, there wasn't one ounce of anything sexual around that suggestion. I'm not really a subtle man, Lainey. If I wanted to say something sexual to you, I would. Kara used to sit in my lap while I did this, that's all. I'm sorry."

Lainey exhaled a ragged breath, barely able to focus on his words due to the hammering between her temples. Damn, but he looked so sincere, and his ministrations had actually been helping…

"Okay," she said, standing and gesturing to the chair. "Plop down. But if this gets weird in any way, I'm out."

The curve of his lips was incredibly sexy in the dim light of the moonlit clouds. As he maneuvered his muscled body into the chair, Lainey realized her mistake. She'd never be able to sit atop his broad body and control her ragged heartbeat. He was too masculine. Too raw. The thought of losing herself to the ridiculous chemicals that always accompanied sexual attraction was terrifying. She'd done that once before, and the consequences had been calamitous.

"Hey," he said, stretching his hand toward her, "it's okay. Come on. If you feel uncomfortable at all, just tell me. There's no way I'm going to piss off the lady who feeds and clothes my men." He shook his hand at her. "Come on, Lainey."

Heart already pounding in her chest, she slipped her hand in his and let him guide her onto his lap. As she shimmied the globes of her jean-clad butt over his fly, she thought she heard him expel a soft hiss by her ear. Trying her best to relax, she aligned her spine with his front, the back of her head resting on his shoulder.

"That's good," he said, placing his fingers against her temple and resuming the measured strokes. "Let the tension go. You're safe. You can turn that busy brain off for a few minutes."

His lips brushed across the shell of her ear as warm breath flooded the tiny channel. God, but this was erotic. Embarrassed her body was a mass of frayed nerves, she tried to shift the focus.

"Tell me about Kara," she said softly, eyes closing as he massaged her head.

Now, it was his turn to stiffen, ever so slightly, where he sat below her.

"If you don't want to talk about her, I understand. It was a lame attempt to change the subject. I'm a bit uncomfortable here, if you can't tell."

The puff of air from his gentle laugh rushed against the back of her neck. "Talking about her doesn't always come easy to me, so I guess that puts us on even ground." The thick pads of his thumbs situated over the two straining muscles in the back of her neck, and he began circling with measured pressure as he spoke softly.

"She was a firecracker," he said, his velvet voice seeming to flow in tandem with his agile movements. "We were so young when we met—I was barely twenty years old. I'd signed up for the Old Rebellion, intent on saving the planet, and had gotten grazed in the side one day during target practice."

"Yikes."

"Yeah, I wasn't always the confident, measured soldier I am today," he said, his chuckle rumbling against her back where she rested atop his chest. "She was the nurse assigned to me in the infirmary, and I told her I didn't need stitches. She told me to sit the hell down and let her work, or she'd have me dishonorably discharged from the army herself."

Lainey couldn't stop her laugh. "She sounds like my kind of woman."

"For sure," he said, thumbs moving to the juncture of her shoulders and neck. The steady circles were doing wonders for her migraine, which she considered a small miracle. "You two would've been fast friends. I'd be terrified for any man who challenged either of you to a bar fight."

"My bar fighting days never really began, but I appreciate the sentiment," she said, smiling as she tilted her head, granting his hands greater access.

"I was mad for her. Completely besotted, but my pledge to the cause was also important. Although it was against army policy, I convinced her to marry me—a feat I'm still amazed by. Old Rebellion soldiers weren't supposed to marry because their partners could be used as leverage and hostages. But I'm a stubborn son of a bitch, so I just plowed ahead anyway. We loved each other so deeply, it was almost combustible. Our arguments were passionate, and our life together wasn't always easy, but she was my world. We were just a couple of kids. It seems like a thousand lifetimes ago."

Lainey let the sentiment of his words wash over her, heart thumping in her chest. She longed to ask him the question flashing in her hectic brain.

"You want to know how she died," he said softly, inhaling a stilted breath.

"I don't want to make you discuss it if you don't want to. I told you, I'm a private person. Sometimes, things are better left in the vault for us to process on our own."

"I'm not sure I agree," he said, his tone thoughtful. "It's not something I enjoy talking about, obviously, but I've told people over the years. It's cathartic, in a way, to remember her with other people." Strong thumbs moved up and down the thick corded muscles in her neck as he continued. "This will probably sound ridiculous to a woman of science like yourself, but I dream of her. Quite often, actually."

"Dreams are usually comprised of memories, so that sounds reasonable."

Lainey felt his nod against her hair. "Sometimes, she speaks stilted words that usually don't make any sense. Other times, she just stares at me, and I want so badly to understand what she wants. The only thing I can surmise is that she wants me to use whatever time I have left here to defeat the bastards who murdered her. So, that's what I'm going to do."

"Oh, Hunter," Lainey said, compassion filtering through every pulsing cell in her body. "I'm so sorry. It's so hard to lose someone you love. I wish it hadn't happened to you."

He exhaled a breath, the action ragged with despair and sorrow. "I was a high-ranking officer in the Old Resistance, arrogant and filled with notions of destroying the New Establishment. I was high on their list for capture. Once they had me, they made sure they made an example of me."

Lainey's chest filled with dread as he continued.

"They set up a firing squad, led by some asshole who reported to Eli. His name was Trace Gibson. What a stupid fucking name. They blindfolded Kara and lined her up with the others, ten hostages in all. I was forced to watch as they systematically shot each person in the heart, one by one. I screamed and struggled the entire time while the guards held me. Kara was so strong. She didn't utter a word. She just faced the bastards head-on and died with dignity."

Tears poured from Lainey's eyes as he recounted the story, unable to comprehend how he'd lived through such pain and carried on. Even the strongest of men would question their existence after such a tragedy.

"I know what you're thinking," he said, his cheek grazing her hair as he shook his head. "She made me promise I wouldn't hurt myself if she died. It was hard at first because I wanted so badly to die, but it's softened to a dull ache over the years. She knew I'd never break a promise to her. I told her I'd live, so I carry on, fighting those bastards in the ways I can reconcile in my conscience. Knowing I might have the chance to go back and set things right brings me some comfort."

Tilting her head, she lifted her face to his. Gray eyes glistened as he gazed into her, unashamed. Cupping his cheek, she struggled to find words.

"I wish I could save her for you too."

"You will," he said, his smile sad as he spoke.

Her thumb trailed back and forth over his cheek, the stubble prickly beneath. "I hope so. I want so badly to save everyone."

His palm cupped her neck, supporting her head as she gazed up at him. "But who's going to save you?" he whispered.

"I've never needed saving," was her raspy reply.

Gunmetal silver irises darted slowly between hers. "I'm not sure that's true." He placed his finger over her lips, cutting her off when she opened her mouth to argue. "But we'll let you believe it for now."

Awareness slammed into her bones, spurred by his warm finger against her lips and his strong body beneath her. Against her will, desire rushed through her veins, culminating in a deep throb between her thighs and a resulting slickness at her core. Unable to control her reaction, her breath became choppy.

Hunter must've sensed the change in her body because he tensed underneath her, his grip growing stronger around her neck. His expression grew pensive as his eyes roamed her face.

"Lainey," he whispered, eyebrows drawing together as if he was considering something. Was he contemplating kissing her?

Deciding that would be disastrous, she chose to change the subject. "I'm not sure I ever granted you the right to call me Lainey. Did we cross that line yet?"

Full lips turned into a smile, contorting his face into something wickedly handsome. "I must have crossed the friend line with that awesome migraine massage, no? Are you feeling better?"

Feeling her brow furrow, she realized the intense hammering had indeed dulled to a slow pulse. "Holy crap, I do feel better." Shifting away from him, she rose from the seat, offering her hand. "I officially declare you a friend, Captain Hunter Rhodes. Henceforth, you may call me Lainey."

He gripped her hand and let her pull him to his feet. "And you may call me Captain Rhodes," he said, teasing her.

"Good lord. Did I sound that pretentious when I forbade you from using my nickname?"

"More so," he said, rubbing the back of his neck as he grinned. "I think Claire thought you might end up flaying me alive."

"I'm sorry," she said, lifting her hands in concession. "I'm a mama bear around here. Have to protect my den. I've learned I have to be tough as nails."

"I get it, and you're really good at it. I was intimidated as hell."

He offered her his arm, and she took it, letting him escort her from the clearing as they slowly walked under the stars. "I'm not that bad," she said, rolling her eyes.

"Okay," he muttered, causing her to punch him softly in the bicep.

When they reached his tent, she removed her arm from his, feeling slightly morose that she no longer had a reason to touch him. "Good night," she said, smiling up at him. "Thanks for the amazing massage."

"Good night, Lainey. Thanks for listening. Like I said, it helps me remember her."

"You're welcome," she said, feeling her throat bob as she swallowed.

He stepped into his tent, zipping the fabric behind him. Left alone, as she was so used to being, she padded toward the entrance of the hub to get some sleep.

Chapter 15

The next morning, Lainey felt refreshed and invigorated. Perhaps it was the fact last night's migraine never really took hold, or possibly because she'd let another person inside her securely-guarded wall, if only for a few minutes. Remembering the feel of Hunter's warm body at her back, she allowed herself to experience contentment.

Once dressed, she headed to the Sphere room to meet Claire and Zach. Claire had already gathered Puss in Boots in the carrier and was gently soothing him with soft words where he sat upon the stool in the middle of the contraption. Marie stormed down the ladder, handing them each a sandwich while muttering something about how they couldn't save the world if they were dying from starvation. The melodrama was quite refreshing.

Once they were full and ready, Zach took his place behind the console, Claire at her side as they observed the Sphere. Giving the order, Zach set the contraption in motion, and the metal rings began to circle. When the lasers were lit, the small wormhole appeared, growing larger until it was wide enough for the feline and the carrier to fit through.

"Engage the fuel rod," Lainey yelled over the noise of the Sphere.

Zach depressed the black button, and a zap of power was jolted toward the center of the Sphere. A swirling suction sound emitted from the machine, and suddenly, the cat and carrier disappeared.

"Shut it down!" Lainey called, desperately trying to see if anything remained atop the stool. From her vantage point, it seemed as if the cat had traveled safely. Once the metal arms of the Sphere were immobile, she approached the center, holding a palm up to Claire to urge her to stay back.

Nearing the stool, she ran her fingers over the circular seat, blood pounding throughout her shocked body. Pivoting to face her team, she lifted her arm, not understanding how she still retained control of her body, now it was visibly quaking.

Noting the time, she said, "Time of first completed time travel with a live being at eight twenty-seven a.m. on August 30, 2075. The subject was a male feline, and transport is confirmed."

Cheers erupted as Claire and Zach rushed to embrace her, the moment so thick with importance Lainey barely knew how to mark it. They celebrated with exclamations of disbelief and proclamations that history had been made.

For the next thirty minutes, Lainey worked with Claire and Zach to calculate the mathematical probabilities of success, based upon what they'd observed and the disappearance of the subject. Each equation could be tweaked so that a subject could be sent to a specific date in the past. In this instance, the Sphere had been set to send Puss in Boots back to March 27, 2035.

Once every equation had been triple-checked and verified, the three of them embraced in a massive group hug, overcome with the knowledge that after all these years and all the heartbreaking failures, they had finally succeeded.

While they rejoiced, a man walked down a small side street in Washington D.C., in the year 2035. The man was angry, for he was embroiled in a secret government mission ordered by President Randolph himself. The mission held great significance, and he wouldn't let it get derailed by a few nosy do-gooders who'd recently discovered the clandestine operation. No, he would ensure the mission succeeded, for humans had become complacent, fat, and lazy, with their endless technology and false information spread by the swipe of a finger in seconds. This man would save humanity from itself even if he had to die to accomplish his goal.

Stopping short, he noticed the wind pick up and swirl some trash that lay on the curb in front of him. Focusing on the tiny whirlwind, he observed a dark point generate out of nothing above the ground. Frozen in disbelief, he witnessed the black orb grow larger until it was the size of a kitchen appliance. Blinking rapidly, unable to comprehend what he was seeing, he watched a black bag emerge from the hole. As quickly as it appeared, the orb made a whirling sound and vanished.

Cautiously advancing toward the bag, which now sat upon the curb, he gingerly touched it and reached for the zipper that held it closed. Dragging the zipper open, a cat with gray and black fur hopped out, startling the man. The cat lifted its nose in the air, sniffing its surroundings, and focused on the man, giving him a meow.

Gingerly scooping up the feline, the man observed it, wondering if he was locked in a dream, although the cat's fur felt soft and warm against his skin.

"Well, hello…" he said to the animal, studying it as he rotated the cat to see multiple angles. "Where in the hell did you come from?"

The cat gave a responding meow, and the man felt his eyes narrow. "I think you and I have some things to discuss, kitty." Placing the cat back in the carrier, he zipped it closed and lifted it in his still-trembling hand. He didn't understand what the hell was happening, but he'd sure as shit figure it out. The ability to make something appear from thin air was all but impossible, but he'd seen it with his own eyes. If the technology existed, he would discover it. It would only help him further his clandestine cause.

Chapter 16

Unfortunately, Lainey, Claire, and Zach's celebration didn't last long. When she emerged from the Sphere room, pops of gunfire could be heard in the distance, and Lainey ran outside to search for Cyrus among the soldiers.

"They're coming," Cyrus said, appearing at her side, expression morose. "Hunter's men scouted the New Establishment soldiers heading down from Terrum. That commune has now been overtaken, and they've set their sights on Solera. We're stuck in between. It's inevitable that they would raid us."

"Damn it!" Lainey swore, hands fisting at her sides. "We just got the blasted thing to work!"

Cyrus's brown eyes grew wide. "You did?"

"Yes," she said. "We sent Puss in Boots back. If they discover the Sphere, I'll have to destroy it. Son of a bitch, we can't let that happen, Cyrus."

"Agreed," he said, scanning the horizon. "We'll do the best we can. Thank god it's in the bunker. Let me help the men. Stay inside and lock the door. Don't open it, not even to save me or anyone else. Got it?"

"I wouldn't sacrifice you—"

"I mean it, Lainey," he said, swinging his rifle over his shoulder and resting his hands atop hers. "This is bigger than me or any one of us. You can't throw everything away for one man."

"Nothing's going to happen to you," she said, her eyes welling with tears. "I won't let them hurt you. I'll kill them myself before they seize this compound."

"There's my scrapper," he said, giving her a warbled smile. "Go on inside. I need to help the men."

Lainey watched him stick his fingers between his lips and give a loud whistle. Several men formed in front of him. Sparing her one last glance, he headed toward the sounds of gunfire.

Filled with dread and a million sparks of anger, Lainey bolted down the stairs and into the hub, securing the locks behind her. She hadn't seen Hunter but assumed he'd already joined the melee. Lainey hoped he would be okay…hoped they all would survive. Informing Claire, Zach, Sara, Luke, and Marie of the escalation, they huddled together in the kitchen, somber and silent as they waited.

Lainey and Zach prepared the explosives in case they needed to detonate them, so the New Establishment wouldn't discover the Sphere. All her work, all the years vying for success, would be erased in moments. God, it was so unfair.

The sounds of war grew closer, urging Lainey to head to the foyer by the hub entrance and observe the security cameras. Flashes of soldiers running and dodging bullets appeared on the screens, and she knew it was only a matter of time.

"Go stand by the bunker," she commanded Claire and Zach. "I'll give the order to detonate if needed. Make sure you close the hatch after you light them, so we don't blow up the whole hub. Go!"

They scurried off, and Lainey told the others to stay in the kitchen. Striding through the hub, she stopped by her office and grabbed the pistol, tucking it into the waistband at her back. Stalking to the entrance, she unlatched the door, unwilling to wait like a calf to slaughter. This was her home, and she would protect it at all costs.

She emerged into a whirl of battle and flying bullets. Still standing on the bottom step of the entrance belowground, she was shielded—for now.

"Stop!" she screamed, clutching the gun and holding it in the air. Encircling the trigger, she fired two shots. "Cease-fire! I want to speak to your leader."

A New Establishment soldier dressed in camouflage must've heard her because he lifted his fist in the air, causing some of the nearby men to halt. Eyes locked onto hers, he stood firm, his gun aimed directly at her heart. As Lainey froze in fear, the echoes of gunfire began to cease. One soldier appeared at his side, then another, until several New Establishment soldiers surrounded the man who still aimed the gun at her.

"She's not a soldier," Cyrus said as he moved around the right side of the hub, the deep baritone of his voice welcome to her pounding ears. Rifle aimed at the man who was pointing one at her, he slowly advanced. "There's no need to escalate this further. Let's lower our weapons and discuss terms."

"An excellent idea," a smooth voice called to her left.

Head snapping, her gaze landed on none other than Eli Hernandez, leader of the New Establishment on the Eastern American Isle. Lainey knew tales of his wrath and ruthlessness from Alora, who'd gathered much intel on the figurehead over the years.

"Hello, Mr. Hernandez," Lainey said. "I have no wish to continue fighting." Gingerly, she lowered her gun to the ground. "I'm not sure what you want but I'd like to discuss it peacefully and civilly, leader to leader."

Dark eyes filled with a sinister humor, and his lips curved into an austere smile under his black hair and sharp nose. "Are you truly comparing yourself to me, Dr. Randolph? That seems a bit overzealous, don't you think?'

"I am the leader of this hub," she said, unwilling to back down. "That's all I've ever wanted, to live in peace with my team."

He glanced at his men, and she noticed the soldier lower the gun. Cyrus did as well, but his body remained tense.

"And to solve time travel, perhaps?"

It took all of Lainey's might not to gasp. Not wanting to give him the satisfaction of a reaction, she shrugged. "Scientists want lots of things. That one would be impossible."

His chuckle was menacing, stretching across the clearing around the hub. "Oh, I think you can figure it out. My little birdies tell me you're awfully close. Isn't that right…Hunter?"

Hunter appeared, sluicing through an opening between the men that had formed in the clearing. Heart pounding, she stared at him, tamping down the confusion. Hunter wouldn't betray her. He'd made a pact with her father. A pact with *her*.

"They're quite close but haven't solved it yet," Hunter said, sparing her an indecipherable glance before he faced Eli. "We'll keep an eye on them until they do. And then, we'll turn the technology over to you."

"You bastard!" Lainey screamed, rage consuming every pore of her quivering body. "I have no idea what the hell you're talking about, but you'll never see one speck of my work! Science stands for freedom. For rationality and goodness. I'll sacrifice myself before I turn anything over to you!"

Eli's black eyebrows lifted, his expression sardonic. "Is she always this dramatic?"

Hunter shrugged. "Depends on the day."

Betrayal, true and deep, surged through her frame. Although she'd only known Hunter for a short time, she'd judged him an ally. Her father had recruited him, and she'd been incredibly moved by his motivation to save his wife. But it had all been a lie. Had he even been married? God, she wanted nothing more than to knee him in the balls and ask him while he cried in pain.

"I'd like to discuss the terms of our occupation with you, Dr. Randolph," Eli said, oblivious to the emotions warring inside her trembling body. "Inside the hub. You can invite me in, or we can force our way in. Your choice."

"You're never getting inside the hu—"

"Over my dead body," Cyrus said simultaneously, lifting his rifle at Eli.

Eli sighed. "Shoot him," he commanded tonelessly, as if he were asking for the time rather than directing his men to kill her friend.

"No!" she screamed, taking a step toward the center of the haphazard half-circle they'd formed. "I'll allow you inside if you don't hurt him. I need your word. If you won't give it, my team will blow up the time machine before we enter. They're observing everything on the security cameras and have their orders."

"Fine," Eli said, sounding annoyed. "You have my word. I won't harm any of your men if you let me inside to discuss what we came here to say."

"Lainey, no—"

"Enough, Cyrus," she said, cutting him off with a hand in the air. "Eli, you may come inside. I expect a cease-fire while we talk. Cyrus will stay out here with Hunter's men and your own."

Eli glanced at his camouflaged troops. "Cease-fire, men. Await further orders until I return."

Her gaze found Cyrus's, so filled with worry, and she slowly pivoted to walk inside. Eli and Hunter followed, closing the large door behind them. Turning, she faced them: the dictator, and the traitor.

"You son of a bitch," she hissed at Hunter. "How long have you been working with him?"

"Yikes," Eli said, his expression droll as he looked at Hunter. "She's pissed."

Lainey gritted her teeth as she glared at Hunter. "How. Long?" she asked, the words stilted.

"Six years," Hunter said, lifting his palms as he began to approach her. "But it's not what you think."

"Don't touch me!" she said, causing him to freeze. "Six *years*? You had a letter from my father. I trusted you!"

"It's all my fault, really," Eli said, flippant as he shrugged. "You see, I've done such a good job at advancing the notion I'm a ruthless dictator that my reputation precedes me. It's gotten out of hand, really. I'm not sure anyone could be as nefarious as the dreaded 'Eli Hernandez' is rumored to be," he said, fingers forming quotes as he said his name.

Confusion coursed through Lainey, and she took a step back. "What the hell are you talking about?"

"Can we sit?" he asked, gesturing to the chairs that lined the room.

"No."

"Tough as nails," Eli said to Hunter. "You said she would be."

Hunter nodded. "Lewis was right, she's a ball-buster. And a great asset to our team."

"I'll never join the New Establishment," she said, furious they were discussing her as if she wasn't there. "I abhor everything they stand for."

"As do I, my dear," Eli said, further enflaming her ire. She was lost in their cryptic conversation, and to a scientist, lack of understanding was probably the most uncomfortable experience imaginable. "I have no love for the regime," Eli continued. "I've fought them since I was young. But all great strategists know that true evil can only be destroyed from within."

"What the hell are you talking about?"

"I'm a spy, Dr. Randolph. Perhaps the best one who's ever lived. I infiltrated the New Establishment in its infancy and worked my way up to become its most powerful leader. Now, it's time to abolish them. Namely, with your time machine."

Lainey gave an incredulous laugh. "You want me to believe you're one of the *good* guys? Are you insane? Your reputation is deplorable."

"As I meant for it to be. I've had to make sacrifices in the name of protecting my identity. It hasn't been easy. One of my greatest regrets is that one of my subordinates killed Hunter's wife before I could stop him. I wasn't able to find a way to prevent her death without revealing my identity."

Lainey glanced at Hunter. "Trace Gibson," she said softly.

Hunter nodded, a muscle clenching in his jaw.

"It was a terrible insolvency on my part. Eventually, Hunter was able to move past it and realize my true intentions. The New Establishment is vast, Elaine. It won't be brought down by one person. All the pieces must fit exactly for it to happen."

"And how do you know this?" she asked, hands flailing in frustration. "A little birdie told you how to destroy the regime?"

"No," Eli said, his tone thoughtful. "Actually, you told me."

Lainey felt her mouth fall open. "Excuse me?"

He gave her a timid grin. "You told me when I was only seven years old. You came to me in the year 2039, looking much as you do now, and told me that I must infiltrate the New Establishment and convince them I'm one of theirs. You detailed the path I would follow and that I should show up to your hub, on this date, in the year 2075, because this was the day you finally succeeded."

Breath hitched in her straining lungs as Lainey struggled to comprehend his words. "We haven't succeeded yet," she lied.

Eli lifted a brow. "We both know that's not true, Dr. Randolph. You sent Puss in Boots back this morning. The chain of events has started."

Shock ricocheted to every inch of her body. "You can't know that," she whispered.

"The cat you sent back to 2035 was found by a very powerful man who observed the wormhole. He was an associate of your grandfather's. He began to put the pieces together and realized there were people from the future attempting to change the past. This man was quite evil and determined to succeed in his quest to reshape the world."

Slowly closing the distance between them, his expression turned conciliatory. "You and I have more in common than you can ever know, Elaine. The man who found Puss in Boots was my father, Victor Hernandez, and I want nothing more than to ensure he never succeeds."

Unable to withstand the barrage of unbelievable information, Lainey fell into the chair behind her. Holding her fist to her mouth, she felt the words coil and digest in her gut.

"I know this is shocking, and I'm sorry for that," Eli continued. "But we need to sit down and chart next steps immediately. There are fifty New

Establishment soldiers outside who have no idea I'm not an evil dictator. I need to give the appearance of seizing the hub."

Lainey squeezed her eyes shut, shaking her head. "It's so much to process. My people's safety is everything to me. I'm supposed to believe, after a two-minute conversation, that you won't harm them? It goes against every instinct I possess."

"I know," Eli said, crouching down in front of her. "Here," he said, reaching into his back pocket and pulling out small, shiny arrowhead. "You said you found this beside the river to the north. You and your father spent hours researching the indigenous tribes of Virginia to figure out who fashioned it. Eventually, you determined it was Iroquoian."

Lainey extended her hand, taking the arrowhead and slowly rubbing her thumb over it. "Yes," she said, her voice as pebbled as the stone. "I would've given you something like this to help you convince me."

"It's back in your possession now," he said, sliding his hands over hers and closing her fingers around the arrowhead. "I wonder if the original still sits on your father's desk, or if this is the only version. It would be a great example of a time travel paradox."

Lainey lifted her gaze from her hand, still clutching the stone. "It disappeared several years ago. I remember being sad because it held significance for me, but Marie is a tornado when she's cleaning, and things often go missing. I didn't think anything of it, really."

Eli smiled. "Perhaps we'll never know its true trajectory through time. It's possible that the arrowhead disappeared as a result of the universe trying to amalgamate space-time. Only one such arrowhead should exist, in theory. Or, perhaps Marie accidentally wiped it into the garbage. As much as I'd love to postulate, Hunter and I need to form a plan with you. We've already wasted too much time."

Anger reared its head, flushing through her body as she stared at the handsome captain who'd gained her trust so easily. Cursing herself a fool, she stood.

"I need to speak to Hunter alone first. Please call Cyrus inside and bring him up to speed. Show him this." She thrust the arrowhead back into Eli's hand. "You," she said, glaring at Hunter, "follow me."

Pivoting, she stalked toward her office, knowing Hunter would follow.

Chapter 17

Lainey pushed open the office door and marched through, holding it open for Hunter as she glared at him. Once he was inside, she slammed it closed.

"Lainey," he said, holding up his hands.

"Don't you 'Lainey' me, you son of a bitch!" she hissed. Coming to stand before him, she fisted her hands at her sides, her nails digging into the soft flesh. "You've lied to me from the first moment you turned up on my doorstep."

"Yes, I lied," he said. The sentiment in his eyes was so genuine, reminding her of how he'd played her. "Everything needed to come to light in its own way. There's a certain sequence of events that have to take place for us to succeed."

"Don't talk down to me, you imbecile! I understand the space-time continuum better than you've ever dreamed of!"

"I'm sure that's true," he said, showing her his palms. His placating tone made her want to punch his handsome face. "But it's possible that if I'd told you I was working with Eli, you wouldn't have trusted me, and I wouldn't have been able to grant you the extra time you needed to get the Sphere to work. You must understand, the compound only remains unoccupied because Eli held them off. Our alliance is instrumental to your success."

"I don't trust him," she said, defiant.

"Honestly, I don't trust anyone. Except you." Closing the distance between them, he tried to place his hands on her shoulders.

"No," she said, stepping back.

Sighing, he dropped his hands. "We can't lose the goodwill we've built here, Lainey. You need me more than you know. I'm imperative in your quest to take down your grandfather."

"Like hell you are," she said, thrusting up her chin. "I had this plan before you arrived, and I can certainly accomplish it without you."

Pinching the bridge of his nose between his thumb and forefinger, he clenched his eyes shut. "My god, woman, you're infuriating. You could drive a saint mad."

"*I'm* infuriating?" she cried, eyes wide as her arms flailed. "You come here, giving me some sob story about your dead wife—"

"That wasn't a lie," he cut in, slicing her with his silver eyes. "Every single thing I told you about Kara was true."

"Then I don't understand," she said, exasperated. "How can you help me prevent the past? You're going back to 2063 to save Kara."

"If you prevent your grandfather's actions, my hope is that the New Establishment will never form, and she'll never be in danger. I was only a toddler in 2035, but I believe the younger version of myself will eventually find my way to her. Unlike you, I believe in fate, Lainey. This older version of myself—my present self now—will warn my younger self of the date of her death. Hopefully, it's not a 'fate paradox,' and she's not destined to die on that date in every timeline. If she is, it will be a huge blow, but I'll at least know I gave my younger self the knowledge to try and prevent it."

"Good lord," Lainey said, "this is preposterous. It upends everything we know about space-time. You're banking your future on something unknown."

"We've been staking everything on unknowns for years, Lainey. Time travel itself is the greatest unknown ever invented."

She scowled at him, unwilling to admit the truth of his words.

His irises roved over her, contemplative. "There's something else Eli didn't tell you."

"Great," she muttered, rolling her eyes as she fisted her hand on her hip. "Go ahead, lay another one on me. Maybe you had an evil ancestor we need to align against too? Hmm?" His lips quirked, and she glowered. "Don't you *dare* laugh at me!"

"I'm not," he said, inching toward her.

"Don't come any closer," she warned.

"Why?" he asked, still advancing, lithe as a cougar. "Because you feel it too? I know you do, Lainey. Believe me, no one was as shocked as I was when Eli told me."

"Told you what?" she asked, her voice breathy. The front of his body brushed hers, and she refused to capitulate. Straightening her spine, she repeated, "Told you what?"

"That we were married."

Her mouth fell open, and her eyes threatened to bulge out of her head. "Excuse me?"

"When you visited Eli when he was seven. He told me your husband accompanied you. *I* accompanied you."

"That's impossible. You're going to save Kara—"

"Going back to 2063 was the only part I fabricated, Lainey. I never intended to go back to that timeline. From the time I met your father, I always intended to go back to 2035 with you and help you stop President Randolph."

"But you love her."

"I'll always love her," he said, his expression relaying his frustration. "But my time with her is over. The best thing I can do now is warn my younger self. I truly believe that once you reset the timeline, the younger version of me will still find her. That version will live with her in the new timeline for however long fate allows. And apparently, this present version of myself is going to continue on and marry you." His features drew together. "Although, I don't quite understand how at the moment. You seem to hate my guts, and I'm not really a big fan of yours right now either."

"Screw you," she hissed, pushing his chest. "I wouldn't marry you if it meant the entire world was saved. You're a traitor and a liar."

Strong hands shot to her upper arms, grasping firmly and giving her a shake. "I'm your greatest asset. My alliance with Eli is going to cement your success. Admit it."

"Never!" Attempting to shrug from his grip, she managed to free an arm and lifted it to strike. He stopped her mid-swing, grabbing her wrist as she gasped, "I hate you!"

Small puffs of air escaped his lips as his body throbbed against hers. "Now, who's lying?" he asked, the silk in his tone causing bumps to rise on her flesh.

Drawing her hand to his face, ever so slowly, he placed a kiss on her knuckles. "Open your hand."

Warring jolts of arousal and anger spurred through her, the nerve endings of every limb crackling with unreleased energy. Unable to cease the tiny huffs of breath, she let them linger between them, the air warm and thick.

"Why?" she whispered.

"Relax your hand," he commanded softly.

As if motivated by an unseen force, her fingers uncurled, slow and shaking, until he placed his lips on her sweaty palm. Eyes locked with hers, he extended his tongue and licked the soft skin. The sight of his wet tongue darting over her flesh, his gaze boring into her, sent a gush of wetness to her core.

"I know it doesn't make any sense," he said, maneuvering her palm to cup his cheek and placing his hand over it, securing it against the scratch of his scruff. "I wondered about it too when he first told me. I've had years to digest it, Lainey. At first, I thought I would never get over Kara."

The words hurt for some reason, and Lainey's features must've fallen, because compassion entered his eyes.

"Wait," he said, his voice holding her by some invisible tether. "Just stay with me for a sec, okay?"

She nodded, hating how shaky she must seem.

"I never had any notions of being with Kara again. I understand how timelines work. I knew I would only ever be able to save her for my younger self and hoped that version of me would find her and be happy. I told myself that was okay because we'd already had a passionate love that lasted for eleven years. I didn't need more."

"I don't know what this has to do with me," Lainey said. She didn't begrudge him his great love, but did he have to throw it in her face? Especially when she was literally dripping inside her jeans and desperately trying to push away the image of his full lips overtaking hers?

"It has everything to do with you," he said, eyebrows drawing together as he slid his palm from her arm to her face. "Because if we truly are married in the future, it means I didn't give up. I opened myself back up to something I thought I never would. That gives me hope."

"I've never wanted to get married," she said, her brain foggy from the intense desire pulsing between them. "I don't believe in love. It's just a bunch of chemicals—"

His lips stole the words from her, closing over hers as he inhaled them. Lainey stiffened, frozen as he nibbled at the sensitive flesh.

"Stop thinking," he said, moving one hand to thread his fingers through her hair, the other sliding around her waist and drawing her flush against his hard body. "And for god's sake, stop talking." Opening his lips, he devoured her.

Lainey melted as his tongue swept over her lips then darted inside the warm confines of her mouth. Unable to control her high-pitched mewl, she clenched onto his shoulder with her free hand. His thick arm pulled her close, aligning their bodies, heat radiating from his chest to the skin bared by the neckline of her t-shirt. Her nipples pebbled, aroused by the pressure against his pecs, and she rubbed them against his chest, sending sparks of pleasure through her body.

His resulting groan vibrated in her throat as he plundered her. Sliding his hand to her ass, he latched onto the round swell, drawing her into his erection. Lest she have any doubt of his arousal, he jutted into her, hard behind his black pants, curving into the juncture of her thighs. Needing more, she parted her legs, bringing one high to wrap around his waist.

Moaning in approval, he bent over her, arching her back and tugging her hair with his hand. She capitulated, head limp, as he traced kisses along her jaw. Coming to rest over the shell of her ear, his lips tickled the sensitive skin before he spoke, low and sexy.

"I know this is a lot to process," he said, blowing into her ear and rimming it with his tongue. Lainey clutched him closer, feeling she might collapse to the floor. "I've had six years. You've had six minutes. After a while, it won't seem so incredible."

Lost to desire, Lainey barely understood what he was droning on about. No—she just wanted more of that delicious tongue. Granting her secret craving, he pushed the tip of his tongue into the sensitive channel of her ear.

"Oh, god," she moaned, spearing her nails into his back.

He hissed, his muscular body tensing further at the coarse contact, and took the lobe of her ear between his lips. Steady and sure, he began to suck it through his teeth, the tip of his tongue lathering the minuscule spot, showing her what he would do to other tiny nubs on her body.

Eventually, he ceased, lowering his forehead to rest at her temple. Exhaling a deep breath, he squeezed her ass in his hand, pulling her tighter.

"I can't keep kissing you. Otherwise, I'm going to fuck you right here on Lewis's desk. I'm not sure that's what he had in mind when he recruited me."

Lainey stiffened, taking stock of her wanton position. Her leg was thrown around his waist, hugging his erection into the juncture of her thighs as she clung to his broad back, nails extended, for dear life. The man she'd professed to hate only seconds ago. What the hell was wrong with her?

Furious at herself, she slowly let go, lowering her leg to the floor and unclenching her fingers from his shirt. Realizing the moment was broken, he gradually released her.

They stood frozen except for the rush of their breath, Lainey wary, Hunter resigned.

"I don't care what type of fate you believe in," she said, striving to keep the anger from her tone. "There's no way in hell I'm marrying you or anyone else." Needing to dismiss him and escape the disaster that just occurred, she lifted her chin in the air and pivoted, stalking toward the door. Once she pulled it open, she turned, finger extended. "And if you ever lie to me again, I'll put a bullet between your ears."

Feeling she'd at least regained one percent of the footing she'd lost during the most explosive kiss of her life, she stormed from the office.

Chapter 18

Hunter ran his hand through his hair, silently cursing himself for the way he'd handled the entire situation. He'd thrown the stunning scientist off-balance yet again, and he knew that was something she detested. Sighing, he acknowledged he needed to return to the foyer to discuss next steps with Eli, Lainey, and Cyrus. But first, he just needed a damn moment.

Hand clutched over his chin, he remembered his first encounter with Lewis. The kind man had found Hunter at his cabin, fifty miles north of Terrum, where he was living off the land, solitary and broken. They'd sat on the weathered couch in the sparse living room, Lewis reveling in the taste of the strong coffee Hunter had served. His wife Mara didn't let him drink coffee anymore—the caffeine wasn't good for his heart—so it was a vice he often longed for.

Eventually, Lewis had explained he had a secret alliance with Eli Hernandez. Hunter's reaction had been to lift his gun from his belt and aim it at the scientist's forehead. After several minutes of calm pleading, Hunter gave the man a chance to explain.

Lewis recounted that Eli had approached him one day when he was fishing in the river that ran north of the hub. The man had irrefutable evidence he'd been contacted by Lewis' adult daughter Elaine in the past, even though Elaine would've only been a child when they made the supposed contact. It all seemed impossible, and Hunter realized he was listening to the rantings of an old and unstable man.

Until Lewis pulled the pictures from his coat pocket. Pictures of a large machine with metal arms, looking like something from the science-fiction graphic novels Hunter's grandfather had loved to read. Pictures of the hub, of pages and pages of scientific equations, and lastly, pictures of his daughter.

Lainey's amber eyes had called to him from the photographs. They held a deep sense of purpose and in some, such unbearable loneliness. The same loneliness Hunter saw each time he stared at his reflection.

"I haven't done well by her," Lewis said, rubbing his finger over her face in the photograph. "I've trained her for one purpose and placed such a burden on her. She doesn't understand love, except in the context of the few people at the hub. In preparing her for the doom of the world, I inadvertently made it her reality." His irises lifted, the same stunning ochre as Elaine's. "Eli has given me information that perhaps this reality will change for Lainey one day, but that is for him to tell you. I've done my piece here."

Rising from the couch, Lewis pulled a letter from his pocket. "I'll tell you not to read this, but you will anyway. You'll wait a few days, but curiosity will get the best of you. That's fine, my boy." Eyes shined as he patted Hunter's cheek. "There is continuity in chaos, and you'll discover that eventually. Love is not linear, Hunter. Take it from an old man like me. I know you mourn Kara terribly, as you should, but you will discover a new purpose, and love will take shape in new ways. Your past was with Kara and the man you used to be. Your future is yours to decide."

He set the mug on the table and circled the scarf around his neck. "Be kind to Lainey. She's cynical but practical. You'll always reach her if you remember that." Tipping his hat, the genial and cryptic man exited the cabin.

Hunter sat frozen, the chill of the air from the now-closed door wafting over his lifeless body. He'd been like this for so long, ever since the New Establishment bastards killed his wife. Deadened. Hardened. Empty.

Resolved to stay that way, he resumed his day, milling about the cabin, chopping wood for the fire. Living the life he'd promised Kara he wouldn't end, even though it was pointless.

But, curiously, Hunter's eyes kept darting to the photographs on the coffee table, situated beside the folded letter the strange man left behind. For days, he convinced himself he didn't care. The rantings of a washed-up scientist had no place in his squalid world.

Until the curiosity won out. Days later, Hunter sat in the threadbare chair spreading the pictures across the table. The time machine was something out of his wildest imagination, causing his eyes to narrow as he studied the photos. Beside them, images of Elaine smiled up at him, and he felt some untenable connection to the woman behind the depiction.

Days bled into weeks as Hunter slowly began to live again. He resumed jogging and lifting the weights that had gathered dust in the corner of his cabin. When his body was strong enough, he assembled supplies and his stockpile of weapons and headed to find his battalion mates from the Old Rebellion. Locating several of them, they formed a rebel squad, their allegiance to themselves and justice. Although they didn't align with the Insurgency, they would help them in battles against the New Establishment they deemed worthy, usually as unknown militias, fighting from behind the trees and in the shadows.

In the year 2069, Hunter made first contact with Eli Hernandez. The New Establishment leader was visiting the troops stationed west of what was formerly known as Washington D.C. They'd built a new compound from whence to spread their evil upon the isle. In a rare moment of privacy, the dictator had entered a small clearing in the forest outside the compound walls to experience a moment of solitude.

The click of Hunter's trigger sounded as he held the barrel of the gun to Eli's head.

"Hello, Hunter," Eli said, his tone nonplussed. "I've often wondered when you were going to find me. Took you long enough."

"Let's get one thing clear," Hunter gritted through his teeth, observing the man in the shards of moonlight that shot between the tree branches and rumbling clouds above. "I'm basing this meeting on information from a man I'm convinced is half-insane, so tread lightly. I'm not above killing you. I have nothing to live for anymore except the promise I gave my wife that I wouldn't end it all. My bar is exceptionally low."

Eli sighed and placed his hands in his pockets.

"Hands where I can see them," Hunter gritted.

Eli pulled them free, rotating them slowly. "It would be nice if you removed the gun from my temple, but I won't push my luck."

Hunter backed away, cautious and wary, but kept the gun aimed at Eli's heart. "Okay, start talking."

Eli recounted the tale of Lainey's visit when he was only seven and the arrowhead she'd left him. He detailed his journey to build a reputation so disastrous, not even the most skeptical would dare assume he wasn't on board with the New Establishment's plans for world domination. Then, he lifted dark eyes to Hunter's, full of sorrow and compassion.

"I searched every scenario possible to prevent Captain Gibson's execution of your wife. For years, I postulated a thousand ways I could manipulate the outcome. In the end, I couldn't do it. Although I am admired and feared, there are powerful men who watch me closely. Any opportunity to take me down would derail my chances of success. Even now, I chose this wooded area hoping this would be the night you made contact, but who knows who's watching? I've learned we never fully comprehend the complete truth of any situation. In the end, I couldn't save her. I'm sorry, Hunter." Eli laid a comforting hand on the man's shoulder even though he was pointing a gun at his chest. "It's one of my greatest failures."

Hunter slowly lowered the gun, letting his guard down as he rarely did. If Eli wanted an opportunity to kill him, it was now or never. But the enigmatic man only squeezed Hunter's shoulder before his arm fell back to his side.

"The only thing I can surmise is that everything happens as it's supposed to. A sequence of events that can't be changed, no matter how many instances of time we travel through. As tragic as it was, Kara's death led us here."

Hunter's gaze dropped to the ground, his grief still raw though it had abated to a dull ache over the years.

"One point of solace is that you'll find happiness again. For that, I am truly grateful."

Hunter's gaze latched onto Eli's. "What does that mean?"

"With Elaine," Eli said, his raven-black eyebrows drawing together. "You were married when she came to me as a child. You accompanied her."

Shock spread through his frame, slow and sticky, as he digested the words. "That's impossible," he said, nostrils flaring. "I will always love Kara. I have no desire to be with anyone else."

Eli's lips quirked. "Lewis didn't tell you. Slimy bastard. He always did leave the dirty work to me." Shrugging, he stuck his hands in his pockets. "Sorry," he said, "it's a habit. I don't have a weapon in my pockets, I assure you." Compressing his lips, he finally said, "I need your alliance, Hunter. We've got to set this right."

Gazing up at the half-moon, Eli's eyes narrowed. "I've already been gone too long. Continue your fight against the New Establishment. In a few years, we will begin seizing the scientific hubs. For now, the regime is intent on keeping the world bereft of technology because they want people kept in the dark. That won't last forever. Once we start occupying the hubs, approach Lainey. She'll be resistant. Lewis told me she's quite distrustful of men thanks to a disastrous relationship with someone in her past. It's best not to tell her you'll eventually marry until absolutely necessary. Her belief that you're still in love with your wife will help ease her cynicism and help you gain her trust."

"I'll always love Kara," Hunter repeated, not understanding how he could ever share something so extraordinary with anyone else.

"I know, but love is not linear, Hunter. I'm sure Lewis told you that. It's my favorite quote of the old geezer's. I hope it's true. Otherwise, what the hell is this all for?"

Hunter felt his forehead furrow, questioning.

"Yes, my friend," Eli said, chuckling. "Even I wish for love. For companionship. I was raised by a beautiful, passionate woman who instilled that in me. Being the vilest dictator in the world doesn't lend to happiness, but I hope I'll procure it one day. For now, I must go."

Extending his hand, Hunter grasped it and shook, finding the man's grip strong and steady. He struggled to speak, unable to process Eli's predictions.

"The more you digest the information, the less insane it will sound. Take it from a once-seven-year-old boy who was visited by a woman from the future and told he must become evil to vanquish it." Granting Hunter one last smile, the New Establishment leader quietly stalked from the clearing.

Hunter returned to his men, shaken to the tips of his boots from their conversation. As weeks bled into months, he did his best to process the snippets of his future that seemed impossible. If Dr. Elaine Randolph was going to solve time travel, he'd just go back and save Kara and resume their life together. Simple as that.

Lewis contacted him again in late 2069, several weeks before his death, the note asking Hunter to meet him by the river while he fished. There, they discussed the paradox of time travel. Even if he traveled back to 2063 to save Kara, Hunter was now almost forty, and she would be years younger. A younger version of himself existed, and that would be the one who would thrive with Kara if she survived.

"I know it's all quite confusing," Lewis said, coughing as he held the rod. Hunter could sense his looming death and he found himself wondering how Elaine would process it. Mara had died a few years ago, leaving her with no one but the few people who lived at the hub. Effectively, she was as alone as Hunter.

Hunter lifted a hand to pat Lewis's back, trying to ease the coughing.

"Eh, I'm fine," he sputtered, waving him off. "Damn old age. It's a bitch." He began reeling in the line, the circling of the spinner soothing. "You can only save Kara for your younger self. To that end, it's best if you go back to 2035 and help Elaine stop my father."

Hunter stared at the water, contemplative.

"She'll need your military competence, along with Cyrus's. You two together will be formidable. When you stop the apocalypse and reset the timeline, you'll have the opportunity to provide the details of Kara's death to your younger self. I suggest a letter," Lewis said, sparing him a glance, "because you should in no way have contact with yourself in a different timeline. It could quite literally set off another apocalypse, one we will never recover from."

Hunter nodded, all of it sounding far-fetched and quite ridiculous.

"But the fate paradox has been theoretically proven, Hunter," Lewis continued thoughtfully. "There is a chance Kara's fate is to die on the same exact date in every timeline. No amount of meddling or space-time travel can prevent it. This is the great beauty and the great curse of knowledge."

"I understand," Hunter said, allowing it all to sink deep into his bones. For the second time in his life, he had to acknowledge and accept that his time with Kara was over. Once when she died, and he knew nothing of time travel. Now, again, when he'd learned people could travel through time—as preposterous as it seemed—but he still could never be with her. The rest of his days in the body he inhabited now would be lived without her, however long they may be. The realization was paralyzing and overwhelming.

"Now, now," Lewis said, patting his shoulder, "I know this is all gloom and doom, but you've got a good heart, Hunter. The fact you were able to love Kara so deeply gives me hope for Lainey." Maple-colored eyes seemed to drill into Hunter's soul. "I only ask you to consider the possibility you are a very lucky man who was destined to love two incredible women, each in very different phases of your life."

"My life has been anything but lucky," Hunter muttered.

"Then change the narrative, son," was Lewis's cheerful response. "Only you can."

Hunter had left him by the river, learning of his death only weeks later. In the years that followed, he kept a close eye on the hub, wanting to ensure its inhabitants were safe, and Elaine could continue her work.

At night, he would study the now frayed photograph, staring at Elaine's amber-colored eyes, not understanding how he could ever open himself up to anyone again. She would stare back, frozen and smiling, and he would wonder. About her. About her desires. About the loneliness that emanated from several of the other pictures Lewis had left sprawled on his coffee table.

Over time, his wonder turned to curiosity. Could he actually find it in his heart to love again? When Kara died, it seemed impossible. Now, it seemed…like a distant notion. Far away and clouded, not quite tangible, but on the edge of possibility.

As the inquisitiveness overtook him, he eventually searched her out. From behind a thick tree hidden in the dense brush, he observed Elaine at the spot where she came to find solace. Two comfortable, high-back wooden chairs sat in the clearing, and she would relax into one and close her eyes. With nimble fingers, she would massage her temples, and Hunter realized she suffered from migraines as Kara had.

Elaine would sometimes reverently stare at the chair beside her and clutch the arm with her hand. Hunter understood she was remembering Lewis, and his heart would constrict as tears rolled down her cheeks in the darkness. He knew it was a violation of her privacy and told himself he should be ashamed, but surveillance was a skill he'd learned long ago. Who better to observe than the woman destined to save the world? The woman two intelligent men insisted was an integral part of his future? His voracious mind craved knowledge of her, and the infrequent yet poignant eavesdropping sessions cemented something inside his broken soul he couldn't quite name.

Not wanting to be a creep and certainly not wanting to be discovered by Cyrus, who monitored the premises extensively, Hunter kept the surveillance sessions short and sporadic. But over time, they became an escape for him. He began to look forward to the nights she would appear long after the moon rose and will away the pain in her head. She would talk to Lewis about all sorts of scientific equations and theories even though he wasn't there. The conversations were a metaphor for her solitude, causing Hunter to wish she had someone to talk to who was real.

The years dragged on, Hunter fighting with his men while his fascination grew. Ultimately, he decided he was open to whatever the future held and would continue to do his best to honor the promises he'd made to Kara, Lewis, and Eli. Kara had often told him that if something happened to her, she wanted him to find love again. In the arrogance of his youth, when he'd believed them invincible, it had seemed a waste of breath. Now, he wasn't so sure.

Finally, the day came for him to approach Elaine. When she stood before him, fiery and defiant, he'd been so proud, for he felt he knew her now, in a way, and he'd seen her at her most vulnerable. Her strength and fortitude were magnificent. The few weeks he'd spent at the hub somehow felt longer, as Hunter reveled in each conversation they had, each touch they shared. Although he still couldn't see a scenario where they were married, considering she'd just threatened to put a bullet through his skull, he could still see…possibility.

It was more than he'd ever hoped for, and he was loath to squander it. Only time would tell what the future held, but for now, he was determined to help the snarky physicist accomplish her goal.

Firm with resolve, he straightened his spine and exited the office, ready to discuss the next steps in their clandestine plan.

Chapter 19

Hunter found Lainey, Eli, and Cyrus in the foyer by the hub entrance. Lowering to one of the chairs that lined the sparse room, he addressed Cyrus. "You've been updated?"

"Yes," Cyrus said, murder in his eyes. He was obviously pissed at Hunter's deception, but their subsequent discussion—or punch in the face, judging by the man's furious expression—would have to wait until later. Time was of the essence and couldn't be wasted.

"Here's what I would like to do," Eli said, leaning forward, elbows on his thighs. "Hunter revealed his deception outside. I'll announce he's aligned with the New Establishment and leave him in charge of the troops I station here."

"Is that really necessary?" Lainey asked.

"Yes. It must appear we've overtaken the hub. I need to leave at least ten men here. It's believable that I'll take the rest of the battalion with me to meet up with our troops outside of Solera. The Insurgency forces are strong there, and the New Establishment needs every soldier possible."

"Along with my twenty men, that will give the appearance of an occupation," Hunter said. "My men know me well. They'll understand my alliance is for show, but no one else can know. Eli's true intentions must be kept secret. They're essential to our success."

"I have to tell Claire," Lainey said, frustration evident in her tone. "And the whole team. They can't believe I've let the hub be seized. It goes against everything they know about my character."

"No, Lainey, we can't chance it," Hunter said.

"Listen, guys, it's non-negotiable. I'm not lying to my team. Some people here seem very comfortable with being bold-faced liars,"—she shot a glare at Hunter—"but if I lose my integrity, I have nothing. I tell my team, or I tell the New Establishment that Eli's a spy. I don't give a crap what can of worms that opens, I won't leave them in the dark."

"Lainey," Hunter pleaded softly.

"Non. Negotiable." The words were stilted through her clenched teeth.

"Fine," Eli said, waving his hand. "We don't have time to argue. Tell your team, but I swear, if they tell another soul, they'll jeopardize everything. Their silence is imperative."

"Understood," Lainey said with a nod.

"I'll leave my men here, with Hunter in charge along with the captain of the battalion I leave behind. The New Establishment's primary goal is to seize Solera at the moment. The science of the hub is secondary. There is vague knowledge you're working to solve time travel, but many believe it's impossible. Although my father knew of its existence, thanks to him discovering Puss in Boots, he eventually became drunk with power and devolved into a hateful old man. His rantings about time travel were considered by most to be delusions. The regime is more interested in your ability to supply power than solve time travel. This gives us a great advantage. You have the time machine hidden in a bunker, correct?"

"Yes," Lainey said. "The entrance is inconspicuous to the human eye. Cyrus helped my father build it. Opening the hatch requires several security codes and knowledge of hidden keypads even the best-trained soldier would be hard-pressed to find."

"Good. Hunter will ensure the compound is occupied while surreptitiously allowing you to continue your work. I'll instruct the men to stay outside and that you'll bring them any supplies they need. Their mission will be to keep you sequestered here until we overtake Solera. What is the next step for you, Dr. Randolph?"

"I need to send our human test subject Luke back to 2035. Once there, he will set up a home base for us in an abandoned warehouse my father identified from when he used to live in Washington D.C. before the apocalypse. My father stockpiled currency from 2035, and Luke will use that to purchase supplies. My team will arrive at the warehouse a week later, and we'll all work to prevent my grandfather's actions."

"I'm sure you've discussed your grandfather's security at length," Eli said. "Getting past the Secret Service alone will be daunting."

"Yes," Cyrus said. "But we have all the knowledge Lewis imparted upon us. He knew many of President Randolph's associates that were embroiled in the apocalypse plan. I'm confident we will find a way past his security."

"I'm sending Luke back to March 25, 2035," Lainey said. "There are specific equations that allow us to set the laser frequency to extreme precision and select the date where we open the wormhole portal. I sent Puss in Boots back on March 27. I'll instruct Luke to observe the portal and hopefully prevent your father from discovering him."

"You can try," Eli said, "but it could be a fate paradox that he was supposed to find him."

Lainey nodded, rubbing her upper arms. "We'll still try. If Luke thinks he'll be discovered, I'll tell him to hold back. The ultimate goal is to prevent my grandfather from destroying the world. He detonated the nukes on September 4, 2035, so arriving in March will give us some time to study him and carry out our plan."

Eli nodded, and Lainey contemplated him in the staid light of the foyer.

"There's something you want to ask me," he said.

"I don't understand what your ultimate goal is here," Lainey said. "You want to prevent your father's actions and stop the New Establishment from forming. Do you want to return with us? I don't understand what you're looking for."

"No," Eli said, his expression resigned. "I have no love for the life I've had to lead to get here. In trying to prevent the maliciousness of my father, I inadvertently became as evil as he. It's a great incongruity of my life and one I struggle with. It's prevented me from having things most men crave: family, connection, love. I hate the person I am in this timeline and won't mourn his demise. My hope is that you can prevent your grandfather's actions, and I will grow up in the new timeline a very different man. For now, my one purpose is to ensure you continue your work while giving the appearance the hub is seized. My men will never disobey my orders. I'm too feared, and the consequences are too great. You'll succeed, and I'll be gone from this wretched timeline. Not a minute too soon, if you ask me."

Compassion swept over her, and she reached for his hand. "I understand the burden that was placed on you as a child. It's overwhelming."

His soft grin was filled with a shared comradery. "Perhaps you're the only one who can."

Lainey contemplated the significance of him choosing to live his life for the cause even if it required less than honorable actions. There was a latent nobleness in his choices.

"Okay," Eli said, standing, "I have to get back outside. I'll be cruel to you in front of the men. Just know, it's not personal."

"Got it," Lainey said, standing too. "Let's get on with it then."

As the four of them headed out, Hunter reached toward Lainey and placed a supportive hand on her lower back so she could exit ahead of him. The scathing look she gave him caused him to drop his arm immediately. Hating that he'd hurt her, he vowed to set things right. Remembering Lewis's words, he brainstormed ways to appeal to her practicality, because they wouldn't succeed if they weren't aligned. Sighing with remorse, he headed into the bright sun.

Alora understood something was wrong the minute she entered the first thicket of trees surrounding the compound. It was quiet, and quiet meant things were still. Frozen. Devoid of life.

Marie was always buzzing around the commune, singing to herself as she hung the laundry to dry or cooked large vats of stew over the bonfire. Not today. Even the birds seemed to have silenced, their song stuck in their throats—from fear or trepidation, Alora could only wonder.

Riding her horse, back strapped with bags full of supplies, she whispered to her and patted her neck. "Tread softly, Zita," she said, the lilt of her South American heritage in the words. "Remember, bad men wish to hurt the ones who react the fiercest. Stay calm, and they will let you live."

The horse carried her through the brush until she entered the clearing outside the entrance of the hub. Several New Establishment soldiers stood firm, rifles in hand, while other men dressed in black blanketed their sides. A man with thick hair the color of midnight and firm, broad shoulders was addressing the group that had gathered. Lainey and Cyrus stood by the entrance, flanked by a man Alora had never seen. He had dark brown hair, with gray at the temples, the same color as his eyes. This man held many secrets—she surmised this immediately—but he didn't seem to emanate malice. No, he radiated...*purpose*. Strong and sure, though surrounded by a mysterious air. Alora digested it and decided he posed no immediate threat, but her guard would remain high.

The man addressing the group? Well, he was another matter entirely. Although she couldn't see his face, Alora would recognize the set of his shoulders and muscular frame anywhere. It was the same as his father's and just as evil.

Gazes lifted toward her as the men slowly became aware of her arrival. The wicked man's body tensed, if only slightly. He ceased talking and slowly turned, deep brown irises shifting to stare up at her where she sat atop Zita.

"Hello, Alora," Eli said.

Her eyes narrowed, and she struggled to remain unaffected. She knew the situation must be handled with great care and she must stay devoid of emotion. Swinging her leg over Zita's back, Alora hopped to the ground, the sound of guns being cocked emanating through the thick air.

"Halt," Eli called softly, holding up his fist and signaling them to lower their weapons. Dark eyes flitted back and forth between hers as he contemplated her. "I wondered when you would arrive," he said, the silken words vibrating in tandem with the blood coursing through her veins.

Alora stayed silent, assessing her surroundings. Lainey seemed to be watching them with her ever-present scientific fascination.

"Yes," she said, chin tilted up, determined to hold his gaze. "It seems I've arrived just in time. I knew it was only a matter of time before you seized the hub."

He blinked, slow and cautious. Alora, usually a master at reading people, sensed there was something lurking in the depths of the black flecks of his eyes, but she couldn't place her finger on it. Eli had always been the one person she'd never been able to fully get a read on. It was maddening.

"I have made an arrangement with Dr. Randolph," he said, his handsome face an indiscernible mask. "We will occupy the hub, and she will provide the men I leave behind with supplies, power, and food. Our primary goal is to overtake Solera. Once we do, they will no longer be able to send soldiers to fight for the Insurgency. Our occupation of the isle will be complete. As long as Dr. Randolph keeps us happy, she and her team have nothing to worry about."

The fucking bastard. Alora wanted to grab his ears and thrust her knee into his perfect nose. God, that would feel amazing. Instead, her lips curved, though they held no amusement.

"How generous of you, Eli. Will you wait to kill them until they've given you all their supplies? Or perhaps just half? I know how hard it is to curb your murderous cravings."

His eyes narrowed, and he stood silent, refusing to rise to the bait.

"I'm sorry, but it seems like you two know each other?" Lainey chimed in. "That would've been really helpful to know, Alora."

"Oh, I'm sorry," she said, her gaze remaining locked on Eli's as she refused to give him the satisfaction of looking away when she uttered her next words. "Didn't I tell you? Eli's father is the one who murdered my family all those years ago, on the South American isle. And the prodigal son here just stood by and watched while they were slaughtered."

His throat bobbed as he swallowed, relaying a small sliver of discomfort only she would notice. Alora imagined plunging her knife into the very spot.

"People who defy the regime will always be made examples of, Alora."

"Oh, yes," she said, smirking. "I believe you said those same words to me when they all lay dead and bloodied on the grass. I was only fourteen, and you were barely a man. Eighteen, perhaps? Do you remember what you said to me next, all those years ago?"

Full red lips drew into a thin line as his gaze drilled into her. "I said, 'We're leaving you alive so you can spread the word to everyone on the isle. If they resist the New Establishment, their family will die.'"

"You son of a bitch," she whispered, her restraint vanishing as she recalled the gory images. Clenching her fist, she struggled to contain the urge to strike him.

"Don't," he said, the command soft but firm as he closed the distance between them. "I can't protect you if you strike me." The words were whispered so only they could hear. "For the sake of your family here at the hub, you need to back down. *Now.*"

The words incited confusion in her furious mind as she attempted to reconcile the notion that the man who'd allowed the massacre of her family had just uttered something about protection. It went against everything she knew about Eli Hernandez and it shocked her into stillness.

He gave her an almost imperceptible nod and turned to address the curious onlookers. "Alora has just returned from a long trip and is quite exhausted. Dr. Randolph, please escort her inside. Soldiers, be ready to depart for Solera in twenty minutes. Captain Parker will remain behind with his battalion and run the occupation here alongside Captain Rhodes. I expect the occupation will be uneventful and peaceful. We will return once we've overtaken Solera and work with Dr. Randolph to develop a new power grid, run by the New Establishment and only given to people who conform with our regime."

The New Establishment soldiers called out a unified, "Yes, sir!" and saluted Eli.

After saluting them back, he addressed Lainey. "Get her inside," he said, motioning with his head to Alora. "I can't have her hatred jeopardizing everything."

Alora opened her mouth to unleash every vile word she'd ever spoken upon the arrogant bastard. Before she could, Lainey rushed to her side, hugging her close.

"Come on, Alora," she said, a warning in her gaze. "We have a lot to discuss."

Sparing Eli Hernandez one last glare of revulsion, she let her friend whisk her inside.

"That conceited, pompous jackass!" Alora exclaimed once she entered the foyer. "I swear to god, one day, I'll chop his head off with a dull knife!"

Lainey stared at the gorgeous woman, who was known for her intense control and ability to remain passionless in even the direst situation. Never had Lainey seen her react this vehemently.

"Alora," she said, rubbing her upper arm, "there's a lot I need to tell you, and perhaps a lot you need to tell me." Lainey's tone softened. "Why didn't you ever tell me Eli's father murdered your family? Or that he was there and witnessed the entire thing?"

Alora sighed, slumping into one of the foyer chairs. "I didn't want to muddle things," she murmured, running her fingers through her long, silky black hair. "It was in the past and became the driving force for my quest to bring down the New Establishment." Her almond-shaped eyes lifted to Lainey's, swimming with anger and pain. "And it's my trigger. The one instance of my life that sends me over the edge. Obviously," she muttered, rolling her eyes and sinking back in the chair. "Goddammit! I hate that I lost my cool in front of the bastard. I let him win."

"This certainly complicates things," Lainey said, lowering into the plushy chair across from Alora.

"And why is that?" Alora asked, eyes narrowed.

Lainey sighed. "Because he's now our ally."

Alora's magnificent brown eyes widened, and her nostrils flared as she digested the statement. "Excuse me?"

"I need you to let me explain, from the beginning, when Hunter showed up. It's a long story, and I don't want to leave out any details."

Urged on by her friend's hesitant nod, Lainey spent the next few minutes bringing her up to speed on Hunter, the progress with the Sphere, and Eli's true identity. When she was finished, she sat back and regarded Alora.

"I know this is a lot to process. I think it's best if you unload your supplies and take the day to digest everything. I'm going to instruct the team to meet at the Sphere at midnight. Hopefully, that will be late enough that we'll go undetected."

Alora twirled a strand of hair around her finger, an absent habit she often employed. "This is all quite incredible, Lainey," she said. "I don't know if I can work with Eli. I hate him with a vitriol I've never felt for anyone else."

"I can understand why," Lainey said.

"But I will take some time to think. Will the troops leave me alone while I unpack the supplies through the back door?"

"Hunter should keep them relatively in check. We'll see. He lied to me repeatedly, and I never should've let my guard down with him. It's like Dalton all over again."

Dark eyebrows arched. "So, you are romantic with him?"

Lainey exhaled a *pfft*. "He wishes. I wouldn't touch him with Lucifer's own hand. Lying bastard."

Alora made the sign of the cross, her Catholic heritage summoned by the use of the fallen angel's name. "You're passionate about him. Off-balance. Be careful you don't become what you profess to hate, for you're lying to yourself that you don't desire him. I've been home for five minutes and the energy between you is palpable."

Lainey scowled. "Passion rarely produces favorable results for me. I think we saw that with Dalton."

Alora stood and extended her hand to Lainey, pulling her into an embrace. "Dalton was an asshole, *querida*," she said, rubbing a soothing palm over Lainey's back. Drawing back, she grasped Lainey's upper arms. "I don't get the same read on Hunter. He seemed filled with resolve and a latent morality, but only time will tell."

Lainey breathed a humorless laugh. "Time. It's the one thing in my life I strive to control but never will. It's my greatest adversary."

"Hey," Alora said, giving her a warm smile. "You kicked time's ass, Lainey! You sent a living being back to the past. Don't let this other crap overshadow that. I'm so proud of you."

"Thank you," Lainey said, pride swelling in her chest. "I did it. I still can't believe it."

"I can. You've always been our shining star. We admire you so much and are so lucky to call you our friend."

"Our *family*," Lainey said, pulling her into another embrace. "I missed you so much, Alora."

"I missed you too. I'll take your advice and unload the supplies while I digest everything."

"Sounds good," Lainey said, releasing her. When Alora reached the front door, her hand froze on the latch, head hanging slightly.

"Holy shit," she breathed, turning to look at Lainey. "Eli is one of the good guys."

Lainey shrugged, still shocked by the knowledge herself. "Eli is one of the good guys. Until he shows us differently."

"War makes for strange allies."

"Damn straight."

Alora drew open the door, sunlight streaming over her striking features, and departed up the stairs. Needing to digest the events of the most momentous day of her life, Lainey headed to her office to strategize.

Chapter 20

Several hours later, Lainey sat at her desk, contemplating the enormity of everything that had occurred in the past twenty-four hours. There were so many repercussions of what she now understood, even her fastidious intellect could hardly comprehend it.

A knock sounded on the office door, and her heart slammed in her chest. Hating that Hunter was the first person who flashed through her mind, she approached the door, opening it a mere sliver.

"Hey, duchess," he said, the curve of his sexy-as-hell lips remorseful and a bit playful. "Marie forced me to bring this sandwich to you. She said, if you don't eat something today, she'll burn in hell for breaking her promise to Lewis." Lifting the plate with what looked to be a chicken salad sandwich, he shrugged. "Do you mind letting me in? I'm terrified of the old bat. I can't let her down."

Lainey scowled, furious that blood was now coursing through her body, the nerve endings in a state of hyper-awareness. Why did she react this way to this man, with whom she so desperately wanted to remain aloof and dispassionate? Human attraction and its chemical reactions were an absolute bitch.

Eyes locked with his, she inhaled deeply, realizing he was determined. Stepping back, she opened the door.

"Fine. But only because I'm starving."

He breezed inside, sitting on the leather couch in front of the bookshelf as she closed the door. Turning, she regarded him.

"Come on, Lainey," he said, gesturing to the plate. "Sit down and eat. Your equations will be there in ten minutes. For a few moments, just relax and be a human instead of the scientist who's going to save us all."

The words were so similar to the ones Claire often spoke to her that she relented, moving over to the couch and reluctantly grabbing the dish. Sparing him a glare, she took a huge bite of Marie's sandwich, eyes closing in ecstasy at the taste. It was heavenly.

To his credit, Hunter sat beside her, ankle crossed over his knee, quiet and relaxed. Yet again, Lainey wondered why their silence was never awkward. Although her vitals seemed to increase at his presence, much to her dismay, she never felt uncomfortable around him.

When she finished, he took the dish and rose, striding to set it on her desk. Slowly rotating, he sat on the edge and crossed his arms over his chest, legs outstretched. Those silver irises darted over her face, but she wouldn't give him the satisfaction of speaking first. No—he had some apologies he needed to make, and she damn well wouldn't make it easy for him.

"I'm sorry I lied to you," he said softly. "I was given a lot of advice from Lewis and Eli about how to handle this situation. Unfortunately, I fucked up. Big time. You have to know, I never meant to cause a rift between us. We need to work together, Lainey."

She sighed, running her fingers through her hair, now thick and wavy since being released from its bun a few hours ago. Desire flashed in Hunter's eyes at the motion, inciting a small fraction of satisfaction. At least he felt the undeniable heat between them too.

"It's just so much," she said, gaze lowering to the fingers twining in her lap. "My father lied to me. You lied to me. Nelson lied to me. I just don't understand why people I care for would choose to deceive me."

His expression was soulful and remorseful, caring and wistful, all at once.

"I mean my father and Nelson, of course," she said, embarrassment causing her cheeks to warm. "I would never accuse you of caring for me. You know what I mean. It just hurts to be deceived. I'm not a fucking idiot. I probably possess the most brilliant mind on the planet, and even with that, others still feel they know best. It's absolutely maddening."

His lips curved, and his muscular body straightened. Lainey's mouth watered at the set of his broad shoulders and confident stride as he came to sit beside her. Leaning back, he stretched an arm over the couch, causing her to turn slightly toward him to maintain eye contact.

"The truth is, Lainey, I do care about you."

"You don't even know me," she said, feeling her eyebrows draw together.

"That, duchess, is where you're wrong."

Scowling, she said, "I don't think I like that nickname."

Hunter breathed a laugh. "I think it fits you perfectly. You're a regal warrior who's going to save the world. You're breathtaking."

The words, uttered so sincerely, literally knocked the air from her lungs. Struggling to speak, she sucked in a breath. "You know what I was thinking before you showed up with dinner?"

He shook his head, body language open as he waited for her to continue.

"That this isn't the first time we've done this. If I truly did visit Eli when he was a child in 2039 then this is part of a new timeline we created. We must've failed since my grandfather still detonated the nukes, and we're here, fighting the New Establishment."

Gray eyes widened as he exhaled. "Heavy."

She nodded, picking at a fleck of nonexistent lint on her jean-clad thigh. "How many times have I failed? How many people have traveled through time? Did the technology of the Sphere fall into the wrong hands? It's driving me mad."

His hand slid over hers, gently grasping and interlacing their fingers atop her thigh. "I don't know. That's what you're here for. I'm just the hired help—grunt work and soldier duty. You're the genius. I was hoping you'd have it all figured out."

A laugh escaped her throat. "Having it all figured out is the opposite of where I'm at. At this point, maybe I should just let the world exist and live out my days with Marie's chickens. I'll eat their eggs and finally drink the damn Malbec I've been saving forever."

His firm lips curved into a smile, and he gently tugged her, urging her to his side. Giving up the will to fight, she slid into his warmth, his arm across her shoulders. With his free hand, he cupped the back of hers, interlocking their fingers from behind as her palm rested on his thigh. Allowing herself to enjoy the comfort of his embrace, she rested her head upon his shoulder.

"Although that sounds interesting, your drive will never let you quit," he said against her temple, his fingers drawing lazy circles on her upper arm where his hand dangled across her shoulder. "From what I know of you, Lainey, you'll never stop trying to save the world."

"You're so convinced you know me," she said, confusion in her tone, "but how could you?"

Warm breath flitted across the hair at her crown while he seemed to contemplate. Then, he told her. About the times he'd met with Lewis and the pictures he'd seen. About how he'd been so broken, but the thought of setting things right resonated with him. It pulled him from despair and gave him a reason to live again. And through it all, he began to feel a connection with her, spurred on by the incredible knowledge they would marry one day even though he'd never met her. It was all quite unbelievable.

"Regardless of what happens between us, if you decide you hate my guts and strangle me in my sleep, I'll still care about you, Lainey. Your gorgeous eyes found me from a tattered photograph across time and they pulled me free from drowning in grief. For that, I'll always be thankful to you."

Such beautiful words, spoken in his gruff and sincere voice. Lainey thought them more apt for a poet than a fighter.

"How does such a hardened soldier have such a romantic side?"

He chuckled. "I don't know. My parents were deeply in love before they both died of pneumonia when I was fourteen. Post-apocalyptic medical care was hard to come by, and they didn't make it. But I remember their passion and the way they used to laugh with each other. I think I've always known I want that too."

"I'm sorry they didn't survive," she said, squeezing their laced fingers.

"Me too," he said. "I was on my own after that and joined the Old Rebellion when I was sixteen. Never looked back. I was determined to save others since I couldn't save them. Told myself it was noble."

She tilted her head back, lifting her gaze to his. "It was," she said, her voice raspy.

"I'm not perfect"—sadness swam in his eyes—"but my intentions are good. I'm so sorry I fucked up, Lainey. I hope you'll accept my apology and that we can move on from this. I'm determined to accompany you to 2035 and help you. I'm pretty stubborn, and even if you hate my guts, I won't be swayed. I'm on your team now, whether you like it or not."

God bless her heart, she liked it. Judging by her body's reaction to the deep rumble of his voice, she *loved* it. Sometimes, the law of attraction made no sense. It was futile to maintain any pretense of anger or betrayal when she didn't have the heart or energy to fight him. Her efforts were needed elsewhere and prolonging a rift between them was a waste of time. Lord knew, she had none of that to spare.

"Okay," she said, nodding up at him. "Let's formulate next steps. I've updated my team, and we're going to meet in the bunker at midnight. I'm going to send Luke back and hope like hell he survives. If so, we'll all transport back the next day. You, me, Cyrus, Sara, Claire, Zach, Alora, and Marie. From there, I have no idea what will happen. Hopefully, we'll save the world."

"Heavy," he repeated, giving her a grin.

"Yeah," she said, gaze sliding to his chest. "Everything is so damn heavy. I hope we succeed."

Lifting his fingers to her chin, he tilted her face so that his eyes locked with hers. "With you leading the charge, I have no doubt." His lips quirked. "*Duchess.*"

His tone was so sexy it almost melted her panties off. She imagined him saying the silly nickname against her skin, worshiping her as his lips trailed across her abdomen and below. Feeling the slickness between her thighs, she began to pant, her breath choppy and uneven.

"As much as I want to kiss you right now, I won't." Strong fingers trailed from her chin to her jawline, eventually cupping her neck. "I don't want this to be one-sided, Lainey. I want you so badly, but I won't be made the scapegoat for forcing something on you. When you decide you want me too, I'll be ready. Until then, let's work together to kick the New Establishment's ass." He placed a gentle peck on her forehead, causing her to shiver. "Good night."

Slowly disentangling himself from her, he stood and placed his hands in the back pockets of his black pants. "Do you want me in the bunker at midnight?"

She shook her head, berating herself for already missing the heat of his body and the bliss of his touch. "I need you and Cyrus outside, making sure the troops don't suspect anything. Hopefully, we can pull this off."

His head tilted in acknowledgment. "Got it. Give Luke my best. He's a good man, and I hope he makes it safely." Pivoting, Hunter left the room, the door clicking softly behind him.

Lainey collapsed back on the couch, groaning in frustration as her flushed body vibrated with unspent arousal. Deciding the world she was striving to save had turned itself upside-down in the most confusing ways, she grabbed the plate and headed to the kitchen to do the dishes. Sometimes, one just needed to do some damn manual labor to feel human. Duchess, her ass.

When she reached the kitchen, she found the soap empty and the sink clean. Well, fine then. Placing the plate in the sink, she left it for Marie to clean with the breakfast plates in the morning. Hunter would have a field day, chiding her for leaving the platter unwashed. Realizing she was beaming at the thought, Lainey finally acknowledged that she reveled in his good-natured poking. Someone as serious as she needed it. In that way, they were a good match.

Rolling her eyes at the direction her thoughts had taken, she plodded to her chamber to grab a cat nap before midnight.

A lora knocked on Cyrus's door in the dim hallway. When it cracked a sliver, she slipped inside. He was bare-chested, wearing only black pants and socks.

"You caught me just getting out of the shower," he said with a sheepish grin. "I'm going to sleep outside with the men tonight, so I can keep an eye on them."

Her eyebrow lifted. "Won't that be suspicious?"

He shook his head. "I fabricated some story about a night training that will commence at two a.m. It will ensure the soldiers sleep during Luke's transport. Hopefully." His broad shoulders shrugged. "We're winging this, Alora."

Giving a tilt of her head, she approached him, laying her palms flat upon his pecs. "*Fabricated*. Your vocabulary is growing, Cyrus. Claire's lessons are paying off."

White teeth flashed as he drew away and strode to the bedside table. "*Where the Red Fern Grows*," he said, holding up a book. "Have you read it? I just finished it earlier. It's my latest assignment."

Her lips pursed as she contemplated. "I think I read it ages ago. It's a classic."

Cyrus nodded, reverently running his fingers over the book. It seemed to hold significance for him, and maybe a bit of…sentimentality? It was something she'd never seen in the stoic and practical soldier.

"I got the supplies you asked for," she said, drawing the bag over her shoulder and setting it on the bed. Digging inside, she brought out three tiny vials. "Green, blue, and some strange shade of orange. I thought she'd like them."

Cyrus took them from her, beaming now as he examined them. "These are perfect. Claire will love them. She was complaining the other day that all her nail polish was drying up. I can't wait to see her face when she opens these." His deep brown eyes sought hers. "Thank you, Alora."

Alora studied him as realization washed over her. "You love her," she said softly.

A large breath exited his lungs. "Of course I do."

She grinned, refusing to let him play word games with her. "You love her as a man loves a woman." Closing the distance between them, she slid her palm up his arm, gently grabbing his chin. Turing his head, she forced him to make eye contact. "It's beautiful, *mi amigo*. I'm so very happy for you."

Cyrus tenderly grabbed her wrist, drawing her hand from his face. "It's not meant to be. I'm too old for her. Too cynical." Placing the book back on the nightstand, he gingerly rotated his hands, studying them. "These hands have killed, sometimes in instances I'm not sure were justified. She's such a bright soul in our dark world. I want her to find someone who can give her a family and a future. Someone who isn't haunted by nightmares and hopelessness."

"You could give her those things, Cyrus. Perhaps you're just afraid."

"Perhaps," he murmured.

They stood silent, digesting the contents of their discussion.

"It's been a long time since I've lain with a man. I thought to come here tonight and perhaps take comfort in your arms. We haven't done that in a while. But I realize now, our last time has already occurred." Lifting to her toes, she gave him a soft peck on the cheek. With her thumb, she rubbed it away, the salve she wore on her lips sticky and glossy.

"I enjoyed the time we spent together, Alora," he said, cupping her cheek. "You're a stunning woman with a brilliant mind. But I..." He struggled to find the words. "I just can't. I hope you understand."

"More than you know, *querido*. I wish to find a man one day who will turn down a hundred willing women for the opportunity to be with me. Do you think I have a chance?" She waggled her eyebrows.

Cyrus chuckled. "I think any man who has the balls to take you on and try to win your heart is a saint and a hero. I hope you find him one day, Alora. You deserve to be happy."

"So do you," she said, allowing herself one more glance at his exquisite chest. She was only human after all, and he was magnificent. "Don't let your fear guide you. I look forward to seeing the polish on Claire. Although, it will only shine half as bright as her beautiful heart. You chose well, my friend. Good night."

She exited the room, lips curved as she smiled in the hallway. Something rustled to her left, and she turned to see Claire frozen outside her bedroom door, tears glistening in her green eyes.

In an instant, Alora understood. Not only had she learned tonight that Cyrus had feelings for Claire, she now comprehended Claire reciprocated those feelings and believed Alora had just slept with Cyrus. What a cluster.

"Hi, Claire," she said, awkward energy sizzling throughout the hall. "I was delivering some supplies to Cyrus."

"Cool beans," she said, her voice devoid of its usual cheer. "I was going to bring him another book, but it can wait till tomorrow. See ya." She ducked into her room.

"Wait!" Alora said, closing the distance between them. "You should take it to him now. I gave him everything he needed."

Alora wanted to strangle herself, realizing the words sounded sexual when nothing of the sort had happened. Claire's nostrils flared, and Alora ached to soothe her.

"It's fine, I'll give it to him tomorrow." Pasting on a fake smile, she said, "Sweet dreams. Glad you're home. I missed you." The door closed with a soft click.

"*Mierda*," Alora muttered, slapping her palm to her forehead. She'd royally screwed that up. Claire, with her kind heart, had still spoken caring words to her even though she believed Alora had just been intimate with Cyrus.

Sighing, Alora headed to her own chamber, stunned at what had just occurred. Cyrus and Claire were in love with each other but neither was brave enough to act on it. Matters of the heart were rarely easily navigated, and Alora decided she'd best steer clear. Hopefully, they would find their way to each other and release their fears. Only time would tell.

Chapter 21

The team gathered in the bunker at midnight, the atmosphere in the room tense and solemn. Luke was sheathed in the lead and zirconium-based orange suit Lainey had fashioned, created to shield him from the radiation. Beneath it, he wore black tactical gear and carried a small backpack. The image reminded her of the astronauts from the Apollo missions. She'd spent countless hours looking at old photos with Lewis, imagining how exciting it must've been to chart a new course in scientific history. In essence, she was doing the same at this very instant. The gravity of the moment permeated the chamber.

Luke hugged Sara one last time before stepping into the Sphere.

"Who knows what will happen?" he asked, teasing her from behind the plastic mask that encompassed his head, attached to the suit. "I might be back here tomorrow looking like an old man. I hope you'll still love me."

Tears shone in her eyes as she warbled, "I'll love you across space and time. Never forget that."

Blowing her one last air kiss, Luke stepped into the Sphere, where the stool stood only yesterday. His backpack was lined with currency from 2035, some apples, and basic tools and clothing. Lainey had chosen not to send him back with any sort of gun, lest the instability of the wormhole ignite the ammunition.

When he was standing firm, arms crossed in front of his body, Lainey gave the command to set the Sphere in motion. Sara observed, fist cemented to her mouth, as Claire hugged her close. Marie and Alora stood to Lainey's left, completing their small family circle. Cyrus and Hunter were outside keeping an eye on the hub and ensuring the men didn't suspect what was happening in the bunker.

Finally, the wormhole opened, and Lainey gave a nod of finality to Zach. He ignited the jolt from the fuel rod, and the rocky walls of the bunker began to slightly shake. They were far enough underground that the disturbance wouldn't be felt above. An untrained observer would categorize it as an animal in the brush or some other mundane occurrence.

Little would they know that scientific history, on a scale unimaginable in the three million years of human evolution, was being charted. The light of the Sphere grew bright, and Luke was enveloped by the wormhole. In an instant, he disappeared.

Lainey called to Zach to close the portal, and the whirling arms of the contraption began to slow. Sara was now fully crying into Claire's shoulder, her orange and green painted fingers stroking the woman's hair.

Approaching, Lainey embraced them both, wishing she could absorb Sara's pain. "Your husband is a hero, Sara," she said, soothing her with strokes on her arm. "You should be so proud."

"I am," Sara said, lifting her head and sniffling. "I just miss him already. I'm terrified for him."

"We all are," Lainey replied, grabbing her hand and squeezing. "This entire endeavor is frightening as hell. But he's strong, and we'll hopefully know by tomorrow what happens to him in 2035. All we can do now is wait for his letter."

Sara nodded, wiping her nose with her arm. "I'll be in my room."

"Do you want me to come hang with you for a while?" Claire asked.

"That would be lovely. Thank you, Claire."

"Sure thing, chicken wing. We'll slumber party in our skimpy PJs and have a sexy pillow fight." Lifting her hand to whisper loudly behind it, she said, "I said that for Zach. He needs something steamy to dream about tonight."

"I heard that," Zach muttered, sending Claire a good-natured glare.

They left the bunker, Lainey once again thankful for Claire's spirit and sense of humor, for they desperately needed it.

Once everyone had retired to their rooms, she met Cyrus at the back door of the hub. There in the darkened hall, she confirmed Luke's transport.

Now, they would wait.

Luke's orders were to perform reconnaissance and gather intel, then write a letter that could be transported through the decades until it reached Lainey on the day after Luke was sent back. Once the letter was received, they would all travel to meet Luke in 2035. They would convene with his younger self, the one Lainey had just sent back. If he survived the decades in between 2035 and 2075, an older version of Luke would exist. That version would live out his days in solace, knowing he helped prevent the apocalypse. If all went well, Sara and the rest of Lainey's team would travel to 2035 and reunite with the younger Luke. It was all quite paradoxical and bewildering, as were most things related to time travel.

"It's done?" Cyrus asked.

"It's done," Lainey said, exhaustion evident in her voice.

Cyrus gave a nod. "You need to get some sleep, Lainey. Take one of Sara's pills if you have to. We can't have you functioning on anything but all cylinders."

"Is that your way of telling me I look like shit?" She grinned and arched a brow.

"It's my way of saying I care about you and need you to rest." He placed a brotherly kiss on her forehead. "I'm heading back outside. Get some sleep. Tomorrow won't wait for you to catch up."

Exhausted, she took her friend's advice and attempted to sleep—in a world where human time travel was now an unequivocal reality.

Lainey awoke to the sounds of bootsteps outside her door. Throwing on a t-shirt, jeans, and sandals, she rushed to the kitchen to assess.

Marie had her hand on her hips, barking at the New Establishment captain, who stood a foot taller than she. "Don't you tell me what to make for breakfast, Captain Parker. I've been feeding this ragtag crew for years, and your men can eat what I prepare just like the rest of us."

"What's going on here?" Lainey asked, wondering where in the hell Cyrus was.

"Everything is fine," Captain Parker said, his frustration evident. "Two of my men are allergic to eggs. I'll need extra bread for them."

"We barely have enough to go around, and you bastards want more? I swear, I'll murder you all myself!" Lainey imagined puffs of smoke emanating from Marie's ears as she scolded the soldier.

"Okay," Lainey said, moving into the room. "Marie will make extra bread." She shot the woman a look, daring her to argue. Marie only scowled and crossed her arms over her chest. "I prefer you wait outside, Captain Parker. We have nothing to offer you here. My understanding is that you're supposed to ensure we don't leave the hub until Solera is overtaken. You can do that just as well outside. We're happy to provide you with food and supplies as long as you treat us with dignity."

Captain Parker's ice-blue eyes roved over her. "That will be fine. For now. When Eli returns, I suspect things will drastically change for you. The New Establishment wants your intelligence, and you will have no choice but to help them. I'll let you enjoy your last days of autonomy, but don't forget who's in charge here."

Cyrus and Hunter strode into the room.

"A fight broke out between Hunter's men and some of the New Establishment troops," Cyrus said, his massive body tense. "We deescalated the situation. Did you need something, Captain Parker? The soldiers were ordered to stay outside."

The New Establishment captain's expression turned cold, filled with disdain. "We don't take orders from anyone but Eli, Montgomery," he said, addressing Cyrus by his last name. "Especially ones of your kind. Remember that next time you open your mouth." With a nasty tilt of his head, he stormed from the room.

"Racist asshole," Cyrus muttered.

"Sorry, man," Hunter said, shaking his head. Looking at Lainey, he said, "We got caught trying to break up the scuffle. Captain Parker's men might have initiated it so he had a chance to get inside and do some reconnaissance. Did he get past the kitchen?"

"No," Marie said with a huff. "I stopped the bastard cold. Grabbed him by his damn shirt and dragged him here. I won't let any of those traitors anywhere near the back of the hub."

"You're the best among us, Marie," Cyrus said, bending to place a kiss atop her white hair. "Thank you."

"It's a crisis averted, but we need to be cognizant of the fact they can overpower us and enter anytime," Lainey said. "Eli's orders to stay outside carry weight, but he's not here, and tensions are high. It's imperative we all go through the Sphere at midnight. I hope word arrives from Luke soon."

"Me too," Marie said, turning to the large pan of eggs frying on the stove. "Now, you all get out of here. I've got a ton of food to make, thanks to Lainey."

"Thank you, Marie," Lainey said. "Hopefully, it will keep them at bay."

As Cyrus and Hunter returned to the men, Lainey headed back to her room to examine the small bag she'd be taking with her to 2035. Its contents included a Swiss army knife, some currency from 2035, a change of clothes and underwear, and something she certainly hadn't packed. Lifting the small box, she opened it to find a collection of condoms and a note from Claire that read:

Hey Boss,

Just in case you need some sexy times with Captain Hotness in 2035. Yes, I snuck into your room to put these in your bag. Don't be mad. Love you!

Claire

Lainey laughed, stuffing the condoms back in the bag. It seemed her creative and well-meaning friend was determined she get laid, even if Lainey had absolutely no intention of the sort.

Feeling nostalgic, which was rare for her rational brain, Lainey took a walk around the hub to her father's office, where she remembered sitting on his knee as he struggled to solve equations. At the bookshelf, her fingers traced over the spines of all the books she'd read with Mara. Her mother had been a voracious reader and had read to Lainey every night until she was ten. Although she'd probably been too old for the ritual toward the end, it was one of her fondest memories of her mother.

She walked outside to the chicken coop, where she'd discovered two of them mating when she was barely eleven years old. Lewis had proceeded to explain in his very scientific manner how animals upon the planet reproduced. She'd thought it disgusting and possibly quite messy. Smiling, the image of Claire's condom stash flashed through her mind. Would it be messy with Hunter? Probably. Sticky and wet and messy. For some reason, it didn't seem so gross in that context. Hmm…

The soldiers milled about, and she found Hunter inside his tent.

"Hey," he said, straightening from packing his own bag. "What do you need?"

"I want to walk to the river where Dad used to fish. I can't go alone. It's not safe."

Setting his pack on the ground, he extended his hand. "Come on."

She took it, thankful for his firm grip and unwavering support. Hunter had no reason to pledge his alliance to her cause except for the greater good. It showcased the nobility he was searching to portray when he'd originally joined the rebellion all those years ago.

They strolled to the river, silent under the rays of the sun, surrounded by chirps of birds and the buzzing of insects on the warm day. When they reached the riverbank, shaded by the overhang of trees, she released his hand and crouched to sit cross-legged on the ground.

He sat beside her, picking up a flat stone and attempting to skip it across the water. It made it halfway before plopping to the bottom of the shallow flow of gurgling water.

"You're sad to leave," he said, leaning back on his palms, gazing over the water.

"This is my home," she said, running her fingers over the soft grass at her side. "It's all I've ever known. I wouldn't be human if I wasn't a bit sad." Feeling the corner of her lip curve, she said, "Even though you and Claire think I'm incapable of being human, I assure you, I am."

He squinted, pondering. "Eh, maybe. Or you might be a cyborg, sent here through time by the New Establishment. We'll never know."

Lainey rolled her eyes. "I'm not that bad."

His warm chuckle washed over her. "You're okay."

She punched him in the arm, causing him to clutch it dramatically. Eventually, their smiles softened, and they both stared at the water. Hunter recounted his last conversation with Lewis upon the spot, and Lainey told him of the many times she'd fished with her father. Eventually, their words ran out, and they sat silent and pensive, understanding that tomorrow would be drastically different—if they even survived the journey in the Sphere at all.

"I have to offer you one last chance to go to 2063 and find Kara. Even if you save her for your younger self, I can't guarantee we'll survive in 2035. If we die there, you might never save her."

"When I make a commitment, I stick to it, Lainey. I made a commitment to your father, and I also made one to you. I'm resolved to help you in 2035 and hopefully help my younger self prevent Kara's death in 2063 if we survive that long. But thank you." He surrounded her wrist, which was straight above her palm that rested on the ground, supporting her weight. Giving it a light squeeze, he released her, and she felt it, a wave of longing and desire so deep inside her very core. She was drawn to this man, who exhibited qualities of loyalty and virtue. To deny it any further would be pointless. Was she ready to act on it? Absolutely not. But digesting knowledge was important in her structured world, and her mind would fit the pieces together eventually. For now, she reveled in his proximity.

"We have to get back."

He nodded. "I'm sure we're being watched. Don't kiss me, okay? They'll begin to suspect we're lovers and they'll doubt my conviction to keep you sequestered until Eli returns."

They stood, each wiping the dirt from their jeans. "But we're not lovers."

His firm lips curved into a smile so sinful her toes curled. "Careful, Dr. Randolph. Time has a way of making liars out of all of us. Pretty soon, that statement won't be true."

His arrogance should've been off-putting. Instead, it sent a rush of heat through her veins. Arching a brow, she said, "You're awful sure of yourself."

Extending his hand, he grasped hers when she offered it. "Just stating the facts, duchess."

They strolled back to the tent, Hunter informing her that he was going to do some target practice with the men to keep up the appearance of unity.

"Are you like this with all the women you seduce?" she blurted, unable to stop the words.

"How many women do you think I seduce, Lainey?" he asked, his grin making her insides quiver.

"I don't know. You must've gotten back out there over the years. Twelve years is a long time."

His gaze raked over her, filled with desire. "I haven't seduced anyone since Kara. My success rate is one-hundred percent when you come to think of it. Wasn't interested in being with anyone else after her." Inching closer, but not too close since the men were milling around, he said softly, "Until you. Don't mess up my streak, okay? I want to stay at one-hundred percent." Giving her an almost imperceptible wink, he stepped into the tent.

Feeling dismissed, Lainey pivoted and entered the hub, striding to the kitchen to check on Marie. Men weren't known to go years without getting laid, even those still in love with their dearly departed wives, and especially those as blatantly physical as Hunter. Possessing yet another snippet of knowledge to be digested, she pondered his celibacy, afraid she would let him down if he broke it with her.

Dalton's words blazed through her mind, the snippet of the last argument they had regurgitating the pain all over again as if it were yesterday.

"You showed up tonight knowing I would be here, Lainey," he said, his expression indecipherable under the faint light from the waxing moon. "What do you want?"

Lainey swallowed. "I just... I didn't want things to end on bad terms. Eventually, we'll both move on, and I'll be gone...to a place that's so different than here. Before I go, I needed to tell you I was sorry."

His eyes narrowed. "Where are you going? Are you moving from Terrum?"

"Yes," she said, the corner of her lip curving as she imagined telling him she was heading to 2035 to prevent the apocalypse. "Once my father is better, we plan to move."

"You can move to Solera with me," he said, inching closer. "We could still try to make this work."

Lainey regarded him, considering his aspirations of power and his vision of the life he wanted. There was no place for her there. Not for the woman who only wanted one thing; who only had one purpose. The woman who was not predisposed for love or happily-ever-afters.

"I'm sorry, Dalton. That's not why I came here. I only wanted to set things right between us. I hate that we ended on such a sour note. I'll always think of you fondly."

Rage contorted his features, and Lainey wondered how the emotion could overtake him so quickly. How had she overlooked it during their affair? Had she naïvely ignored it, overcome by the new experience? Suddenly, his arm shot out and he roughly grabbed her chin, forcing her to meet his gaze. She swatted his arm away, already feeling the bruise from on her jaw from his forceful grip. He stared at her, nostrils flared, as his fists clenched at his sides.

"I should've known you were just a whore looking for some excitement. When I met you, I thought you were so stunning." Dalton scoffed, his face an ugly mask of wrath as they stood under the stars. "But fucking you was like screwing a dead tree. What a waste of time. At least I saved myself from spending my life with a frigid bitch."

Lainey recoiled at his words. She'd always thought their loving pleasurable, although nothing she couldn't live without. Since sex was a function, just like any other bodily activity, she didn't expect it to be mind-blowing.

"You're saying this to hurt me. I'm sorry it didn't work out, Dalton. I truly am."

"To think I spent all these months intent on marrying you. Fuck you, Lainey. You never pleased me. Thank god I won't have to spend my life trying to get my dick up around you. You're pathetic."

Lainey forced the cruel memories from her brain, pushing them back inside, deep where they wouldn't surface. She understood that Dalton's words sprang from fury, but did they hold any truth? Would Hunter think her frigid? Was being with him even worth taking the chance? She'd most likely die of embarrassment if he found her lacking in bed. She already struggled so vehemently to not be thrown off-balance around him.

And why was she contemplating sleeping with him anyway? They were traveling four decades to the past later this evening, on an important mission that would leave little time for a game of wandering hands. Good lord, Claire had gotten in her head for sure. All her talk of sexy times and the wad of condoms—she'd fallen prey to suggestion.

Telling herself to stop being an idiot, she set about living the last hours of her life at the place she'd always called home. And only thought of Hunter about a million times—or maybe even a few more than that…

Chapter 22

T he woman approached on horseback, her stallion's hooves quiet upon the warm ground. The late afternoon sun was low on the horizon, and she wished she'd arrived earlier. But battles between the Insurgency and the New Establishment scattered the fields and meadows she traversed along the way, and she'd been careful to avoid them.

Entering the clearing that housed the scientific compound, the sound of rifles being cocked flitted through her ears. Gandalf rode slow and steady below her, and she lifted her arms, palms forward, to show she wasn't a threat.

A man with hate-filled eyes entered her path and asked, "Are you lost? You're trespassing on the site of the scientific hub of the Eastern American isle."

Elle pulled the hood from her head, swinging her blond hair free so it could wave in the summer wind. "No, I've traveled here from Terrum. My mother is very ill, and I thought I might be able to procure some medicine. If I don't, she will die."

The man lifted a gun from his belt, pointing it at her horse. "Sounds like something a spy would say."

"Okay, Captain Parker, that's enough." A man with much gentler gunmetal gray eyes approached, coming to stand beside the captain. After giving him a scowl, Captain Parker lowered his weapon.

"What is your name?" the kinder man asked.

"Elle Huber. I'm unarmed and desperate. I hope you wouldn't kill an innocent woman."

"No one is ever completely innocent," Captain Parker mumbled.

"I'm Captain Hunter Rhodes. I think it's best if you hop off the horse for now. Cyrus will help you."

A large man with smooth russet skin lifted his arms to her. Elle had never seen muscles bulge as they did from his extended arms. "Ma'am," he said, urging her along, "I'll help you down."

She let him assist her, her sandaled feet touching the ground. Once balanced, she regarded the three men.

"I've written the supplies I need on this paper." Rustling inside the brown bag slung over her shoulder, she pulled out the parchment. "I understand you have a nurse here."

"We do," Cyrus said with a nod. Looking at the other two men, he said, "She doesn't seem to pose a threat. We could at least let Sara look at her list and offer her some water."

"No," Captain Parker said. "Eli was clear. No intruders, no exceptions."

"I don't want to cause any trouble," Elle said, eyes downcast as she had practiced so many times. Submissive actions usually calmed even the angriest of men. "I'm happy to stay here while your nurse looks at the list. I've written my mother's symptoms and everything she ate and came into contact with. Hopefully, your nurse can scrounge together something that will help."

Cyrus took the document, gaze filled with comprehension. Good. He was a quick learner. They'd need that in 2035.

"I'll take this inside and return with some water. Please, wait here."

She nodded, folding her hands in front of her abdomen to appear demure. Eventually, Captain Parker lost interest, stating in his gruff tone that he was heading to check on some of the men cleaning rifles at the rear of the hub.

Captain Rhodes approached her, lifting an arm to pet the horse's neck, effectively hiding his face from the other men in the distance.

"Do you carry news of Luke?" he asked softly.

"Yes," Elle said, her lips barely moving. "It will be devastating to them."

Hunter's muscular body stiffened. "He didn't make it."

She gave an almost imperceptible shake of her head.

Inhaling a deep breath, Hunter gave Gandalf one last stroke. "What's your horse's name?"

She told him, inciting a smile from his firm lips.

"Lord of the Rings. A story that traverses time and space."

"That it does," she said, giving a wistful grin.

There they waited, in the waning sunlight, for the inhabitants of the hub to read the words Luke had sent through time.

Lainey lifted her head when Cyrus bounded into her office. He usually knocked, so she immediately sensed something was wrong.

He thrust the letter toward her, explaining where it came from. Rounding her desk, she sat on the edge and unfolded the withered paper. With shaking hands, she began to read.

Lainey,

I'm writing this letter from a prison cell near Washington D.C. on April 3, 2035. Katonah Prison lies in Eastern Virginia, but I urge you not to try and save me. I'm set to be executed tomorrow and realize the justice system was broken long ago in this strange sliver of space-time. Due process is a distant memory for anyone who jeopardizes the plans of President Randolph or his associates. Chalk my death up to a fate paradox—I already have. I can't see a future where I survive past tomorrow.

Your grandfather's network of nefarious associates is vast. Many upon each continent are working to ensure the apocalypse. Afterward, most will go on to form the New Establishment. Eli's father, Victor Hernandez, is one of the vilest. I saw him discover Puss in Boots and followed him back to his townhome, where several armed guards were waiting to take me into custody.

Lainey, somehow, he <u>knew</u>.

Knew who I was and everything about me and you and the future. All I can surmise is that we're on an unending loop. Each instance you send me back convinces us we conquered time travel for the first time, but in reality, we've actually done all of this before. Powerful men, consumed by malice, will always be one step ahead, already foreseeing our every move.

Throw out your previous plans. Do not meet me at the warehouse in D.C. Instead, you must chart an entirely new course. Only with the element of surprise will you succeed. My brain is too muddled from the constant beatings and the fear of death to help you form a strategy, but I know your brilliant mind will triumph.

I'm giving this letter to one of the guards I've deemed trustworthy. His son was killed in the latest war President Randolph sanctioned in

Afghanistan, so he's no friend of the regime. He also believes your grandfather's power has grown too vast, and I believe his assignment to my cell block to be my last grant of good fortune. If so, he will pass this letter to his children and perhaps their children, for them to carry through time on its journey to you. I have given instructions for it to be delivered before sundown on September 1, 2075, the day after you sent me back in your timeline.

Lastly, I've written a note for Sara on the second page. I would ask that it be for her eyes only, but doubt that will happen due to the numerous hands this letter will inevitably touch. Regardless, I ask this of you: Help her move on and ensure she gives herself permission to love again. I can't die knowing she lived in self-imposed loneliness for the rest of her life. That would break my soul more than death ever could. Encourage her to find a husband who can cherish her as I was so lucky to do for the few years we had.

Godspeed, Lainey. May you prevail over the evil that has overtaken the world. I fear you are the only hope we have left.

Luke

Lainey inhaled a large breath, allowing Luke's words to wash over her. Tears stung her eyes as she handed the letter to Cyrus, and he began to read. Lainey knew Claire had been teaching him for years now, something that warmed her heart.

"You're able to read it?" she asked softly.

"Yes," he said, his broad features laced with sadness. "I get the gist." He handed the letter back to her. "What are you going to do?"

Lainey stood and raked her hand through her thick hair. "I'm not sure yet, but I'll tell you one thing. There's no way in hell I'm letting Luke die. Our first priority will be to save him. I'll readjust the settings on the Sphere so we go back to the day after he arrived. That way, we can warn him and work together to bring down my grandfather's regime."

Cyrus's lips curved. "Damn straight. I'm on board." His dark eyebrows drew together. "Do you think he's right, that we've done this before? Possibly multiple times?"

Lainey sighed. "Honestly, yes. I began to understand we were on some strange, unending space-time loop when Eli gave me the arrowhead. It's baffling. As much as I want to process it, at this point, I just need to take action. Prepare the team—we're heading back to March 26, 2035, tonight at midnight."

"What about the girl?" Cyrus brought her up to speed on Elle Huber.

"I need to sit down and asses her intentions. Obviously, if we leave her behind they'll kill her. Let's bring her inside, and you and Hunter can help me question her."

Cyrus nodded. "Captain Parker is suspicious of her."

Lainey's eyes narrowed. "Captain Parker is an asshole. I trust you and Hunter can figure out a way to get her inside. I'll leave you to it."

He gave a nod and exited while Lainey sat at her desk. The news about Luke was devastating, but she wouldn't allow herself to mourn. No—she would save him and prevent his imprisonment and eventual death. Resolved that this would be the ultimate outcome, she braced herself to tell Sara the news. Once she was ready, she headed to find the sweet nurse and deliver the update.

E lle sat before Dr. Elaine Randolph, Captain Rhodes, and Cyrus Montgomery at the circular table inside the hub. Gingerly ingesting the soup they'd set before her, which tasted amazing, she eyed them.

"Sorry to inhale this," Elle said, swallowing another spoonful. "I've just had a long journey and I'm starving."

"Of course," Elaine said. "Our associate Alora is taking care of your horse, and he will be fed as well."

"Thank you," Elle said.

"We don't want to bombard you, but time is of the essence," Captain Rhodes said. "We need to ask you some questions."

Picking up the bowl and slurping down the last of the contents, she pushed the dish aside and folded her hands atop the table. "I'm happy to answer anything you need, Captain Rhodes."

"Hunter is fine," he said, smiling. "Although, call this one Dr. Randolph,"—he jerked his thumb toward where Lainey sat beside him —"or she'll lop your head off."

"Lainey is fine, Elle," she said, darting a look at Hunter. Elle immediately sensed the seething sexual tension between them. "So, if you don't mind, I'd like you to start at the beginning. Are you a descendant of the prison guard Luke befriended in 2035?"

"Yes," Elle said with a nod. "My grandfather, William Huber, was assigned to Luke's cell block at Katonah Prison in April of 2035. My mother was very young then, but she eventually had me, and being her only child, I was tasked with delivering the letter to you. My uncle John died in President Randolph's final Afghanistan war, and my grandfather and mother hated him for instituting the draft. Their disdain for him cemented their allegiance to your cause."

"Not to be a cynical scientist, but the mysticism the letter carries with it is almost incomprehensible," Lainey said. "I wonder how your grandfather and eventually your mother and you came to believe Luke's story. I can only surmise that if I was Luke's guard, I would probably think him insane."

Elle laughed. "Yes, tales of time travel and alternate timelines are considered quite strange. The thing is, my grandfather was enthralled with Luke's tales in the short time he knew him. He spoke of things that seemed so fantastical, but there was an element of realism in his retelling of the rise of the New Establishment. I think Grandpa Will felt he was a part of something bigger than himself and wanted to contribute in some small way. His last words to me were to assure I would complete the mission." She lifted her hands in a shrug. "And here I am. I was born outside of Terrum in 2051. My mother moved to the compound in 2053, when my Grandpa Will died and when my father left her to join the New Establishment. Yet another reason she wanted you to succeed, Lainey."

"Is your father still with them?" Cyrus asked.

"Honestly, I don't know," Elle said. "I haven't had any contact with him since he left. It's possible, but I was so young I don't remember him. My mother destroyed every photo of him and she never spoke of him again. Jeffrey Cannon was his name. My mother chose to go by her maiden name, and so do I."

"Is your mother truly sick?" Lainey asked. "If so, we could attempt to send a courier with medicine to Terrum."

"My mother is dead," Elle said. "Lost to drowning when she was doing laundry in the river outside Terrum. It's possible she committed suicide, or perhaps some New Establishment soldiers came along and murdered her. I'll never know. Some local nomads brought her body back, and I buried her several years ago. Since then, it's just been me."

"I'm so sorry," Hunter said, compassion in his silver eyes. "You're quite young. You must've barely been a teenager."

"I was sixteen when she died," Elle said, lifting her chin. "Old enough to understand the world and what needs to be done to exist in it. I won't claim my life has been easy, but I possess a knowledge of how to thrive as a woman in this dark existence and believe I do quite well at it. However, I do have one wish I hope you will grant in exchange for me delivering Luke's letter."

"What is that?" Lainey asked.

Straightening her spine, Elle spoke the most important words of her short life. "I want you to take me back to 2035 with you. I'm resilient and smart. I can help you prevent your grandfather's actions and pledge my loyalty to you. I have no wish to stay in this timeline where everyone I love is dead."

"I understand your desire to start over, Elle," Lainey said. "I'm not opposed to taking you back with us, but I'll admit that I'm wary. We don't know you and don't have the time to vet you properly. It's possible you came upon the true descendant of the guard Luke befriended and stole the missive so you could deliver it yourself. Luke didn't mention the guard's name in his letter, as you must know. It's possible you're a spy for the New Establishment, intent on traveling with us to warn your counterparts in the past. You must understand that I have to protect my team at all costs and am distrustful of anyone I haven't thoroughly vetted."

"I understand," Elle said, determined to prevail. "I will do whatever it takes to prove myself to you. You only need to ask."

Lainey nodded. "Let me discuss with Cyrus and Hunter. For now, I'll grant you access to one of the vacant sleeping chambers. It has a small but functional shower and a warm bed. You must be tired from your travels. Zach can show you the way."

A tall, lanky man with shaggy light brown hair and light green eyes entered the kitchen, his smile bright. "Hey, Lainey, sorry. I wasn't eavesdropping, just starving. Was hoping to grab some food."

"Sure," Lainey said, standing. "But can you show Elle to the vacant room next to Alora's first? Elle, this is Zach, and he'll escort you. Please, don't go anywhere in the hub except for your room or common areas like the kitchen and foyer."

"Got it," Elle said, standing and grabbing her bag. "Thank you, Lainey."

Zach's grin was warm and his eyes kind, something Elle had rarely seen during her two decades on the planet. "Nice to meet you, Elle," he said, extending his hand.

She shook it, realizing he must be a scientist because it was smooth instead of calloused like a soldier or laborer.

They strolled down the hallway until he motioned to a door on the left.

"Here you go."

Stepping inside, she regarded the sparse room with a twin bed and desk and a door off the side.

"That's the bathroom," Zach said. "The water only stays warm for a few minutes, so shower fast. There should be some soap in there, but if not, just come find me."

"Thank you," she said, taken by the air of innocence surrounding him. In her experience, men were harsh. Rough. Angry. Sexual. He didn't seem to be any of those things, and curiosity began to curl in her gut. Was it still possible to be born in this dystopian world and retain an aura of innocence and innate goodness? Perhaps it was after all.

"My office is a few doors down on the right. Claire and I are usually in there crunching numbers. Just come find me if you need me." With a tilt of his head, he closed the door behind him as he left.

Exhaling a large breath, Elle collapsed on the bed. Reaching into her bag, she pulled out the old photo of her father, the only one her mother hadn't destroyed. He wasn't who she told them he was, but she felt that didn't really matter in the long run. Eventually, all would come to light. For now, she was craving a shower.

As the water sluiced over her, she wondered if she should feel guilty for lying. Deciding guilt was futile, she toweled off and brushed her teeth. Keeping her father's identity secret would help her get back to 2035, and that was her ultimate goal. One thing Elle had learned was that one had to look out for themselves, even if it meant perpetuating lies.

In the end, she would succeed no matter the cost. And then, she could join her mother in heaven, or wherever one went when they died, for she had nothing to live for once she accomplished her one singular goal.

Resolved and determined, she lay down on the bed to rest for an hour before resuming her fight to join the team of ragtag time travelers who were intent on saving humanity.

Chapter 23

At midnight, the members of the scientific hub gathered in the bunker, the gravity of the journey upon which they would soon embark heavy in the air. All were dressed in the "bunny suits," as Claire called them, to prevent radiation poisoning.

The Sphere could only send back two travelers at a time, so Lainey and Hunter would be first, followed by Claire and Cyrus, Sara and Elle, Marie and Alora, and lastly, Zach. Lainey had offered to transport Ivan and Steven, but after a lengthy discussion, both had chosen to stay. They had family members in the current timeline and felt an obligation to remain and fight with the rest of Hunter's men who would stay behind. Lainey found the decision extremely noble.

She'd ultimately decided Elle would accompany them to the past, although she was still wary. The woman would have little protection in the current timeline, and Lainey felt an obligation to ensure her safety. Hopefully, she wasn't a spy who would destroy everything they'd worked for. Only time would tell.

The team lined up around the Sphere, Lainey and Hunter entering together. She gave the nod to Zach, and the metal arms began to spin. Hunter grabbed her hand and squeezed, thick through the material of the suit, and she smiled at him through the plastic head cover, so thankful he was with her. Regardless of how she'd first insisted she would remain aloof toward him, and even though it had only been a short few weeks, she now felt an unbreakable connection with him. Perhaps even her cynical heart could accept that they were fated to meet and form a bond so they could partner on this journey.

She squeezed back, her throat swelling with fear and excitement as the wormhole opened behind them.

When the pressure grew, and Lainey's teeth were clenched as firm as her grip around Hunter's hand, she closed her eyes, knowing their entrance to the time portal was near. Suddenly, she felt a tugging sensation at her backside, and all went dark. Struggling to breathe, she attempted to open her closed lids.

Seconds that felt like eternities passed as she existed in a vacuum lacking time, space, air, or particles. And then, as quickly as it had appeared, the darkness vanished.

Sucking in massive gulps of air, Lainey tugged the plastic helmet from her head, squinting against a bright light. Realizing it was the sun, she searched her surroundings, pushing her body up with her arms on the soft grass. Locating Hunter beside her, she crawled over and helped him remove his helmet. He gasped for air and then proceeded to rest his palms on the ground and vomit.

Lainey rubbed his back, letting him get it all out. When he was done, he rolled to a sitting position and rested his forearms over his knees.

"Holy shit," he said, still breathless. "That was some journey."

"Zero G's aren't for the faint of heart."

His eyes narrowed. "You did fine."

She shrugged. "I'm a natural. Scientist and all." He gave her a morose scowl. "What? I have a strong constitution. Don't worry, I won't tell anyone you puked your guts out."

"Thanks," he muttered, surveying the surroundings. "Where are we? Did we make it?'

Lainey unzipped the suit and removed it, then pulled the compass from her bag. "Yep. We're in the forest I identified outside of Washington D.C. Hopefully, we arrived on March 26, 2035. We'll wait for the rest of the team to arrive and then we'll get to work. Zach will be last, once he shows Ivan how to push the buttons in sequence on the console and send him back. Then, he and Steven will blow up the bunker and destroy the Sphere." She frowned as she absently ran her hand over the blades of grass.

"I know it's hard to demolish your masterpiece," Hunter said, grasping her hand, now free of his suit as well, "but it has to be done. We can't chance it falling into the New Establishment's hands."

"I know," she said, sighing. "At least you'll all be with me."

Hunter smiled, consoling her as they waited.

And waited.

Until, eventually, they accepted the truth. No one else was returning to 2035 that day. Minutes turned into hours while Lainey and Hunter sat stoic, understanding something had gone terribly wrong. None of the members of her team appeared.

Finally, they stood, knowing they couldn't wait any longer, exposed in the grassy clearing. Together, they headed to the abandoned warehouse to find Luke. On the way, Lainey pushed away the tears. This was a time for strength, not emotion.

When they reached the warehouse, set in an abandoned industrial park about a mile from the forest where the Sphere had placed them, they found Luke on the second floor.

"Hey, guys!" he said, jogging toward them, his limp pronounced. "You're early. I made it, Lainey! Can you believe it?" He gestured around the squalid concrete structure. "Where's everyone else? Where's Sara?"

Lainey opened her mouth then closed it, unable to tell him she had no damn idea.

"We don't know, man," Hunter said softly. "They were supposed to follow us back, two by two, but they never appeared."

Luke's features collapsed into a mask of worry. "Do you think something happened to them?"

"I don't know," Lainey said, emotion swirling through her body. "But we can't stay here. It's a long story, but I don't believe this is the first instance of time travel. We're most likely in danger. We need to find a different place to stay and change our entire plan. Otherwise, you're going to be executed in a week."

Luke started. "How do you know this?"

Lainey pulled a folded letter from her bag. "You wrote it to me in this letter. I'll let you read it later. For now, I think the best thing to do is to head to a crowded place. That way, if we start disappearing, people will be more likely to file police reports. Police reports lead to investigations, and the last thing my grandfather and his associates want is people sniffing around. I know we discussed staying off the grid before, but everything has changed, especially now we have no idea what happened to the team. We have to employ new tactics."

"I agree," Hunter said. "I like the idea of making connections and not hiding. If they already know we're here, let's stick it to them. Let's shove our middle fingers right in their faces. Luke, did you scout the area?"

He nodded. "Honestly, if we're going to do this loud and proud, I say, let's get a hotel downtown. Can't be more conspicuous than that."

"I agree," Lainey said. "Let's go."

Luke pulled a device from his pocket. "I can call us an Uber."

"Uber?" Lainey said.

Luke smiled. "So, I bought this pre-paid cellular phone yesterday," he said, shaking it in his hand. "The lady at the store was nice enough to show me the basics. It has these applications where you can summon things on demand. I bought some pre-paid Uber cards—it's a service where you tap the phone, it pings your location, and the driver comes to pick you up."

"I've lived in a world without technology for so long," Hunter said, staring at the device in Luke's hand. "This is going to be really interesting."

"No doubt," Luke said. He swiped his finger a few times on the screen and smiled. "Javier in a Silver Camry will be here in five minutes."

"Well, damn," Lainey said, eyes wide. "Welcome to 2035. I can probably recite every equation that makes that thing work, but I've never actually used a cell phone myself. Incredible."

Luke nodded. "We'll get to the hotel and then we can discuss next steps, right? Obviously, I want to figure out what happened to Sara."

"Yes," Lainey said, exhaustion latent in her tone. "We have to figure out what happened to all of them."

Hunter must've noticed her tearing up because he placed a supportive arm across her shoulders. "Come on, guys. Let's not keep Javier waiting." Letting him lead her down the dirty concrete stairs, they headed toward the car and to the unknown future that awaited them.

They settled on an economy hotel on the outskirts of downtown Washington D.C. They visited three hotels before they found one that would let them pay in cash, but eventually, they prevailed. Lewis had saved his old driver's license, and Zach had created forged IDs based on the specs from Lewis's for each of the hub members months ago, in anticipation of being sent back. When Lainey had approved Hunter's travel to 2035, Zach had made one for him as well. The only exception was Lainey, who was using her mother's old ID. She and Mara could pass for each other, although Lainey had inherited Lewis's hazel eyes and not Mara's light green ones.

"We need to find a way to get a credit card," Hunter murmured while they waited for the desk clerk to finalize the two rooms.

"Yes," Lainey said. "I know my mother's social security number and can most likely get one that way. I'll work on it tomorrow. First, I need to get my hands on a laptop."

When the rooms were secured, they traveled up the elevator, Lainey stopping at the door next to Luke and Hunter's room. "Let me wash up and brush my teeth, and I'll meet you guys in your room in ten."

Entering the functional, two queen room, Lainey pulled her toothbrush from her bag and commenced freshening up. Staring at herself in the mirror, she noticed the dark circles under her eyes. Man, her face looked like it had lost a fight with the wrong end of a shovel. Was it a result of traveling four decades in only an instant? With her fingers, she manipulated the skin around her eyes, willing away the small wrinkles that lived there. Almost forty, with what to show for it? Her team was missing, her journey to prevent her grandfather's disastrous actions had only begun, and she was stuck in a time that wasn't hers.

Sighing, she forced herself not to dwell on the negatives, for they were vast. Heading next door, she sat with Luke and Hunter at the round wooden table in their room, discussing their path forward. They would need to make contacts, perform reconnaissance, and do their best to figure out what had happened to the others, all while ensuring Luke didn't get sent to prison or executed. Each task was a huge undertaking in its own right.

Finally, exhausted and irritable, Lainey acknowledged she needed sleep or she'd never be able to help anyone. Excusing herself, she headed next door and threw on the soft, worn boxer shorts and t-shirt from her bag.

A knock on the door jolted her, and she eyed the peephole. Hunter stood outside, eyebrow arched.

"Let me in, duchess."

She barely opened the door, somewhat embarrassed for him to see her in the faded sleepwear. "I'm in my PJs," she said, giving him a glare.

"Lucky me," he murmured. "Come on, Lainey. Let me in for a sec."

She relented, drawing the door open and letting him enter. When it clicked behind her, she turned. "I'm tired, Hunter—"

"Hey," he said as his fingers encircled her wrist. Pulling her to the bed, he gingerly sat and drew her between his legs. "I know, Lainey, but I needed to check on you. You're always so damn strong. Don't get me wrong, it's amazing. But sometimes, we all just need to be comforted."

"I don't," she said, feeling like a petulant child but too exhausted to filter it. "I just need a few hours' sleep. After that, I'll be fine." Withdrawing from his grip, she headed to the bedside table in between the two beds and removed the tie that held the bun atop her head. Mahogany waves fell down her shoulders, and she fluffed it out, combing it with her fingers. The motion reminded her of all the times Marie had done the same, combing her slim fingers through Lainey's hair before braiding it when she was young. Unable to squelch the emotion, she buried her face in her hands and began to cry.

Hunter was there, his strong arms surrounding her waist, the warmth from his firm chest against her back. He held her as she shook, her cries sometimes violent, and whispered words of comfort into her hair. Hugging her against his steady body, he consoled her.

"Where the hell are they?" she sobbed, her body quaking. "What if they're dead?"

"No," he said, turning her and lifting her chin with his fingers. His other arm supported her lower back, holding her against his muscular frame. "I won't let you think that way. We're going to do everything we can to figure this out and set things right."

"My entire life has been dedicated to setting things right," she said, chin trembling, "but I always seem to accomplish the exact opposite. What the hell am I doing, Hunter?"

"Shhh…" He smoothed the pads of his fingers along her wet cheek, drying her tears as his silver gaze bore into her. "You're right where you need to be. I told you, I believe in fate, Lainey. I don't know how, but there has to be a reason for all of this."

"I don't believe in fate."

"Then I'll believe for you."

The words lingered between them, spoken in his deep timbre, and the dull thud of Lainey's pulse pounded through her veins as it always did in his presence. They stood frozen except for their breathing, eyes locked as their hearts beat in tandem.

She lifted her hand, sliding it over the stubble on his cheek. His eyes closed as he whispered her name.

"Why does it feel this way with you?"

His lids opened slowly, and his eyebrows drew together slightly. "What way?" he murmured.

"Like I just ran a marathon and I'll never catch my breath."

"I think that's called chemistry, duchess. You should be an expert in that."

"I should be, but I'm not." She shook her head. "Hunter, we can't. With everything that's going on, we can't."

Concerned irises darted over her face as his fingers threaded through the hair at her temple. "I didn't come over here to make love to you, Lainey. I came here to comfort you. But sometimes, those two things are one and the same. I think it might actually be beneficial for you to let go, if only for a few hours. For you to remind yourself that you're alive and fighting to ensure your family stays that way too. But only you can decide. Do you want me to leave?"

The words inspired a jolt of disappointment so severe her breath caught in her throat. The thought of him removing his arm from her waist, of losing the heat from his warm body, was…unthinkable. She craved him so vehemently, she wanted to crawl into every crevice of his muscular frame and let him soothe her with his velvet touch.

"I'm not good at this," she said, her voice raspy.

"At what?"

"At, you know, sex. I've only done it with one person, and he was less than thrilled."

"Then he was an absolute idiot. No one can be with a woman as passionate as you and not be satisfied unless they're only worried about putting themselves first."

"What does that mean?"

"Did he touch you, Lainey?" Hunter asked, sliding his hand from her temple to thread his fingers through the hair at the base of her neck, cupping her head. "Did he take the time to make sure you were ready?" The hand at the small of her back drifted lower to cup the firm globe of her ass, palming it as he began to knead the flesh there.

"Did he make you come, over and over, before he sought his pleasure?" His fingers slid from her bottom, around her thigh, to cup her mound, causing her to gasp. "Did he take care of you here?" His fingers rubbed in concentric circles over her shorts, showing her what he would do if she was spread wide before him.

Lainey breathed his name, unconsciously pushing her mound against his fingers.

"Yes," he hissed softly, the cadence of his breath quick and choppy. "That's what you need. Someone who draws out your pleasure. I want so badly to please you, Lainey. You only have to tell me yes."

"How can we take pleasure when the others are lost?"

"Whether we make love or not, nothing will be accomplished tonight. You're not a bad person if you let me comfort you for a while. Honestly, we'll probably sleep a lot better if you ask me, but I'm biased." His lips quirked.

Her eyes flitted back and forth between his as she searched the depths of his soul. "I won't be a substitute for Kara," she said.

He stiffened, a deep shaft of pain washing over his handsome features. "Wow. Way to kill the mood. Are you serious right now?"

Irritation surged along with a hefty dose of guilt, and she stepped out of his embrace. "It has to be said, Hunter. You obviously loved her and always will. I don't need avowals of love from you since I believe romantic love is just a jumble of chemicals in our overheated brains, but I won't have you imagining you're with her while we're together. I have too much pride for that."

Hunter collapsed on the bed, hands resting on his thighs as he exhaled a large breath. "You really are something, woman. I swear to god." He rubbed his eyes with one hand in a frustrated motion. "Where in the hell do you get the idea that I'd even think of another woman when I'm with you? Are you fucking insane?"

"You spent the entire inception of our acquaintance talking about your wife, Hunter. It's only natural to question whether I'll be compared to her in your mind."

He muttered something about *stubborn women* and rubbed his hands over his face. "I won't let you castigate me for loving my wife, Lainey." The words burned, the irrationality of the reaction causing her jaw to clench as she observed the anger in the set of his broad shoulders. "I loved her for the time that we had, and I spent years gathering the fortitude to forgive myself for moving on. For surviving when she didn't. *Years,* damn it!"

Standing, he pointed a furious finger in her face. "And the one woman who I have the courage to even *attempt* to open my heart to accuses me of being stuck in the past? Well, excuse me, but I think you've got it turned around here, duchess. I moved on because I had to. Because I was so tired of feeling dead inside. You hold on to this past relationship like a sick vice around your neck. I'm sorry love didn't work out for you that time around. News flash, love hurts, and it sucks sometimes. It ripped my entire soul open when I lost Kara, and I sure as hell won't let you do the same. Screw you, Lainey. You're a coward, and frankly, a pretty big asshole to accuse me of comparing you to her."

His words were so pointed, so deep, she felt terrible for even bringing it up. She'd only wanted to state a point since he'd confided in her that he'd been celibate for so long. She didn't want him to expect some fantastic lovemaking session, as he'd most likely had with his wife all those years ago.

Instead, she'd hurt him tremendously. The man who'd pledged his loyalty to her and her cause and who'd been nothing but a gentleman each time he'd touched her. Shame washed over her as he stewed.

"Screw this," he muttered, shaking his head and starting for the door.

"Wait!" she cried, grasping his forearm. "Hunter, please."

"Please, what? Stay here and let you tell me what a jerk I am? No, thanks." He tugged, attempting to pull from her grasp.

"Stop," she said, holding him tight. "Just stop. I—" Rubbing her forehead with her fingers, she struggled with what to say. "I'm sorry," she said, eyes closing as she searched for the right words. "I don't know how to process it when you speak about her sometimes. I wonder about your relationship and how connected you must've been. I don't understand that type of connection. It's just so foreign to me. I'm sorry."

He sighed, resting his forehead in his hand. "You talk about yourself as if you're a damn robot, Lainey. That's just programming. I assure you, you're as capable of passion and intimacy as anyone else."

"Uh, yeah, not to beat a dead horse, but I'm pretty sure I suck at all that crap."

Breathing a laugh, he sat on the bed, tugging her to sit beside him. "I don't think so, sweetheart," he said, taking her hand. "Lewis really did a number on you, didn't he?" He placed a kiss on her knuckles.

"I don't blame him. It's just how I am." She shrugged. "I'm sorry. I wasn't trying to be an asshole. I just don't want to disappoint you."

"Disappoint me? I'm mad for you, woman. It's baffling to me that someone as brilliant as you doesn't understand that."

"I want to understand," she said, turning to face him. Bringing both legs on the bed, she laced one behind his back and glided one over his thighs. Sliding her palms over his pecs and shoulders, she clutched her hands behind his neck. "It's just all so unfamiliar to me. My feelings for you confuse the hell out of me," she said, nuzzling the stubble by his ear with her nose, "but I'd be lying if I said I didn't want you. Don't make a liar out of me, Hunter."

His head slowly rotated so that his lips brushed against hers. "Tell me, Lainey," he whispered against her lips. "Tell me what you want."

She licked her lips, reveling in his shiver when the tip of her tongue barely grazed his. "I want you to take me to bed."

His teeth nipped her lower lip. "Are you sure? I don't do short-term, Lainey. Making love is a commitment to me. If we do this, you're mine. Do you understand?"

"Who else's would I be?" she asked, smiling against his smooth skin. "I don't know anyone here."

"Funny," he said. His tongue darted out to swipe her lower lip, causing a rush of moisture deep at her core. "I mean it, Lainey."

"Okay, but I'm not marrying you. I don't want to get married."

His grin was so sexy, she dug her fingernails into her palms, attempting to squelch the throbbing at the juncture of her thighs. God, he was gorgeous.

"We'll see, sweetheart. Now, be a good girl and open those pouty lips. I'm going to fuck that smart mouth with my tongue."

"Wow, someone likes to talk dirty," she teased.

"Just wait, duchess. I'm only getting started." Spearing his hands into the hair at the base of her neck, he opened his mouth over hers and consumed her.

Chapter 24

Hunter breathed in the scent of her, desire flooding every pore in his straining body. For so long, he'd imagined this. Holding Lainey. Touching her. Making her scream his name as he loved her gorgeous body.

Celibacy had been relatively easy, although he desperately missed being touched. He'd met women along the way and had considered lying with them in an attempt to prove to himself he'd let go of the past, but he'd never been able to carry through. Never until *her*.

The high-pitch whimpers she made as his tongue searched the depths of her mouth sent sparks of arousal to his shaft, straining and hungry under his black pants. Pulling her close, he thanked every god above that she'd already straddled him and situated her atop his straining erection. She squirmed, the opening of her center straight above his cock, and he rested his forehead against hers.

"Don't stop," she said, searching for his lips with hers.

"I don't want to blow it," he said, jutting into the juncture of her thighs. "It's been so long. I usually use my hand for this, and it's definitely not as pretty as you."

Her smile was so cute that his heart melted, causing his chest to heave. "I've always wondered if I was attractive. I have a symmetrical face, and that's usually the first factor in human attractiveness."

"Are you going to spout science to me the entire time we do this?" he asked, teasing her. "Because I can't decide if it's hot or if I need to practice counting on my fingers faster. That's how I do math, by the way," he said, feeling his lips twitch.

Lainey laughed, her head falling back, exposing the smooth skin of her neck. Unable to resist, he pressed his lips there and began to trail kisses along her vein. "Oh, god," she breathed, clutching him closer with the fingers threaded through his hair. "Science is lascivious, my friend. I assure you, it's hot."

Lifting his head, he grinned. "Show me."

She bit her bottom lip, the action causing his dick to twitch in his pants. Fuck, she was so damn sexy.

"Well, most sexual reactions are purely scientific." Reaching to grab the hem of her shirt, she pulled it over her head, tossing it to the floor. Her bare breasts jutted toward him, small and round, with hardened nipples begging to be touched. He realized she must sleep without a bra, since she was in her pajamas, and growled in approval.

"You see," she continued, cupping one breast and lifting it. The areola was dark against the surrounding pale skin, the tiny nub in the center puckered and hard. "My breasts grow heavy when you kiss me. It's a result of blood rushing toward the erogenous zones in my body. Nipples possess clusters of nerve endings, which is why they're so sensitive. And why it feels so good when they're licked and sucked."

He may not be a scientist, but Hunter was no fool. Listening to his lover's words, he lowered his head, nudging his nose against her nipple. She breathed his name, the word a plea from her lips, and he opened his mouth. Rimming the soft skin of his lips around the little bud, he felt her shudder in his arms.

"You're teasing me," she said, nails digging into the back of his neck, driving him wild.

"Yes," he said, blowing on the sensitive spot. "I want you dripping and mindless before I ever push one inch inside you." Extending his tongue, he swiped against her nipple, causing her to moan. "If you can still recite science, I'm doing something wrong."

He licked again, feeling small drops escape the head of his shaft at her high-pitched mewls. Deciding he'd teased her enough, he slid his lips over her areola, closing down on the tight nub. Hollowing his cheeks, he sucked her, back and forth, his tongue working a frenzied pace as his mouth created suction.

Her hips began to buck over his, and he grabbed her ass with his broad hand, attempting to hold her still. If she didn't stop, he'd blow his load right there.

"Hunter…I can't…it throbs…"

"I know, baby," he said, kissing a wet trail to her other breast. "It's supposed to. The build is the best part." Closing around her other nipple, he began to suck, loving how she clenched his hair, his neck, his shoulders. Her hands slid everywhere, looking for a stronghold, but he wouldn't allow her that. No—he wanted her off-balance, drowning in desire, so that when he was finally inside her, her walls would be down. Those gorgeous amber eyes were the windows to her soul, and he wanted them filled with hunger for him.

As he flicked her nipple, she slid her hand down until it rested at the waistband of her shorts. Whimpering, she pushed her hand inside, beginning to rub herself as he lavished her breast.

"Yes," he whispered, securing an arm up her back and supporting her head, as he lowered his other hand to join hers. His fingers slid between the folds, finding her wet and slick, and he rimmed her opening with the tip of his finger while her own finger drew circles over her clit.

"I like watching you rub yourself," he said, inching his finger inside her tight channel. "It's so sexy, sweetheart."

Her hips gyrated into his finger, undulating as she took it deep, the walls of her core squeezing him. Needing to see her face, he lifted his head from her breast, staring at her stunning features. Eyes closed, mouth open, breath panting from between her quivering lips… She looked like a goddess. One he'd worship forever if allowed.

He retracted his finger and reached up, encircling hers, stopping the motions on the engorged nub. Her eyes flew open, and she whimpered. "No…"

Gaze cemented to hers, he laced their fingers, his palm cupping the back of her hand. Drawing them lower, he urged her middle finger to the damp opening. Ensuring his finger was aligned with hers, he pushed them in, watching her reaction as he impaled her with both of their fingers.

"Does that feel good?" he asked, searching her face for signs of pleasure.

"Yes," she whispered, her hips pushing back and forth against their two fingers inside. "I've never—"

"You've never fucked yourself like this?" he asked, marveling at how responsive she was.

"No," she rasped, her cheeks flushed. "I usually just rub my clit."

"Hmm…" he said, increasing the pace of their fingers. Wanting to please her, he rested the heel of his hand against her swollen nub, grinding against it while he stroked her with their fingers. "Sometimes, there are spots back here," he said, simulating a hooking motion so they massaged against the walls of her swollen core. "They feel good if stimulated."

Her head arched back so far he had a fleeting thought it might snap. Remembering to support her, he cupped her head. "You still with me, duchess?"

"Yes," she croaked, "oh, god, yes. It's so…right there…please, Hunter."

"Fuck, you're so close." Increasing the hooking motion of their fingers against her innermost place, he intensified the pressure on her clit with the heel of his hand. "Let go, Lainey. I've got you. *Come.*"

Lowering his head, he closed his lips around her nipple, sucking it so deeply it curled into his tongue. She gave a wail, her body still in a deep arch, and exploded all over him. Deep shudders wracked her body as moisture flooded their fingers, sweet and slick, as he continued pushing them deep. Growling against her nipple, he let her come apart, reveling in the beauty of seeing her so raw and open.

When her tremors faded to quivers, and her muscles seemed to turn to jelly, he stilled his fingers and lifted his head. Her arms fell to the bed, limp and sated, and he chuckled as he laid her on the soft comforter.

"You're laughing at me," she mumbled, eyes closed as she panted on the bed. "I don't care. Oh, god, I might never recover. I'm done."

He stretched over her, resting his head on his hand, elbow on the bed, as his body bracketed hers on the side. Giving her time, he pushed the hair from her temple in a slow, gentle caress.

Eventually, her eyes slid open, staring up at him with wonder and sated desire. "Wow."

He chuckled, lowering to place a peck on her lips. "I've imagined making you come so many times. I was dying to know if you were a screamer or a wailer."

She beamed at him, causing Hunter to wonder if he'd ever seen her smile so broadly. "Well, what's the verdict?"

"Wailer, for sure. So high-pitched and sexy. I didn't know you had it in you, duchess."

"Should I be embarrassed? Because I literally don't have the energy."

His laugh washed over them, and Hunter experienced the joy of sated sexual energy for the first time in twelve long years. It was beautiful, and he was humbled to be with her this way.

"You don't have to be embarrassed with me. But I do reserve the right to tease you."

She bit her lip again, causing his still-hard shaft to twitch. Her eyes darted to his crotch and back up again.

"Hang here a sec, okay?" she asked.

He nodded, wondering where in the hell she thought he'd go when she was half-naked in a hotel room. As far as he was concerned, this was paradise.

She picked up her bag from the chair by the window and rummaged inside. Striding back to him, she held up a box.

"Condoms. Claire stuffed them in here in case I couldn't control my rampant desire for you." The words held humor, but Hunter saw her gaze fill with worry at the mention of her best friend's name.

"Hey," he said, maneuvering to sit on the edge of the bed and pull her between his legs. "I know. Tomorrow, we'll begin the quest to save them. Right now, I need you here, so we can finish what we started and get some sleep. Okay?"

She nodded, although concern still lined her features, which was entirely understandable. "Okay," she whispered.

Setting the box of condoms on the table in between the two beds, she latched onto the waistband of her shorts and shimmied them down her legs. Tossing them aside, she stood naked and unashamed in front of him.

"I'm not twenty-five anymore," she said, shrugging. "I have cellulite and stretch marks and a hundred other blemishes you're going to see, so look your fill, and let's get on with it. I hope you don't mind I'm not perfect."

In response, he stood, pulling his shirt from his chest and throwing it to the ground. Kicking off his boots, he unbuckled his belt and divested himself of the rest of his clothing. Standing naked before her, he grasped her wrist, bringing her hand to rest on a large scar beneath his left pec.

"I have blemishes too, duchess," he said, studying her expression as she traced the scar. "And worse ones on my back. I haven't lived an easy life."

"But you're insanely gorgeous," she said, fingers trailing down, over his six-pack, scratching the tiny black hairs that lined his chest and stomach.

"So are you." His hands wafted over her hips, thumbs tracing the thin white marks at her hip bones. "Stretch marks and all. Trust me, Lainey, a few flaws here and there won't distract from the beauty I see when I look at you."

"You're trying to make me feel better."

"Never," he said, grinning down at her. It was true—she had some dimples around the tops of her thighs, and several small stretch marks lined her hips. The swell of her abdomen below her navel was a bit more pronounced than her flat stomach, but to him, she was perfect. Every dip and hollow was one he longed to taste with his tongue, and he committed to ensuring he would during the course of their affair. However long it lasted. Hopefully for a *very* long time, if he had anything to say about it.

"I was shy around my first lover. I never let him see me naked. But with you, I feel…free. Open and unashamed. Why is that?"

He lowered to the bed, sitting on the side and tugging her toward him. "Because we're going to grow old together, Lainey. Haven't you realized that yet?"

Tears formed in her eyes as she smiled down at him. "You're awfully optimistic for a man who's stuck four decades in the past without a time machine in sight."

He winked. "It's easy to be optimistic when an exquisite woman is standing naked in front of me. I like my chances."

Her lips quirked, and she reached over to grab the box, pulling out one of the condoms. "They're lambskin, as all condoms from 2075 are. If we're going to keep doing this, we should probably buy some latex ones. They're more effective."

He took the condom, unwrapping it as he spoke. "Was that science again? I can never be sure with you." His cock was semi-hard, due to the break they'd taken, and he stroked himself until he was stiff. Hands trembling slightly in anticipation, he began to roll the condom over the sensitive head. Lainey seemed enthralled, and he asked, "Do you want to do this? I forgot you like to study every damn thing imaginable. Have you ever put a condom on a man before?"

She shook her head.

"Here," he said, grasping her hands and drawing them to his shaft. "Make a circle with your thumb and forefinger and roll it on." She followed his instruction, causing him to hiss out a breath as her fingers worked the thin layer of protection over him.

Finally, he was sheathed and raring to go. His cock stood proud, searching for the warmth of her core. She inched closer to him and hesitantly placed one knee on the bed beside him.

"I like where this is going," he rasped, loving how tentative she was. She was so strong and stubborn for her team, but here, in the small hotel room, she was shy and curious. "Don't stop, duchess. Put your other knee on the bed and ride me. I think you'll like it that way."

She obeyed, her knee resting on his other side as she placed her arms around his neck. Lifting his face, his lips searched for hers. They found them, soft and supple, his tongue plundering the depths of her mouth as she loomed over him. Moving his hand to her center, he found her still wet. Gathering her silken juices on his finger, he dragged it up to the nub barely hidden by her swollen folds.

She broke the kiss, staring into him as he circled his finger around her clit. Her hand trailed down his chest to the base of his shaft, and he groaned when she encircled it with her fingers. Positioning her opening over the head of his straining cock, she gently began to ease down.

His hips worked into her—slowly, so he didn't hurt her—as her body gradually adjusted to him. Glazed amber eyes stared into his soul, and he thought he might drown in them if he didn't look away. But he couldn't, no matter how hard he tried, for she had bewitched him beyond rational thought.

Hunter moved his hands to the sweet mounds of her ass, clenching one in each hand and pulling the lips of her sex apart with the tips of his fingers so she could ease further onto him. Each slow slide was torture on the most magnificent scale, and he wondered if any man had ever died of pleasure when making love to a woman who consumed him. If not, Hunter might be the first. Lainey was every dream he'd ever had rolled into this one fantasy that just so happened to be real.

When he was fully sheathed in her tight channel, his hands encircled the globes of her bottom. "I'm going to move you over me, okay?" She nodded, clutching his shoulders. "Hold on tight. It might get rough."

He began spearing his shaft into her wet folds, clenching her ass as he jerked her up and down. The muscles in his arms strained as he lifted her, over and over, forcing his hips into the juncture of her thighs. She rode him passionately, bucking and gyrating, squeezing every nerve ending in his cock with her swollen walls. Blood surged to his shaft, causing him to grow blind with desire, his breathing so labored he thought his lungs might burst from his chest.

The sounds of their skin slapping together, sweat-soaked and sticky, echoed in his ears, and he fought like hell not to come.

"God, I want to fuck you forever. How do you feel so good?"

She purred, the sound visceral as she clutched his hair. "You're so deep inside me."

He clenched his teeth, struggling to draw out the pleasure. "Damn it. Hold on." Grasping her tight, he flipped her around, throwing her to the bed before he maneuvered atop her flushed body. Lifting her leg, he held it high behind her knee. "Tell me if you want me to stop."

"Never—"

Her words were cut short when he impaled her, hard and deep, pulling back out before surging again. His hips began a maddening pace, moving back and forth so fast he thought his legs might give out. Her breasts jiggled in an uneven motion, making his mouth water as he watched her moan. Lifting her hands above her head, she surrendered completely, her body open and limp, letting him take her hard and fast.

His balls slapped against the smooth skin of her ass, beginning to tingle as he felt the orgasm form. "Fuck, I'm going to explode inside you," he said through gritted teeth.

Those gorgeous dripping-maple eyes opened above her cherry red lips, gaping and wet. She uttered one word, and he was lost.

"*Hunter.*"

His body snapped, the orgasm releasing like a bolt of lightning, up his engorged shaft and into her sweet body. Sheathed by the condom, he emptied himself, calling her name as he quaked and shuddered. Her arms surrounded him, hugging him close, and he collapsed over her, burying his face in her neck as he spurted into her. Slow and sure, his tense body eventually relaxed, and he twined his fingers in her hair. Nuzzling a path with the tip of his nose from her neck, across her jaw, and eventually to her lips, his gaze found hers.

Open-eyed, he kissed her, gentle and lazy, as she stared back with emotion-filled eyes. Lifting his hand, he brushed her hair from her forehead.

"Lainey," he whispered against her lips.

"That's Dr. Randolph to you," was her silken reply.

Overcome with laughter, he rested his forehead against hers, so thankful he'd finally lain with the woman who'd consumed his thoughts for six long years.

"Are we the best at sex of anyone who's ever lived?" he joked.

"Most likely, although we'll need to experiment many times to formulate a solid hypothesis."

"God, I love science," he said, pecking her on the lips. Easing away from her, he withdrew, already anticipating the next time he'd be inside her sweet warmth. Giving her a wink, he headed to the bathroom to dispose of the condom and wash up.

When he returned to the bed, she took his place in the bathroom and returned a few minutes later. He'd already situated himself under the covers and reached for her. Taking his hand, she let him pull her into bed. Loving how she snuggled into his side, he stroked her hair while her cheek rested on his chest.

"I'm not good at sleeping with other people," she said, yawning before continuing. "I find it uncomfortable."

"Well, if you want to roll away, I won't be offended. I actually enjoy a good cuddle after sex."

"I swear to god," she mumbled into his chest, "you're way too romantic for a soldier. It hurts my practical brain."

The deep chuckle rumbled through his chest. "I'm just an idealist. You should know that by now."

He stroked her thick hair, reveling in her palm against his heart and her silken leg thrown over his thighs. Her breathing evened out, and he glanced down at her.

"Lainey?" he whispered softly.

It was too late. The woman who professed not to like cuddling was dead asleep against his pecs. Smiling, he shut off the bedside lamp and held her in the darkness before giving in to his own exhaustion.

Chapter 25

Lainey awoke to Hunter dressing in the soft light that filtered through the curtains. "Already making a getaway?" she asked.

He smiled, tugging his shirt over his head and sitting on the side of the bed. "No way, lady. You're stuck with me." He palmed her cheek. "I'm going to head next door and shower. After that, we need to find you a laptop and formulate next steps."

She bit her bottom lip. "Luke will know."

Hunter chuckled, smoothing the pad of his thumb across the lip she'd just indented with her teeth. "Luke will know," he said. "Does that bother you?"

She blinked, realizing it didn't. "No. I just don't want him to think we're focused on anything but finding Sara and the others."

"He knows. You've dedicated your whole life to keeping them safe, Lainey." Lowering, he placed a peck on her lips. "It's okay for you to have the best sex of your life once in a while, with the sexiest man you've ever seen."

Lainey rolled her eyes. "*Pfft.* Go away. I need to shower."

His smooth grin would've singed her underwear off if she were wearing any. "See you in a bit, duchess." Aligning his lips with her ear, he said in his silken tone, "I think you're pretty sexy too."

She pushed him away, laughing as he rose and headed for the door. Once there, he gave her a wink and left, ensuring the door clicked behind him.

Groaning, Lainey pulled the covers over her head. She'd definitely had some great sex last night. With Hunter. Holy shit.

While she showered, she allowed herself to be happy, doing her best to forgive herself for taking a few hours of enjoyment when her team was missing. Once dressed, she met Hunter and Luke in the restaurant of the hotel lobby.

"Hey," she said, sliding in the open booth across from them. "How did you sleep, Luke?"

"Honestly, not great," Luke said, his expression worried. "I hate being stuck here when Sara's so far away. Although, I can't wait to reunite with her and show her everything about the year 2035. It's freaking unbelievable."

"Everything's so bright," Hunter said. "I never imagined the night sky could be so illuminated. These people don't understand how amazing it is to have technology and electricity at their fingertips."

"Uber and cell phones are just the beginning, guys," Luke said, grinning. "Not to diss Marie, because I love her cooking, but you can get chips with barbeque and cheese flavoring right out of a machine in the lobby. They also have these things called Skittles, which taste like heaven on your tongue."

"Dad told me so many stories about this era, trying to prepare me. It's still a shock though," Lainey said. "I'm sure we'll discover a thousand new things every day that will blow our minds. In the meantime, any ideas on where I can get a cheap laptop?"

"Yes, but I'd like to say something first," Luke said, his grin sincere and knowing. "Just to air things out, I'm happy for you and Hunter. I always wanted you to find what Sara and I have. I figured I should get it out in the open, so you don't feel weird."

"Thanks," she said, gaze traveling to Hunter, who looked completely normal and unaffected.

Unfazed, he slid a toothpick between his teeth, giving her a glib wink. When had the annoying habit become sexual? Lainey didn't know, but Hunter's tongue around a toothpick did all sorts of things to her insides.

Returning her gaze to Luke, she cleared her throat. "I don't feel weird. Now, let's get crackin'. We've got some people to find."

In a stroke of fate, there was an electronics store two blocks from the hotel. Lainey purchased a functional yet basic laptop and returned to the restaurant. Using the hotel Wi-Fi, her fingers tapped furiously over the keys.

"How do you know how to use that thing?" Hunter asked.

"My father salvaged several laptops in faraday cages before the EMPs were detonated," she said, her eyes never leaving the screen. "He knew it would be imperative that if he solved time travel, whoever traveled back would need to understand the technology of 2035. Voila," she said, turning the laptop so they could peruse the screen. "Look who I found."

"Is that Nelson?" Luke asked.

"Yep. Our own Dr. Nelson Longwood. He lived in D.C. before moving to Australia in 2036. He and my father are research partners. If anyone can help me find the others, it's Nelson."

"Wouldn't it be better if we just approached Lewis?" Hunter asked.

"No," Lainey said, shaking her head. "He's too closely related to me. Approaching a relative in a different timeline can throw the entire space-time continuum off-balance. It's better if I make contact with Nelson."

"Okay then, we'll start there in regard to finding the rest of the team. In the meantime, what do we do about Puss in Boots' arrival today?" Hunter asked.

"We need to observe it but put parameters in place so Victor's men can't take us into custody. No one needs to go to prison today. I'll be damned if anything Luke wrote in his letter comes true."

"Thank you, Lainey," Luke said, encircling her wrist and giving it a squeeze.

"Absolutely. Let's get to it. We've got a lot to do today."

Hours later, the three of them stood in the shadows of the narrow alley, watching the spot where Lainey was certain Puss in Boots would appear. Footsteps echoed on the pavement, the sounds stark as they traveled down the passageway.

A gust of wind lifted some of the scattered trash lying against the curb, and the man whose footsteps they'd heard stopped before the small whirlwind. A dark orb appeared, and the pet carrier a few seconds later, the wormhole closing behind it.

The man lifted the cat from the carrier, slowly rotating it and studying it. Wanting to see more, Lainey stepped forward. Hunter grabbed her wrist, his eyes warning her to be careful. She nodded and stretched her head to observe the dark-haired man.

"You'll hurt your neck if you keep straining like that, Dr. Randolph," the man said, his deep voice calm and laced with a latent cruelty. "It would be easier if you just showed yourself now."

Terror coursed through her body as she realized he was already one step ahead of her. How many times had they met at this very spot? How many conversations had she already had with him?

Determined to find out, she forged ahead, stepping into the alley. Hunter grabbed her wrist again, and she turned to face him.

"No, Hunter," she said, gently disengaging. "We can't run from them anymore. I have to figure this out, and you have to let me."

Hunter's gray eyes were solemn as he released her wrist. "Luke and I won't let anything happen to you. We're right here."

She nodded, so thankful Hunter was on this journey with her. No matter the circumstances or her shock when she'd realized Lewis had secretly recruited him, she now knew her father had chosen the right man to travel with her through time. Lainey had never felt safer with anyone than with Hunter, except perhaps Cyrus. Filing that away for her scientific mind to dissect later, she turned to face the man who was entwined with her destiny.

"Hello, Victor," she said, stepping onto the paved stones of the alley.

"Hello, Elaine." He held Puss in Boots in his long, coat-clad arms, stroking him like an evil genius from the old James Bond movies Lewis had loved. Dark hair, pronounced eyebrows, and austere features mimicked Eli's, proving beyond a doubt that they were father and son.

"Don't worry," he said, the smirk on his face causing her to grit her teeth. "I won't shoot you. Hunter and Luke are behind you, and you're safe. For now."

"We've put parameters in place to ensure our safety that have nothing to do with you," she said, chin lifting. "The local police have been tipped off that a possible assault will occur in this alleyway in"—she lifted her wrist to examine her watch—"exactly four minutes. I suggest you speak quickly, before they show up."

Victor's lips quirked. "You're always so cunning, Elaine, I'll give you that, but your fundamental flaw is that you don't realize the truth."

"And what is the truth?" she asked, lifting her hands. "Tell me."

His fingers stroked the feline's fur. "You're playing a different game than we are, my dear. You're not even on the same field. It's sad, really." His gaze lowered to Puss in Boots. Giving him one last rub, he lowered him to the ground. Straightening, he wiped his hands on his coat. "The New Establishment is all-powerful, Elaine. We control every inch of space-time and know every move you're going to make before you can even anticipate it. I'm sorry,"—his shoulders shrugged—"but you're going to fail every time."

"I'd rather fail than ever give in to an evil regime who doesn't believe in democracy and freedom!"

"Democracy," Victor scoffed. "Democracy is a notion of unevolved men, Elaine. We're past that now. Humans are weak creatures. Only the best among us should rule. This is how it was for thousands of years, and this is how it will be again."

Lainey struggled to understand his cryptic words. "What the hell are you talking about?"

"Science eliminated natural selection, Elaine. With the advent of vaccines and modern medicine, weaker people who should've been exterminated were allowed to thrive. The New Establishment does not accept that all are equal. We believe in Darwinism and the idea that the weakest among us should be allowed to perish if they can't survive on their own. Your grandfather supports our cause and will ensure the world is restored to order. Your father, in his own way, will help when he detonates the EMPs. Lewis thought it best to destroy power and electricity so it didn't fall into the hands of the New Establishment, but in the end, he created a world in our image, where only the strong survived. I'm incredibly thankful to him."

"My father wanted nothing more than to save this planet," Lainey said through gritted teeth. "And he and I firmly believe all humans are created equal and deserve the same opportunities to thrive."

"Yes," Victor said. "It is our fundamental disagreement and the reason why we're stuck in this endless loop. Only your determination to stop us has prevented us from succeeding. You now understand that we've had this conversation countless times, each one of them slightly different. I can only imagine the first time I walked down this alley and found Puss in Boots, knowing nothing of what I know now. The cycle is maddening." Showing a sliver of weakness, he rubbed his eyes.

"But it has to end," he continued, his dark gaze cemented to hers. "We are committed to stopping you, no matter the cost. You'll continue to create new timelines, and we'll always be one step ahead. Eventually, we'll find the upper hand that exterminates you. Once that is done, the New

Establishment will reign over its people. People who *deserve* to live and prosper on this planet."

"You're insane," Lainey breathed.

"Perhaps," he said, giving an absent shrug. "It doesn't really matter anymore. I see the end so clearly. You and the people you love so dearly will drown in a pool of their own blood. If you know what's good for you, I suggest you find Dr. Longwood and have him send you back to 2075. Return to the day when Hunter arrived on your doorstep and destroy the Sphere. Live out the rest of your life with your family at the hub. Eli will seize it, but he will ensure you don't suffer. He will let you grow old and die there, if you dedicate your life to supplying the New Establishment with power and knowledge. It's the best outcome your life can have from this point forward. Otherwise, your family from the hub will perish. You must already wonder what happened to them. I can sense your fear that they're dead. They aren't yet, but it's only a matter of time."

"You son of a bitch!" she exclaimed, fisting her hands at her sides. "Where are they? I swear to god, if you lay one finger on them—"

"They're insignificant to me, Elaine," he interrupted. "I don't care whether they live or die. Only you can make that choice. End your quest to prevent the rise of the New Establishment. That is the only way you can ensure they survive."

"Sorry to chime in here, but fuck you, asshole," Hunter said, taking his place at her side. He grabbed her hand, and Lainey squeezed, grateful for his support and protection. "We'll never stop fighting you bastards. If you've met Lainey before, you know she's not scared of slimy filth like you."

"Ah, the noble soldier. Still in love with his dead wife but willing to fuck *her* for the greater cause," he said, gesturing with his head to Elaine. "You fall for him in every timeline, Elaine. It's embarrassing. Have some pride, for god's sake. You must know, you'll never be able to give him what Kara could. You're a shell of a person, bred for one reason. You have no idea how to love someone."

"Don't listen to him, Lainey," Hunter said, constricting her hand. "He wants to drive a wedge between us. It's a proven manipulation tactic even the most basic soldier understands. Is that all you've got, asshole? Because we're smarter than that."

"We'll see," Victor murmured. "Her doubt about her own humanity is one of her greatest weaknesses. We plan to exploit it until she fails. Even now, the seeds have been planted."

Lainey struggled to remain calm, admitting his words were true. Doubt regarding her ability to give Hunter anything but tepid emotion and sex infiltrated her veins. Heavy and thick, it pervaded her body as she digested Victor's words. Hunter had experienced great love with Kara, and Lainey had realized long ago that she just didn't possess a proclivity for romantic love. Honestly, she didn't want to. It detracted from her purpose, and that was her sole reason for existing. There was no room to focus on anything else.

Sirens wailed in the distance, cutting off her thoughts.

"Well, that's my cue to leave," Victor said. "For this go-round, at least. I wonder what will happen next time we have this conversation. It will be had by different versions of ourselves, so one can only wonder. Stay on your toes, Dr. Randolph. The New Establishment is always watching."

"Why don't you just kill me now?" she asked, hands thrown in the air with frustrated resignation. "If you want so badly to be rid of me?"

"I have, several times," he said, arching a sardonic brow. "Luke always sends the information to you in the future and then subsequently prevents your death. I've given up trying at this instance of time. It isn't meant to be. We haven't discovered your fate paradox yet, the day you're destined to die. Believe me, when we do, we will take full advantage."

Lainey digested the information, thankful there were still some unknowns.

"We've now accepted that it is your fate to convince Dr. Longwood to help you rebuild the Sphere in this timeline. We won't interfere, but we'll be watching. The New Establishment wants nothing more than for you to complete your work."

"I'll never let the Sphere fall into the hands of evil men. I'll destroy it before I turn it over to you or anyone else."

Victor sighed. "Your stubbornness is misplaced, Elaine. As I said, we've already won. But clutch on to your principles if you must. Your fighting spirit is admirable."

Lainey felt her eyes narrow, hating the man who spoke in such maddening riddles. "You said my team isn't dead," she said, tugging her hand from Hunter's and stepping toward Victor. "Where are they? Please, tell me. If they're insignificant to you, what harm will it cause?"

Victor's head turned toward the approaching sirens before his gaze landed on hers. "The Sphere was raided while Cyrus and Claire were in transport. They're sequestered in a different time. The others are still in 2075 in Eli's custody. He protects them, for now, but my son walks a precarious line between good and evil. As things are manipulated here in 2035, I can't account for what will happen to them."

He closed the distance between them until only a foot separated them. "I don't begrudge your beliefs and your conviction, Elaine, although I believe them to be wrong." His irises were filled with a reluctant, compassionate admiration. "If I'd had a daughter, I would've wanted her to be exactly like you. You are the worthiest opponent I've ever faced. When I finally defeat you, in some future timeline, I will bow to you with the reverence you deserve. For now, I'll leave you to fumble along. Goodbye."

"You're not going anywhere," Hunter said, stalking forward to halt his retreat.

Victor pulled a gun from his coat, aiming it at them and cocking it. "That, my friend, is where you're wrong." The three of them stood frozen, unable to do anything but watch him exit the causeway.

The sirens grew louder, and Lainey saw a shadow scurry away out of the corner of her eye. Puss in Boots was lost to them now. She hoped he found a loving home.

A police car swerved into the entrance of the alley, and she gestured to Luke and Hunter to hide behind the large dumpster. Approaching the car, she plastered on a smile.

"Hello, Officer. I was out taking a walk. Is everything okay?"

A tall officer with smooth russet skin approached her. "We received a call about a possible assault in this alley, ma'am. May I see some ID?"

"Of course," she said, pulling her mother's ID from her purse. "I hope everything's okay."

He studied the ID before handing it back to her. "You're quite a long way from LeDroit Park, ma'am. You said you were taking a walk?"

"Oh, yes. My husband Lewis is going to come and pick me up on his way from work. He knows I love the greenway over there."

The officer turned to look at the far-off park. "I would suggest you stay near the park, Mrs. Randolph. It's much safer than the alleyways."

"Thank you," she said. "Sometimes, I try different paths. I'll be sure to do that though. Better safe than sorry." Lainey studied the young man, his face somehow familiar. Reading his nametag, she said, "I appreciate your help, Officer Montgomery."

A strange feeling washed over her as she processed the name.

"Ma'am?" he called, jolting her from her musings.

"Oh, sorry," she said, waving her hand. "I just knew someone once with your last name. Cyrus Montgomery. I was just reminded of him."

The man's eyebrows drew together. "You know Cyrus Montgomery?" he asked.

"Yes. Or, uh, I did, a long time ago."

"Well, ma'am, Cyrus Montgomery is my father."

Lainey felt her eyes almost pop from her head and struggled to remain calm. "Oh, imagine the coincidence. I'm sure they're not the same person though."

"Maybe not. Was the Cyrus you knew married?"

"No," she said, relief washing through her though the coincidence was still exceedingly strange. "He was single the entire time I knew him."

"Oh, well, then it definitely wasn't the same person. My father's been married to my mother for thirty years. Claire and Cyrus. They're still as in love today as they were when they got married. My mom tells me all the time." White teeth flashed as he grinned.

"Claire," Lainey repeated softly. "What was her maiden name?"

He seemed startled but answered anyway. "Finch. Claire Finch. Why?"

Struggling to breathe, she shook her head. "Just curious. Thank you, Officer Montgomery. I'll be on my way now. Keep up the good work."

"Good luck, ma'am," he said with a nod. Striding to the car, he sat behind the wheel and drove down the block.

Slowly pivoting, as the conversation replayed over and over in her brain, she headed toward the dumpster.

"Hey, duchess, you okay?" Hunter asked, his and Luke's expressions filled with worry.

"I think I know where Claire and Cyrus are," she said, her voice filled with wonder.

"Where?" Luke asked.

She squinted, calculating in her head. "Somewhere in the past. Most likely, the early 2000s."

"What?" Hunter asked, confused.

"Come on," she said, rubbing her temples as a migraine threatened to form in her brain. Great. Just what she needed. "We've got work to do."

In the brisk afternoon air, they returned to the hotel as Lainey updated them on her conversation with Officer Montgomery.

Chapter 26

They waited until evening to approach Nelson and Lorna. The couple would be at home, and that location was more private than the university. Hunter and Luke would keep watch outside while Lainey explained everything to them and asked for their help.

Under the cool March breeze and cloudy early-evening sky, Lainey knocked on Nelson's door, the sound mimicking the dull thuds in her brain. She'd taken some caffeine pills earlier in an attempt to ward off the migraine, but it still lingered along with her annoyance at its existence. Nelson opened the door, and Lainey looked at his beloved face, so much younger than she'd ever seen it.

"Hello," he said, his smile welcoming. "Can I help you?"

"Yes," she said, attempting to appear as non-threatening and normal as possible. "My name is Elaine, and I'd like a few minutes of your time if possible."

"We already have everything we need, dear," Lorna said, appearing behind Nelson. "We're agnostics who read everything online, so we have no need of religion or newspapers."

Lainey couldn't help her laugh. Lorna always was a tough old bird, although she was exceptionally gorgeous in her youth, with her blond hair and deep blue eyes. Lainey knew she was roughly thirty-five in this timeline, and Nelson only two years older.

"I'm not trying to sell you anything, I swear. But it would be really helpful if you let me inside. I assure you, I have no wish to do anything but sit and talk. I believe you know one of my associates, Dr. Lewis Randolph."

"He's my partner at the university," Nelson said. "I'm sure he would've mentioned you, Ms.…." The sentence trailed off as Nelson waited for her to supply her last name.

"I'd rather we speak inside. It's possible we're being surveilled. You're both very intuitive people. I know this is strange but hope your curiosity will prevail. Nelson, you gave Lewis a lamp that was inscribed with the words, 'May the light shine until all your answers are illuminated.' It would be impossible for me to know that if I wasn't his associate. Please," she said, eyes searching theirs, "let me inside. I promise, I wish you no harm."

Nelson looked at Lorna, and she gave a hesitant nod. Opening the door wider, he invited her into the foyer. They led her to a sitting room lined with a comfortable couch and two chairs. Sliding into one, she addressed them when they were seated on the couch.

Inhaling a deep breath, she rubbed her palms on her jean-clad thighs. "I have no idea how to say this, but I'm a practical scientist, so I'm just going to put it out there."

"Say what, dear?" Lorna asked, her expression perplexed.

Straightening her spine, she said, "My name is Dr. Elaine Randolph. I am the daughter of Dr. Lewis Randolph and the granddaughter of President Edward James Randolph. On September fourth of this year, 2035, my grandfather will launch nuclear weapons upon the Earth, eventually thrusting us into a post-apocalyptic society. Scientists will band together to form scientific compounds on a few continents, my father running the one west of here, in the foothills of Virginia. You two will leave on one of the last boats to Australia, to help form the scientific hub on that continent. It's where you'll live the rest of your days.

"You and my father are currently working on solving time travel at the university here. Eventually, it will be elucidated—not by Lewis, but by me, in the year 2075. Lewis dedicated his entire life to training me so I could decipher time travel and return here, to this timeline in 2035, to prevent my grandfather from detonating the nukes. Unfortunately, there is an evil regime that has also learned to manipulate time travel, and we are stuck on an unending loop, attempting to prevent each other's actions. I need your help so I can rebuild the Sphere and create a functional time machine in this timeline. Are you with me so far?"

They sat still upon the sofa, looking a bit stunned but not as much as Lainey had expected. Her fingers writhed together in her lap as she waited.

Finally, Lorna said, "Why don't you go get the old cell phone, darling?"

Nelson nodded and stood, walking over to rustle in a bin atop the desk in the corner of the room. Striding back, he pushed a button on the side, and the phone illuminated.

"We met a couple on a cruise several years ago," Nelson said, his finger swiping over the screen of the phone. "They were lovely, and we felt a bond with them since they were also an interracial couple. The man had the bartender take a photo of the four of us and he texted it to me. Here," he said, handing the phone to Lainey.

Lainey's eyes grew wide as she observed the photo. Nelson and Lorna sat with Cyrus and Claire, older than she knew them but smiling and happy. "Go ahead," Nelson said, "read the text he sent along with the picture."

Minimizing the photo, Lainey read the text.

Cyrus: *So nice meeting you both. Claire and I had a lovely time. She misses talking about science, and I can't give that to her, so I thank you both for that gift. Seeing her smile is the one thing that warms my heart more than any other. In return, I will give you a gift. It might seem strange, but remember, most things are explained in time. If a woman approaches you asking you to help her with the Sphere, please do not dismiss her. She is a friend and an avid science lover as well. You told me you like riddles, Nelson, so I'll leave it at that. Phones are disposable in this technological world, but please keep this one so this message is saved. I believe it will serve a purpose one day. Claire and I wish you all the best.*

Lainey lifted her eyes, her irises darting back and forth between Nelson and Lorna. "Wow. Good lookin' out, Cyrus," she muttered.

"I didn't have the heart to throw that phone out when I replaced it a few years ago," Nelson said. "When I texted the number back, it was disconnected, and we haven't seen or heard from them since. It was all so bizarre, but I love mysteries, so I kept it, much to my wife's chagrin."

With a sheepish grin, he continued. "I'm confused as hell, being that I just saw Lewis a few hours ago, and he and Mara don't have any children I'm aware of. But you have his eyes, and I'm no fool. What do you need me to do?"

There, in the den of the Washington D.C. townhome, Lainey explained her plan in detail. They would work nights, in the abandoned underground lab of the university, reconstructing the Sphere until it was functional. Then, she had many feats to accomplish.

She would travel to the past to save Claire and Cyrus and help them travel to 2035.

She would transport to 2075 to find Sara, Zach, Alora, Marie, and Elle and ensure they safely conveyed to 2035.

Then, she would work with Cyrus and Hunter to thwart her grandfather's actions, all while maintaining a low profile and putting safeguards in place that assured the New Establishment couldn't interfere. The scope of her efforts over the next few months was massive.

"How did you figure out future time travel, Elaine?" Nelson asked. "Lewis and I only theoretically proved one could travel to the past, not the future."

Lainey shrugged. "I didn't. The Sphere I created was only capable of traveling to the past. I saw no need to create a portal to the future. I was resigned to live the rest of my days in 2035 once I'd stopped President Randolph. Now, I realize how short-sighted that was. We need to create a portal that will transport us both ways."

"Future time travel is rife with paradoxes, Elaine. It's fraught with many theoretical inconsistencies. I hesitate to encourage your belief in it. It's possible we'll fail."

"Failure is something I'm intimately familiar with, Dr. Longwood. Believe me, it's been the cornerstone of my entire existence." Her gaze dropped to her hands in her lap, remembering all the times she'd let everyone down. Determination to succeed burned in her pores. She'd made a mess of things thus far, but she'd be damned if she let the New Establishment win.

"I don't want to sound like an overbearing mother hen here, but are you okay, Elaine? This is a daunting endeavor to undertake. Do you have someone to support you?" Lorna's kind eyes swam with concern.

"Yes," Lainey said, standing and plastering on a smile she hoped was convincing. In truth, Victor's words about Hunter in the alley had rankled her, and that, along with the drumming migraine, made her feel unstable.

Pushing the thoughts away, she said to Nelson, "I'll meet you at the university tomorrow night, at eleven o'clock. We have a prepaid cell phone. Please text me directions to the underground lab." She recited the number of Luke's phone while Nelson tapped it into his contacts. "I appreciate your willingness to help me, Nelson. You were a father figure to me in the future, and I hope I can recreate that same bond here. With both of you." She smiled at Lorna. "With that, I'll say good night." Pivoting, she strode toward the front door.

"Wait, dear," Lorna called. Rushing toward her, the woman pulled Lainey into a warm embrace. "You're not alone," she whispered in her ear, causing tears to sting Lainey's eyes. "Please, call on me if you need me."

"Thank you, Lorna," she said, sniffing. Willing the tears away, she gave the woman a nod and exited the townhome. Hunter and Luke appeared at the bottom of the stairs.

"How did it go?" Hunter asked.

Lainey lifted her chin. "We're meeting at the university at eleven o'clock tomorrow night. We're going to recreate the Sphere."

"Thank god," Luke said, eyes closing as he exhaled with relief. "I knew you'd do it, Lainey." He regained his composure and rubbed her arm. "I knew you'd find a way to locate Sara."

"Yes," Lainey said, suddenly overcome with exhaustion. "We'll find her."

"Let's get back to the hotel," Hunter said, his piercing gaze roving over her, assessing.

As Luke summoned the car from his phone, Hunter pulled her to his side, squeezing her waist. "Are you okay?" he asked softly, head tilted close to hers.

"Fine," she said, her smile so fake he must've known she was forcing it. "I just have a migraine and need to rest."

His hesitant nod indicated he was suspicious, but she was too exhausted to care. Sliding into the rideshare, they rode back to the hotel.

CHAPTER 27

Lainey was sitting at the round table in her hotel room computing equations when a knock sounded on her door. If they were going to travel to the future as well as the past, she needed to figure out the math and figure it out fast. It was an almost insurmountable task, and she didn't have Zach or Claire to help her, so their entire future rested on her brain, which was currently experiencing dull pulses from her never-ending headache.

She approached the door, already knowing she'd find Hunter on the other side. He breezed through as if he owned the place, stirring her ire.

Arching a brow, she asked, "Can I help you with something?"

He glanced at the scattered papers lying across the table. "You're getting an early start on the equations."

"Yes," she said, shrugging. "We don't have time to waste."

He studied her, his expression wary. "It's after nine o'clock, Lainey, and it's been an…*eventful* day, to say the least. I think you should cool it with the equations for now—I can tell you have a migraine. I'd like to help you with it, if I can."

Lainey sighed, feeling drained. "Thanks, but I'm good. I'm going to finish up what I was working on and head to bed."

Anger flashed in his eyes, and her body tensed, ready for a fight. For some reason, she wanted him mad, out of control, so she could send him away and crawl into a hole of nothingness where she would be numb. For a practical scientist, experiencing the wide gamut of emotions she'd felt lately was maddening.

"I've been a soldier for a long time, Lainey," Hunter said, the words piercing the silence. "One of the first things they teach you is to create tension between your opposing battalion's members. It's psychological warfare 101." Taking a step toward her, he continued. "You're the smartest person I've ever known, but you see things in black and white. It makes sense because that's how Lewis raised you. But I assure you that you are quite capable of loving someone *and* saving the world, and I know you understand that deep inside. You need to take a deep breath and let Victor's words go. They're toxic, and if you're not careful, you'll give him exactly what he wants."

Every single word he spoke was true, but Lainey couldn't bring herself to believe them. It broke something within her because her practical side knew she was being irrational, but emotion was overwhelming her. It was so unlike Lainey that she felt unbalanced, like a caged animal desperately wanting to escape. It was embarrassing, but she couldn't muster the will to control it.

"I don't want to argue with you, Hunter," she said, rubbing the space between her eyebrows with the pads of her fingers. "Meeting you has overturned every belief I ever had about myself. Every justification for why I was put here…for why I exist at all. The truth is, I'm not capable of loving you like Kara did, and that's extremely unfair to you. I don't believe in romantic love. I really enjoyed having sex with you, but that's all I can give."

He sighed, head drooping as he rested his hands on his hips. "Goddammit," he muttered. "That son of a bitch. He knew exactly how to manipulate you. I should've foreseen it."

"He was right!" she said, fury coursing through her at his dismissal of her justification for him to leave. "I have one goal. I always have. You've known this all along."

"What do you want from me, Lainey?"

She studied him, the heart she'd convinced herself was wooden and incapable of love splintering in her chest. "I think I just need some space."

His head lifted, and those gorgeous eyes darted over her face. "Fine," he said, shaking his head, "I'll give you space." Closing the distance between them, he stood before her, only inches separating them. Reaching up, he brushed a tendril from her temple that had escaped from the bun on her head.

"I keep telling myself, I've had years to fall for you, but you've only had weeks. It's hard, because I'm not a man who likes to wait. When I identify something I want, or something I need as desperately as I need you, I usually seize it with every ounce of will I possess." His hand cupped her cheek, turning her face toward his since he stood to her side. "But I need you to hear this, Lainey. I deserve to be with someone who is strong enough to love me back. Do you think this is the last time someone will try to manipulate us against each other? If I was the enemy, I would do everything to ensure we hated each other. It's a smart play on their part."

Lainey swallowed thickly, absorbing his words.

"We have to rise above that. Otherwise, we're no better than they are. Animals who believe in the worst humanity has to offer. I know we can do better, Lainey. Don't let them win." He brushed a kiss across her lips, soft and full of promise. "You need to decide if you want me as your partner in every sense of the word, or if you just want me as a member of your team. I'll accept either verdict, but I won't live my life straddling a line where you continually deny what we have is real, that it isn't just as important as your goddamned mission. I'm someone who loves with my entire soul, and that requires a firm commitment. I know you can give me that. The question is, are you willing to?" Releasing her face, he left the room, the door sounding an ominous thump behind him.

Exhausted, Lainey collapsed on the bed, wondering what the hell she was going to do.

Lainey threw herself into rebuilding the Sphere, working long nights with Nelson and performing equations by day. Hunter and Luke were tasked with surveilling the nuclear plant thirty miles outside of Washington D.C., in Eastern Virginia. Eventually, they would pilfer one of the spent nuclear fuel rods to power the Sphere with the jolt of nuclear energy it needed to function. Since it was highly reactive, Lainey would ensure they had proper protective suits, and she worked with Nelson to build a protective zirconium casing that would house the rod in the Sphere.

They found a small, two-bedroom apartment near the university and rented it, although Lorna offered to let them live at the townhome. Lainey felt that would put her and Nelson in too much danger, and she also wanted the visibility of staying in a busy place. She believed the New

Establishment wouldn't be bold enough to attack her in front of multiple onlookers, although she was always on high-alert. Hunter performed a sweep of her room every morning when she returned from the lab, checking for bugs and securing the windows. From the corner of her eye, she would watch him while she muddled through equations, longing to get lost in his arms again. But she didn't allow herself to cave, reminding herself over and over that she had a job to do. *One* job, and it didn't include getting tangled up with a man who would distract her from her purpose and who deserved so much better than she could offer.

After a few weeks, the Sphere was coming along nicely. The underground lab had been abandoned years ago when the building was remodeled, and not even the janitor or maintenance crew entered the secluded wing. Nelson had added extra locks to the door and held the only keys. For now, they were secure.

Lainey returned home one morning to find Hunter in her room.

"Hey," he said, his hand tracing the window frame. "Just finishing a security check. Everything's good."

A wave of sadness overtook her, and longing swelled so deeply in her chest she couldn't resist. Approaching him, she slid her arms around his waist as he faced the window. Stiffening, he lowered his hands, placing them over hers atop his abdomen.

"I miss you," she whispered, forehead pressed between his shoulder blades.

He turned, hands cupping the back of her head. Tilting her face toward his, he gave her a sad smile. "I've given up on trying to understand why you're punishing both of us, Lainey. I just figured you'd come to me when you were ready."

Her gaze drilled into his. "I tried loving someone once. It was a fucking disaster. It almost crumbled everything my father worked so hard to build."

The corner of his lip curled. "That bad?"

She breathed a laugh. "Full-on catastrophe."

"I'd love to hear what happened, if you're open to telling me."

"Okay," she said. Reaching for his hand, she led him to the bed.

Lainey slid over the mattress and plopped up the pillow, leaning her back against it. Hunter did the same, placing his arm around her shoulders. She rested her head in the crook of his neck, overcome with joy at being in his embrace once more.

Inhaling a deep breath, she began recounting the story, all the way through to its heartbreaking conclusion…

"You're so fucking pathetic, Lainey. What an incredible waste of time."

The hurtful words spurred something in her, and before she even comprehended the action, her hand connected with Dalton's face. His eyes grew wide, angry breaths puffing from his lungs as he loomed over her.

"Touch me again, and I'll kill you," he murmured, the tone of his voice murderous.

"You're such a child," she said, hating that she'd given herself to him so freely. "There are things in this world bigger than you, Dalton. Bigger than us! Don't you understand?"

"Nothing is bigger than what I plan to accomplish. I'm closer than ever to infiltrating the New Establishment. If that bastard Eli Hernandez can find his way to power, so can I. And I'll be a merciful leader, loved by all. That's bigger than anything your small mind can imagine."

She scoffed. "You have no idea who I am." Pointing her finger in his face, she spat, "What I was born to accomplish!"

Dalton grabbed her finger, his other hand encircling her neck. "Is that so?" he asked, his fingers tightening.

Lainey struggled, her hand tugging at his grip as she fought to breathe. Suddenly, a gun cocked.

"Let her go, or I'll shoot," Cyrus's baritone said in the darkness. "You have two seconds."

Dalton froze, his fingers slowly uncurling from Lainey's throat. In that moment, she realized how stupid and selfish she'd been. She'd jeopardized their entire mission, and for what? The opportunity to experience sex? The ability to have something that was hers? Feeling like the child she'd accused Dalton of being, she quietly thanked Cyrus.

He nodded, pulling the restraints from his belt with his free hand. They walked back to the hub in silence, Dalton following behind them, bound and constricted. When they reached the hub, dawn was flirting with the treetops.

"Go inside and get Lewis," Cyrus commanded.

Nodding, Lainey went inside and woke her father. He was livid, of course, but knew there was no time to waste on anger. They decided the best course was to turn Dalton over to the Old Rebellion and inform them of his aspirations to infiltrate the New Establishment and seize control for his own objectives.

Once Cyrus began the trek to the Old Rebellion camp, Dalton in tow, Lewis turned to Lainey, placing his hands on her shoulders. "This is the last time you keep secrets from me, Lainey," he said. "I expected better from you."

"I know," she said, drowning in the disappointment and anger in his gaze. "We can't keep secrets from each other. You would never do that to me."

Something flashed across his face, spiking her curiosity.

"Dad?" she asked, wondering if he had his own confidences he hadn't divulged. "Whatever it is, you can tell me. I swear, I'll never keep anything from you again. I've learned my lesson. My focus is on our work and what you and Mom created me for. I promise. No more distractions."

His expression was impassive. "Okay, sweetheart," he said, placing a soft kiss on her forehead. "Let's move on. After Marie makes breakfast, we'll test the new equations."

Lainey headed inside her home with her father, the person she revered above all others, determined to make him proud, no matter that it denied her the things others craved. Saving humanity was a noble sacrifice, and she was more resolute than ever.

"Of course, I realize now, he had so many secrets he never told me," Lainey said. "This was only a few years before he sought you out."

"And what happened to Dalton?" Hunter asked.

Lainey shook her head, the motion solemn. "Sadly, he never made it to the Old Rebellion encampment near Solera."

"Why?" Hunter asked.

Sighing, she clenched her eyes shut at the dreadful memories. "About a mile into the journey, Dalton tried to attack Cyrus, even though he was bound, and Cyrus is so massive. It was a terrible decision." She shook her head. "Cyrus struggled with him, and somehow, Dalton managed to grab the knife from his belt. Cyrus had no choice. He drew his gun and shot him."

Hunter exhaled a deep breath. "Wow."

"Yeah," she said, her chin trembling. "Even though things had gone so wrong between us, I didn't want him to die. Cyrus brought the body back, and we held a funeral for him. Cyrus was a wreck for weeks. He's a hardened soldier but he's no murderer. He beat himself up for shooting for the heart instead of just wounding him in the leg. In the heat of the moment, sometimes, your basic survival instincts take over. I think he still carries so much guilt, even today. And it's all my fault."

"What are you talking about?" Hunter said, sliding a hand over her hair.

She lifted glistening eyes to his. "I knew better. I wasn't put here to experience clandestine love and stolen kisses. I was put here to save the world. It was a hard lesson to learn, but I got the fucking message."

"Hey," he said, eyebrows drawing together. "That's an intense story. I get why you're torn up about what happened, but does it mean you have to close yourself off from the possibility of ever trying to love someone again?"

"Yes," she whispered. "It reaffirmed everything I already knew. I have to stay focused on my goal."

His eyes darted over her face as he studied her. "Is it possible for you to think, for just a moment, that you weren't meant to do this alone? That everything happened for a reason? Lewis recruited me knowing who I was and that I would dedicate myself to helping you succeed. I also believe he recruited me because he understood he'd instilled this belief in you that your sole purpose was to save everyone else. Maybe he wanted me to relieve you of that accession, Lainey. It's not serving you anymore. You need to let it go."

Her shoulders lifted in a poignant shrug. "I don't know how."

Compassion marred his expression as his gaze roamed her face. Breathing her name, he slid his hand to cup her head and lowered his lips to hers. She sought them like a thirsty desert traveler seeks water, and opened to let him in. Wrapping her arms around him, she pulled him in, her back lowering to lie on the bed. His wet tongue swept every inch of her mouth as he grabbed the hem of her shirt, divesting her of the garment before unclasping her bra and tossing it aside.

His mouth lowered to her breast, devouring it, as she tugged the shirt from his chest. Eager hands fumbled with his belt, unclasping it and pushing his pants down while he struggled to maintain contact with her breast.

Lainey tore the button of her jeans free, huffing in frustration as she tried to maneuver them off her legs.

"Let me take these off, sweetheart," Hunter said, straightening. He removed the rest of his clothes then shimmied off her sneakers and tugged the jeans from her legs. With eyes full of desire, he placed his palm between her breasts, sliding it down her abdomen, across her navel, to rest above the small thatch of hair at the juncture of her thighs.

"Beautiful," he whispered, the reverence in his tone breaking something inside her. Perhaps it was the long-held notion she was incapable of love. Perhaps it was the wall that encased her innermost fears. Whatever it was, she felt shattered as he breathed heavily above her.

Grasping the hem of her panties, he drew them off her legs. Lowering beside the bed, he grabbed the backs of her knees and glided her toward him. There was no buildup this time, no space for lingering kisses and whispered words. Instead, he draped her legs over his shoulders and buried his face in her wetness.

Lainey moaned, overcome with pleasure, as his tongue began a series of long, thorough strokes from her opening to her clit and back again. Over and over, he tasted her, causing her body to quiver atop the mattress. With his fingers, he spread her swollen folds apart, allowing him greater access. Spearing his tongue inside her, he lavished her with intimate, loving strokes. Lainey had never been so open with anyone. It was terrifying and thrilling all at once.

She thrust her fingers into his hair, pulling him deeper into her, his resulting growl proving he reveled in the action. His strong jaw worked his mouth over her, resulting in pleasure on levels she didn't even know existed. Focusing on her clit, he began a maddening sequence of different sensations, flicking the tip of his tongue over the nub then sucking it between his strong lips, then lathering it slow and languidly. Feeling her body tense, she opened her eyes, staring into his.

He bore into her, those magnificent eyes locked onto hers, as he licked and sucked her most sensitive spot. Never had she seen desire burn as it burned in his gorgeous eyes. Unable to look away, she mewled, taken with the image of his masterful tongue flicking her repeatedly. Every inch of her skin was flushed, and she clutched his hair tighter.

His eyes pled with her, begging her to come, and finally, she snapped, her body bowing as the dam of her arousal broke wide open. She called his name, his face buried in her core, bucking against his torturous mouth. Wave upon wave of pleasure threatened to drown her as she gasped for air, her lungs straining beside her pounding heart.

Unclenching her fingers from his hair, her body relaxed upon the bed, hands falling to her sides. Hunter caressed her inner thighs, causing her sated body to quiver. Slowly, he stood, bending to pick up his pants and dig in the pocket. Pulling out his wallet, he opened it.

Out of the corner of her eye, Lainey saw it. A picture stuck in the porthole of his wallet, opposite the compartments. A woman with blond hair and a lovely smile was immortalized in the photograph. A woman who wasn't emotionless or unable to fathom romantic love. How could Lainey give him those things she didn't possess?

Oblivious to her thoughts, Hunter withdrew a condom and tossed the billfold to the floor. "I bought some latex ones," he said, grinning sheepishly. "Just in case you couldn't control your rampant desire for me."

Lainey smiled at the words, the same she'd used the first time they made love. Lying there, sated and limp, she couldn't muster the energy to reconcile her thoughts. There would be time for that later. For now, she watched him as he rolled on the condom and crawled over her, his muscled body hard and stunningly gorgeous.

"You with me, duchess?" he asked, looming over her.

She cupped his face. "I'm with you. Fuck me, Hunter."

The corner of his lip curved, melting every part of her body that wasn't already mush. "Who likes to talk dirty?" he teased.

Lainey drew him to her, searching for his lips. They consumed her as he reached down and spread the folds at her center. Aligning the head of his cock with her wetness, he began to jut inside.

Inch by inch, he pushed, gaze cemented to hers as he searched for her reaction. "Good?" he asked, fully seated inside her deepest place.

"So good," she whispered, pushing her hips against his. "Please, Hunter."

Anchoring his hands on either side of her head, he began undulating his hips, spearing into her, the pace increasing as beads of sweat formed on his forehead.

"Lainey," he moaned, his movements so raw and sexy as he loomed over her. "You feel so good, sweetheart."

She let the current take her, sliding her hand between them to stimulate her clit as he hammered into her.

"Yessss…" he hissed, his body a straining mass of muscles as he clenched his jaw. "Make yourself come with me."

He lowered further, their sweat-soaked skin sliding against each other's, one hand gliding to clench her hair. Entwined, they rode each other, slippery and intimate, until Lainey felt her orgasm on the horizon.

His straining shaft was hitting a spot deep inside, and that, combined with the motion of her fingers over her clit, sent her over the edge. Throwing back her head, she began to come.

"Fuck, you're milking me," he groaned into her ear. "I can't…oh, god —" With an urgent cry, he lost control, his hips spearing into her as he began to spurt his release. Lainey clutched him close, loving how uncontrolled he was, needing to feel as much of his skin against hers as possible.

His firm body shuddered and quaked atop hers, his groans so sexy to her ringing ears. He uttered unintelligible words along with ones she understood, like, "Lainey," and, "duchess." Reveling in how raw and open he was, she hugged him to her ravaged body.

Long moments later, he grunted into her neck, face buried against the mattress. "I have to be crushing you."

She laughed, running her nails through his hair and over his scalp, loving his resulting shiver.

"Mmm, that feels good," he murmured.

They lay that way, lazy and sated for a while, her fingers trailing through his hair. Eventually, he padded to the bathroom to dispose of the condom. Returning to the bed, Hunter rested his head on his fist. Smiling down at her, he traced her lips with his finger.

"Thank you for telling me about your past," he said, his gaze reverent. "I want you to tell me everything, Lainey. I want to be your partner, not only in your mission, but in your life."

Tears stung her eyes as she studied him. "I gave up on love after Dalton. I convinced myself it was a stupid chemical reaction and resigned myself to the fact my happiness would be derived from preventing the apocalypse."

His smile was sad but hopeful. "I understand why. We both closed our hearts at different stages of our life. It took a long time, but I was able to open mine again. I hope you can too, Lainey. You deserve to be loved."

"You sound like Marie," she said softly.

"The old bat is onto something. I'd never doubt Marie."

Lainey laughed. "So true."

His gaze flitted over her face. "What are you thinking in that busy brain of yours?" he asked softly.

"That I just don't know how to do this," she said, shaking her head against the mattress. "I don't know if I can."

He placed a sweet kiss on her lips. "How about we hold off on trying to figure everything out right now? I know that's hard for your equation-solving mind, but why don't we just hold each other for a while? I've missed holding you so much, Lainey."

She nodded, overcome with the emotion that swam in his eyes.

They shifted, Lainey stretching out beside him and resting her cheek against his chest. Throwing her leg over his thighs, she reminded herself that lying entwined with another person was uncomfortable and not at all practical.

But then again, lying entwined with Hunter, against his magnificent body, came so naturally to her. Too tired to process why, she closed her eyes and fell into slumber in a matter of minutes.

Chapter 28

L ainey's lids opened to a shaft of sunlight streaming through the window. Groaning, she reached for Hunter, finding the bed cold. Assessing the room, she saw a note on the bedside table, the scrawl thick.

Went to the coffee shop to see where Luke's at with the research. You looked so peaceful I couldn't wake you. Hope you're dreaming of me. –H

She fingered the note, his words causing butterflies to stir in her belly. Needing to take some time to process, she dressed and headed to the park across from their apartment. She probably should've checked in with Hunter and Luke, but she needed space though the park was full of people. Two cops stood near the paved walkway covered by a black arch, and she felt safe. If Victor or one of his cronies was going to attack her, their chances of being discovered were vast, and she knew they preferred the shadows. Hiding. Lurking until they could destroy the world.

The grass was soft under her sneakered soles, gaze lowered as she trailed over the greenery. A pair of large feet encased in black running shoes obstructed her line of vision.

Slowly lifting her head, she whispered, "Cyrus?"

He smiled, brown eyes set deep under brows spattered with gray. A white goatee lined his chin, but his head was still bald.

"Hey, Lainey. I missed you."

She launched herself into his arms, reveling at his deep chuckle in her ear. Tears flooded her eyes as she clutched him to her.

"I was so worried!" Standing back, she gripped his biceps, wide-eyed. "Are you okay? Where's Claire? You guys are married? Holy crap, Cyrus. I almost lost it when I met your son! I need to know everything."

His laugh filtered over her. "Of course you do." Lifting his hand, he trailed his fingers over her cheek. "You look just like you did when you entered the Sphere all those years ago."

Lainey bit her lip. "You look like the old man Claire always accused you of being."

White teeth beamed. "Yep. She never let that one go. That's what I get for marrying a younger woman. I turned seventy-six a few weeks ago."

"It's unbelievable, Cyrus. I was floored when I figured it out but thrilled for you both. You two are my favorite people on the planet, and I'm so happy you fell in love. Your son, I mean…you have a son! Holy shit."

"Jamal," he said with a nod. "And we have a daughter too. We named her Elaine."

The tears in her eyes fell down her cheeks in a trail of humble wonder. "You did?" she warbled.

He nodded, his smile so warm.

"Oh, Cyrus. That's…well, I'm honored. I love you both so much."

"I know. It's why I'm here. You have to let us go, Lainey. I know you're rebuilding the Sphere and you're dead set on coming back to 2002 to bring us here." He grasped her hands, squeezing them as he stared down at her. "But Claire and I made a life together after I stopped being an idiot and let her wear me down." His lips quirked. "It's more than I could've ever imagined from my bleak beginning in the stark world we came from. You don't need to save us, Lainey, but you do need to rescue the others. They're sequestered in a very dark timeline now the loop has begun, and it's very important you bring them to 2035."

"How do you know this?" she asked, eyebrows drawing together.

He shrugged, grinning as he shook his head. "Time travel has a way of ensuring you know many things. You'll know everything one day. For now, I need you to focus on the others."

"How many times have we had this conversation?" she asked, eyes darting between his.

"Several. You came to 2002 a few times before I realized I needed to meet you here in 2035, before you ever take the trip back, and talk you out of it. You eventually give up on us, thank goodness."

"I'll never give up on you," she said, laughing through the pain. And oh, how it hurt, knowing this would most likely be the last time she saw the man with whom she'd shared so much. "I'm not ready to let you go. Where's Claire?"

His gaze fell to their joined hands. "She's sick, Lainey. It happens to the best of us. We're fighting it, and I'm going to spend every last second with her until she leaves me. And then, I'll eventually join her. Such is the cycle of life. She sends her love and also sent me with a message for you."

The news was devastating, and Lainey struggled to breathe. "I'm so sorry, Cyrus." Willing the sting of tears from her eyes, she said, "Go on and give it to me. Knowing Claire, it's a doozy."

Glancing at the sky and squinting, he contemplated. "Let me make sure I get this right. Her exact words were, 'Tell Lainey she's being an ass and needs to marry Captain McHotty Pants immediately.'"

Laughter surged from Lainey's throat as she swiped wetness from her cheek. "Yep. That sounds like Claire."

Cyrus breathed a laugh as well. Growing somber, eyes filled with love, he asked, "What are you doing, Lainey? Why won't you let yourself be happy?"

She stared at the grass, wishing there were words to explain the jumbled mass of emotions in her mind. "I'm so scared," she said, swallowing thickly. "That loving him will detract from my purpose. That I don't understand love or how to even begin building a life with someone else. You know better than most, after everything that happened with Dalton, I'm terrible at this, Cyrus."

"What the hell are you talking about?" he asked, exasperation in his tone. "You've pushed aside your own prosperity to secure everyone else's safety. And I mean *everyone*. You're intent on saving the world. Don't you think you deserve a little happiness for yourself?"

Sighing, she shook her head. "He still carries a picture of Kara in his wallet. Will I be able to give him what she could? I'm not sure it's possible. I'm not sure I want to. What if it hinders everything I've tried to accomplish for all these years? What would my father think?"

"Lewis was devastated he denied you the ability to experience love. He would be thrilled. I know it."

Inhaling a large breath, she pondered. "Maybe he would."

"Look, I understand pushing your feelings away for something you deem bigger than yourself. I fought my feelings for Claire with every inch of my being. In the end, I couldn't prevail. She's my soulmate." Smiling, he continued. "You know, I always thought Lewis recruited me away from the Old Rebellion for you. Now, I understand your father saw so many things clearly. Now, I believe he recruited me for Claire, comprehending that we would someday figure out our souls were puzzle pieces always meant to fit together. And I'm firmly convinced he recruited Hunter for you, wanting someone who was capable of great love to bestow it on you. Your father was wracked with guilt that he didn't instill you with a desire to secure your own happiness. I think he felt Hunter would change that for you. I hope he does."

Lainey nodded, nostrils flaring as she inhaled a deep breath. "My feelings for him evolved so rapidly. I feel so connected to him, Cyrus. It throws me off-balance."

"Love is not linear, Lainey," he said, squeezing her upper arm. "Lewis must've said it a thousand times."

Love. Such a strange concept. It motivated people to do such horrendous and wonderous things. Considering the gravity of the word, thoughts whirled in her head as she tried to make sense of her feelings for Hunter.

"You'll get there. I know you will." Sliding his arms around her, he pulled her into a warm embrace.

"Will I ever see you again?" she asked.

He stroked her hair as she breathed his scent, already knowing the answer.

Drawing back, he swept away the lone tear on her cheek. "I love you, Lainey. We have so much history between us. The future will be hard at times but also so magnificent, if you allow it to happen. Be strong enough to be happy. Okay?"

She nodded, sniffling as the reality of their farewell washed over her. Wetness glistened in his eyes, and he placed a kiss upon her forehead.

"Goodbye, Elaine. My life was better because I knew you." Releasing her, he stepped back a few paces, gave her a wave, and turned.

Emotion choked Lainey as she watched him leave, the cold breeze ruffling her hair. When his large frame had faded into the distance, she straightened her spine, looking to the afternoon sky and attempting to process her thoughts.

Something nudged her deep inside, urging her to accept to Cyrus's words. Would she have the courage? Inhaling the spring air into her lungs, she headed back to the apartment.

Chapter 29

Hunter finished up the research with Luke and glanced at his watch. Lainey should be awake now and she was probably starving. He'd inadvertently taken over Marie's role of meal watchdog since Lainey barely remembered to eat half the time. Heading to the nearby deli, he ordered them both some sandwiches and returned to the apartment.

Knocking on her bedroom door, he held up the bags when she opened it. "I have lunch. Or dinner." Shrugging, he said, "Since you're working with Nelson at night, I can't keep the eating schedule straight."

She smiled, and Hunter sensed something was off. Pulling back the door, she gestured him in. He set the bags on the table, throwing his wallet beside them, and turned to give her a peck on the lips.

"Let me wash up, and we can devour these, okay?"

She nodded, her eyes guarded, and his sense of unease grew. Had something happened while she was sleeping? Striding to the bathroom, he closed the door and took care of business. When he opened it, he noticed Lainey standing by the table, his wallet open in her hand.

She was studying the picture of Kara through the clear plastic. Her shoulders were slightly hunched, her frame frozen.

Approaching her, not even attempting to discern her mood, he gently slid his arms around her waist and propped his chin on her shoulder. She traced her finger over Kara's picture.

"She was beautiful," Lainey said, her voice gravelly.

"She was," he said softly, clutching her back to his front.

"And she wasn't born with the sole purpose of saving the world."

He chuckled. "Nope. She was just a regular person. We can't all be Einsteins like you, Lainey."

Setting the wallet on the table, she slowly rotated in his arms. Lifting her hands, she cupped his cheeks, his breath catching at the emotion swimming in her eyes.

"I have no idea how to do this," she said, her words laced with hesitant concern. "I'm terrified I'll push you away, and you'll give up on me, so let me be crystal clear."

Hunter felt his lips curve, although her tone was extremely serious.

"I have a planet to save, but before I can, you had the courage to implore me to make a choice. I need to find the fortitude to stop straddling this line of indecision I'm so precariously balancing on. I think of everything that lies ahead, rescuing our team, preventing my grandfather from detonating the nukes, ensuring the New Establishment doesn't prevail even if we stop him. It's an almost insurmountable mission. But I think I'm finally ready to accept that I need your support in every possible way in order to succeed."

The pads of her fingers caressed his jaw. "The truth is, Hunter, I think I'm in love with you." Joy flooded him as she shrugged. "I don't understand it, and that's really hard for my scientific brain, but I have an extremely daunting task in front of me, and all I know is that I want you by my side. As my partner and my lover and my anchor. It's a lot to ask for someone like me, who doesn't really understand love at all. I hope you're willing to take the journey with me."

Hunter released a deep breath, thrilled at her words and the genuine sentiment in her amber eyes. Sliding his fingers into the soft hair at her neck, he grinned, studying her gorgeous face.

"I'm so ready to take this journey with you, duchess. I've been ready for several years now. It's about time you caught up."

His knees almost buckled at her brilliant smile. "Time travelers aren't known for their expediency. Occupational hazard."

His chuckle surrounded them. "Noted." Glancing down, his gaze rested on the open wallet. Reaching for it, he slid his finger behind Kara's picture to pull out a different photo. Lainey's own face smiled back at her.

"I keep them both in here," Hunter said, "so I can remind myself how lucky I am. I've loved two amazing women in my life. It's more than I could've ever imagined."

Placing the wallet and photos on the table, he turned back to her. Cupping her face, he smoothed his thumbs over her cheeks. "Every time I look at you, I realize that every step I took in my past led me to you. You're my future, Lainey. You always have been. I love you so deeply I feel it in my soul. Every time you look at me with those stunning eyes, I send a prayer of thanks to every god you don't believe in." She giggled, and his heart swelled. "I'm so honored to be your partner, and I won't let you push me away, no matter how hard you try. You're stuck with me, duchess."

Gliding her palms over his pecs, her red lips curved into a mischievous smile. "Sounds perfect to me. But I'm definitely not marrying you. I don't want to get married."

Hunter rolled his eyes. "She doth protest too much. I think you're secretly dying to marry me."

"No way, buddy. And I definitely don't want kids. Child-free all the way. I have enough on my plate."

"I'm forty-three, woman," he said, unable to stop his chuckle. "I don't want kids now. I'd break a hip trying to play with them. Are you crazy?"

"At least we're on the same page with that. But still," she said, holding up a finger, "no marriage either. Mark my words."

"We'll see, sweetheart," he murmured against her lips.

"We'll see," she repeated, swiping her tongue across his bottom lip. It drove him wild.

Lowering his hands to her ass, he lifted her, and she yelped, encircling his waist with her legs. He carried her to the bed, throwing her on top and devouring her neck. Her hands were everywhere, in his hair, tugging at his shirt, pulling his belt buckle.

Hunter stood, yanking his shirt over his head and unclasping his belt. Lainey sat up on the edge of the bed, her fingers tangling with his, as the metal unlatched and he shimmied his pants and underwear to his knees.

His erection strained toward her, and she gripped his shaft, eyes wide and curious. Always the ever-present scientist, she stroked him, slow at first and then increasing in pace as he gritted his teeth. Needing to touch her, he entwined his fingers in her hair, and her gaze lifted to his.

"I want to kiss you here," she said, running her thumb over the tiny hole at the head of his shaft. It was wet with tiny droplets of arousal, and she spread the moisture over his sensitive skin.

He groaned, the ministrations of her thumb so pleasurable as her dripping maple eyes stared up at him, filled with a slight hesitancy. "Yes, sweetheart," he whispered, cupping her jaw with his free hand. "I've dreamed so many times about having your smart, sexy mouth around me." She grinned, causing his heart to skip a beat. "I promise you, anything you do will feel good."

She contemplated for a few seconds more and then lowered her lips to his shaft. She fluttered his straining skin with kisses, eliciting a deep rumble from his chest as he clenched her hair. Tentative and thorough, her wet tongue darted out to stroke his cock, from the hard base to the tingling tip, and Hunter clenched his jaw so tightly he thought it might break. Determined to let her explore at her own pace, he gritted words of love and encouragement to her.

Finally, she opened her mouth, sliding over his length while she jerked the base of his shaft. Hunter felt his eyes straining, his body a taut mass of nerves and pleasure. Never had he seen anything as magnificent as his resplendent scientist lavishing his most sensitive place with her exquisite mouth. As her lips worked the smooth skin, over and over, he felt his balls begin to tighten, the orgasm starting to form. Exhibiting a control he would surely lose if she kept up the ministrations, he gently pulled her away.

Amber irises were filled with hesitation. "You want me to stop?"

"I want to be inside you. *Now*. Clothes off." He pushed his pants to his ankles, jerking off his shoes and tossing them aside.

Lainey removed her clothes, her actions as frantic as his, and lay back on the pillow, her mahogany hair fanning behind her. Striding to his wallet, Hunter grabbed a condom, noticing how badly his hands were shaking as he slipped it on. Returning to the bed, he crawled over her, searching for her tight channel.

"Are you wet?" he asked, gliding his fingers between her folds. She nodded, looking so cute as she bit her bottom lip. "Oh, yeah," he said, sliding his finger inside her plushy walls as she purred. "You're dripping. Did you like sucking me, honey?"

"Yes," she said, hips arching to meet his finger. "I would've finished you that way. You didn't have to stop."

"I want to be right here when I come," he said, retracting his finger and aligning the head of his shaft with her opening. Looking into her eyes, he pushed into her, so thrilled to be joined with her so intimately.

When he was seated deeply in her snug warmth, he began to move, resting on his forearms as his fingers delved into the thick hair at her temples. "Lainey," he whispered, feeling so connected to her as they moved together on the bed.

"I love you," she whispered, cupping his face as tears glistened in her eyes. The moment was so profound, he wondered how his heart was still beating inside his chest. She'd reduced him to nothingness, unable to even say the words back. Wanting to so badly, he was suddenly incapable. Hoping she understood, he lowered his lips to hers, sweeping his tongue around the warm hollows of her mouth, mimicking the movements of his straining length inside her fiery depths.

Hating that he'd lost all control, he broke the kiss, burying his face in her neck. "I can't hold back. I'm so sorry, baby. I want to make it good for you."

"Don't hold back," she cried into his ear, her warm breath sending shivers down his body. "I love you like this, so raw and open. Please, Hunter. Let go."

The words broke something in him, and a jolt of pleasure shot down his spine. Feeling his hips buck, he growled against her neck as spurts of arousal began to shoot from his shaft. Lost in the intimacy of the moment, he emptied everything inside her, all his years of loneliness and heartache swept away by her gorgeous body and loving words. For a man who'd lived years without knowing peace, it was something akin to heaven.

Eventually, his shudders subsided, his body sated and heavy over hers. Lifting a shaking hand to her cheek, he rubbed his thumb over her swollen lip. She smiled, her face free of the worry and concern it so often carried. She looked young. Happy. It shifted something inside him, knowing she could be so vulnerable with him.

"I love you too," he said, stroking the hair at her temple. "So much, Lainey. Thank you for opening your heart to me. I promise, I'll keep it safe."

"I know you will," she said, kissing his thumb.

He gave her a soft peck on the lips and pulled away from her delectable body to dispose of the condom. When he returned to the bed, she padded to the bathroom and came back to snuggle against his chest a few moments later.

"You always go to the bathroom after we have sex. Should I be worried?"

Lainey laughed, her fingers tracing a pattern over the hairs on his chest. "You should always pee after sex. It lowers the risk of getting a urinary tract infection. That's Science 101, Hunter."

"Ah, yes," he said, hugging her to him. "How could we make love without you spouting science to me? I'm wondering if I can even get hard without you reciting equations first."

She slapped his chest, rolling her eyes at his teasing. "It's sexy being with an intelligent woman. Just you wait. I'm going to make a science lover out of you yet."

Smiling into her eyes, he pulled her close, loving how her nipples flattened against his chest. Gliding his hand over the soft skin of her inner thigh, his fingers searched for her folds. "I need to make you come," he said, circling his finger around her opening. "Let's see how long you can spout science while I play with you."

Giving him a mischievous grin, she parted her thighs. "I like this game. Let's do it." She waggled her eyebrows.

Loving how unguarded she was, the protective walls she'd built all but shattered, he undertook the challenge. And Hunter was thrilled to note his stunning physicist exploded in his arms rather quickly, seemingly unbothered that science was long-forgotten.

Lainey trailed her fingers over the scratchy hairs on Hunter's pecs, reveling in the rise and fall of his chest while he snored beneath her. For the first time in her life, she had two missions: to save the world, and to build a future with someone. Letting the dual purpose settle over her, she contemplated the road ahead.

She and Nelson were close to rebuilding the Sphere. If all went well, it would be capable of time travel to both the future and the past. This opened up a world of possibility for her to save her family at the hub.

Since Cyrus had instructed her not to travel to 2002, she reluctantly accepted his assertion that he and Claire had built a life where they were happy and whole. Love for her two dearest friends washed over her, and she wondered how they'd fallen in love. Perhaps she would hear the story one day. Oh, how she longed to hear the ways in which Claire had worn down the stoic soldier. No one was as determined as Claire when she set her mind on something.

Her brow furrowed as she thought of Alora, Zach, Sara, Marie, Elle, and Eli, still trapped in the 2075 timeline. Cyrus's warning had been ominous, and Lainey was desperate to save them. That would be her first mission, once she and Nelson had recreated a functioning Sphere.

After that, the future was unknown. Or perhaps the past was unknown. In truth, it was all quite maddening if she focused on it for too long. There were so many possibilities, so many timelines that could be created. Were they destined to see the rise of the New Establishment no matter her efforts to prevent it at all costs? She didn't know.

In the end, all Lainey could do was try her damnedest. Forge ahead with everything she'd learned and everything still unknown, in hopes of creating a better Earth. A brighter future for humanity.

In the past, she'd always been so consumed with fear that she would fail. Now, for some unfathomable reason, she felt calm, assured—confident, even.

Hunter stirred below her, and his hand swept over her hair. "Hey," he murmured, his eyes swollen from sleep. "Whatcha thinking?"

"That we have a lot of work do to." Her tone was solemn but firm, indicating her resolve.

"Then we should probably get to it, duchess."

She nodded. "We should. Hunter?" she called softly, running her fingers over his chin.

"Yes, sweetheart?" he said, his thumb trailing over her cheek.

"Let's go save the damn world."

As his soft laughter washed over her, she realized why she felt so assured. *He* was the reason she felt so confident. She now had a partner on her journey to fulfill her destiny, and neither of them would stop until they accomplished their goal.

The New Establishment be damned.

Dr. Elaine Randolph was armed and ready for battle.

Epilogue

The Year 2039

Lainey stood under the thick oak tree, watching the children play. It was a warm day in Florida, perfect for the pick-up soccer game that had begun spontaneously. One of the children kicked the ball with might, and it rolled toward Lainey on the ground. Crouching, she picked it up as the boy approached her.

"Thanks, miss," he said, holding out his hands.

"You're welcome," she said, smiling and handing him the soccer ball. "What's your name?"

"Eli," he said, his dark eyes curious. "Do you live here?"

"Nope," she said. "I live in Virginia. Do you know where that is?"

He nodded, black hair swishing. "My dad lives in Washington D.C. That's next to Virginia."

"Wow. You're smart. How old are you?"

"Seven," he said, glancing over his shoulder. "I'm not supposed to speak to strangers. My mom will be mad."

"That's true, but I'm not really a stranger. My name is Lainey, and we've actually met before."

"When?" he asked.

She felt her lips curve. "It a long story but a really good one. Do you come to this park a lot?"

"Yes. My friends and I play soccer here. Our moms said it's okay if we stay in a group." One of the children called his name from across the meadow. "I have to go."

She nodded. "I'd like to tell you my stories one day. I'll be here tomorrow and hope I see you then. My husband will probably be here too." Lainey gestured with her head to Hunter, sitting on a bench about twenty feet away. "His name's Hunter, and he loves soccer."

"Cool," Eli said. "See ya." Pivoting, he ran back to join his friends.

Lainey stood, wondering how many times she'd done this before. How long would it take her to earn Eli's trust before she gave him the letter in her pocket? The one that explained who the New Establishment was and that even though her team had manipulated some aspects of past and future timelines, the regime was still a threat. Eli was a huge part of preventing their rise to prominence and must follow a specific trajectory. Only time would tell.

Hearing the ground crunch behind her, she felt Hunter's arm snake across her waist. "You made first contact," he said, drawing her close.

"Yep. I'll come back for the next few days and slowly explain everything to him. Then, I'll give him the letter filled with stories from the future. A future that is no longer certain but still needs to be managed. Such a paradox."

"Yes," he said, placing a kiss to her temple. "All we can do is follow the leads we have and do our best to produce a favorable outcome. I have faith it will happen."

Inhaling a deep breath, she lifted her gaze to his. "I told him you were my husband."

A slow smile curled across his face. "Did you now?"

She shrugged. "When Eli told me about our meeting, he said I called you my husband. It's important I try to recreate past events with exact precision."

"But I'm not your husband. *Yet*," he said, winking.

Turning in his arms, she aligned her front with his, palming his cheek. "Well, don't make a liar out of me, Hunter."

He growled, pulling her tight against his muscled body. "What are you saying, Lainey?"

"Marry me, you damn fool. I'm asking you to marry me."

Throwing back his head, he laughed, the rumbling shakes washing over their bodies. Locking his gaze with hers, he arched a dark eyebrow and said, "Well, duchess, a romantic you are not."

Chuckling, she shook her head. "Nope. But I think you'll still marry me anyway."

Placing his forehead against hers, he pressed a soft kiss to her lips. "My brilliant scientist. I love it when you're right."

There, under the white clouds and blue sky, they sealed the commitment with a kiss, sweet and full of promise. Lainey had never been enamored with the idea of marriage, but during their time together, she'd come to understand it held great meaning for Hunter. In the end, she so desperately wanted to make him happy and was honored he craved that level of commitment with her.

Love was a series of compromises, each person striving to place the other's happiness above their own. He'd taught her that and so much more, and she was extremely thankful for every lesson learned. His strength was her guidepost; his love for her more magnificent than anything she'd ever imagined. Knowing that together, they would shape the future, she kissed him with every ounce of emotion in her pounding heart.

Lifting her lids, she murmured against his mouth, "Let's get it over with. We've still got to prep Eli for the future and travel to a different timeline to ensure the world doesn't fall apart."

"Yes, ma'am, Mrs. Rhodes," he said, nipping her lips.

"That's Dr. Rhodes to you."

The boom of his laughter echoed across the open meadow, filled with joy and love. Fingers entwined, they began a slow walk across the field, thus beginning the next chapter of their lives.

Thank You!

Thanks so much for reading **A Paradox of Fates**! I hope you enjoyed Lainey and Hunter's journey as much as I enjoyed writing it.

Want to know how Cyrus and Claire fell in love in 2002? You can read their book, **A Destiny Reborn**, right now!

Dying to know what happened to Alora, Zach, Eli, Elle, and the others stranded in 2075? Find out in **A Timeline Restored**, the exciting conclusion to the Prevent the Past trilogy!

In the meantime, if you'd like to try another one of my books, check out **The End of Hatred**. Inspired by my love of J.R. Ward and Nora Roberts novels, it's a fantasy romance series with a Metallica-loving Slayer princess and a sexy, stoic Vampyre king. Their attraction is forbidden but they both crave peace. Happy reading!

ALSO BY REBECCA HEFNER

Prevent the Past Series
Book 1: A Paradox of Fates
Book 2: A Destiny Reborn
Book 3: A Timeline Restored

The Etherya's Earth Series
Book 1: The End of Hatred
Book 2: The Elusive Sun
Book 3: The Darkness Within
Book 4: The Reluctant Savior
Book 4.5: Immortal Beginnings
Book 5: The Impassioned Choice
Book 5.5: Two Souls United
Book 6: The Cryptic Prophecy
Book 6.5: Garridan's Mate
Book 7: Coming soon!

Acknowledgments

I'm so thrilled to be starting this new series. I always knew I'd write a time travel romance with a theoretical physicist heroine one day! So, first, let me thank my awesome mom for letting me go to Space Camp when I was fourteen. It was such an amazing experience and showed me that being a science-loving geek was actually pretty cool!

Thanks to all my friends for their tireless support! There are so many that I'm worried I'm going to forget someone, but I'll certainly try. *Inhales deep breath*: Thanks to Jaime, Aleks, Shelby, Lori, Margaret, Tracey, Stacey & Jo, Stacey & Donna, Vanessa, Lina, Liz, Melissa, Kristen, Jacquie, Nikki, Trang, Brooke, Susan, Judith, Colleen, Misty, Teresa, Chelsea, Lourdes, Dorothy, Grace…oh, man, I'm probably forgetting so many, and I apologize from the bottom of my heart. You all are so supportive and help me get through this crazy ride I've ventured upon.

Thanks to my awesome neighbor, Michael Valentino, for being my unofficial science advisor. Check out his YouTube channel, I Like to Science! It's amazing.

Thanks to Megan McKeever for the fantastic editing, especially on this novel, which is a bit of a curveball. Thanks to Bryony Leah for being one of the most amazing people on the planet (and also a pretty darn great proofreader!). And thanks to Anthony O'Brien for the smokin' cover!

Thanks to all the amazing bloggers/reviewers who read and review these books. You'll never know how much it means that you take the time to get to know the people who live in my head.

Here's wishing you the best in all your endeavors. May they find you on the path of seizing your dreams and living your best life!

About the Author

USA Today bestselling author Rebecca Hefner grew up in Western NC and now calls the Hudson River of NYC home. In her youth, she would sneak into her mother's bedroom and read the romance novels stashed on the bookshelf, cementing her love of HEAs. A huge Buffy and Star Wars fan, she loves an epic fantasy and a surprise twist (Luke, he IS your father).

Before becoming an author, Rebecca had a successful twelve-year medical device sales career. After launching her own indie publishing company, she is now a full-time author who loves writing strong, complex characters who find their HEAs.

Rebecca can usually be found making dorky and/or embarrassing posts on TikTok and Instagram. Please join her so you can laugh along with her!